The Matchmakers by Kimber
Maggie Weston is going on
with her two great-aunts. Thinking she is along to help
look after their needs, she soon learns this has been a ploy
to fix her up with the aunts' bachelor pastor, who is lead-
ing the church's senior women's group on the trip.

Troubled Waters by Linda Goodnight
Carrie and Greg Bridger have everything, including a troubled marriage. As a last-ditch effort to mend the rift, they
agree to an island vacation in Bermuda. En route, their private plane crashes in the ocean and they are adrift in a
lifeboat. Can they survive a battle against the elements?
And even if they do, will their marriage survive, as well?

By the Silvery Moon by JoAnn A. Grote
Ryan Windom is shocked when feminine Chrissy Bonet
accepts her brother's challenge to join them for a wilderness
canoe trip in Minnesota-Canada Boundary Waters. It is a
true wilderness. And Ryan is betting that Chrissy won't
survive one day. The trip will be ruined. Or, will it. . . ?

Healing Voyage by Diann Hunt
Victoria Chaney is looking forward to a summer of rubbing
elbows with the rich and influential of the medical field.
She is furious when her parents force her to take a term
aboard the mission ship, *Providence*, in the Philippines. She
finds herself partnered with Dr. Benjamin Meyer and nursing the poorest people she has ever known. A haunting vow
and recurring nightmares cast a shadow upon the handsome doctor, while Victoria's selfishness forces her into a
surprising decision.

LOVE AFLOAT

*Drifting Hearts Find Safe Harbor
in Four Romantic Novellas*

Kimberley Comeaux
Linda Goodnight
JoAnn A. Grote
Diann Hunt

BARBOUR BOOKS
An Imprint of Barbour Publishing, Inc.

The Matchmakers ©2001 by Kimberley Comeaux.
Troubled Waters ©2001 by Linda Goodnight.
By the Silvery Moon ©2001 by JoAnn A. Grote.
Healing Voyage ©2001 by Diann Hunt.

Illustrations by Mari Goering.

ISBN 1-58660-134-2

Published by Barbour Books, an imprint of Barbour Publishing, Inc., P.O. Box 719, Uhrichsville, Ohio 44683, www.barbourbooks.com.

 Member of the
Evangelical Christian
Publishers Association

Printed in the United States of America.
5 4 3

LOVE AFLOAT

The Matchmakers

by Kimberley Comeaux

Dedication

To Kristy Kennedy, my sister and friend.

Chapter 1

Seven days suddenly seems like seven years, Magnolia "Maggie" Weston thought as she followed her two elderly great-aunts onto the large cruise ship. While they were precious women and Maggie loved them dearly, she didn't know how much of their constant chatter she could take.

So far she'd heard them read through the cruise itinerary three times, their packing list twice because they were sure that they had forgotten something, and finally the inventory of the medications they'd brought along—just in case they caught a tropical illness or got seasick.

All she wanted to do was take one of the many novels she'd brought along, find a nice quiet place to read, and get a little sun.

Maggie lifted her face into the ocean air, letting the salty breeze fluff her medium-length, light brown hair. She was there to watch after the aunts and relax. . .but obviously, the aunts had other plans.

"Oh, Amelia, I heard they had shuffleboard. How long has it been since we played, Dear?" Aunt Isabel asked her sister. Both she and Amelia were dressed similarly in their "cruise wear" of bright print blouses and culottes. Perched smartly on their stylish, gray hair were green sun visors.

"I think the last time was in '41, right before the Pearl Harbor incident. It was at that country club down in Minden. Remember all the fun we had there before it was struck down by that tornado in '49? But anyway, I had a mind to wander up to the Ping-Pong tables in the game room."

"Oh, for heaven's sakes, Amelia! You can hardly walk, much less run around, trying to hit a little ball. Tell her, Magnolia—remind her of her arthritis!"

Maggie raised her eyebrows with interest. "Why Aunt Amelia, I didn't know you'd ever played Ping-Pong."

She sniffed. "I haven't, but I have a mind to try it out."

"We'll see, Sister. We'll see," Isabel told her with exasperation. "We haven't asked Magnolia what she wants to do. I just know you'll want to swim in that beautiful pool we saw in the brochure, or maybe you'll want to visit the art exhibit that's featured on board."

Maggie quickly shook her head as she adjusted the strap of her carry-on bag. "Oh, no. Don't you two worry about me. You just go and have fun."

Her aunt Amelia turned and smiled at her sweetly. "Of course we worry about you, Dear. We're not going to let you just sit around reading. You're here with us to have fun!"

Maggie blinked. "How did you know that's what I planned to do?"

Amelia patted her on the shoulder. "We know you, Dear. It's our mission to help you get out of your shell on this trip. You stay in that bookstore of yours, day in and day out, and you never have fun."

Maggie was about to protest that she had to work hard to make her bookstore and coffee shop a success, but they'd reached the information desk. They found out where their cabin was located, and with key cards in hand, they were on their way. But something about what the lady behind the desk had told them unsettled Maggie.

"Uh, Aunt Isabel, what did she mean when she asked if you were with the Cottonridge Baptist Group?"

Isabel shrugged nonchalantly. "Oh, she means our little senior women's group. There are about ten of us in all who signed up. We'll meet them later."

Now Maggie was very confused. . .and a little suspicious. "I thought I was here to look after you! If you have eight friends here, why did you ask me to come?"

Isabel gave her sister a conspiring look. "Did we say that we needed looking after?"

"Well, no. . .but—"

Amelia looked wide-eyed and innocent. "Why, I don't think we've been looked after since our husbands passed on, have we, Sister?"

"Not that I recall, unless you want to count the time that you had your gallbladder taken out, and you were in the hospital, and—"

"Then why am I here?" Maggie interjected, confused.

"To have fun!" the aunts replied together as they pulled her down the narrow passageway.

Maggie wondered for a moment if her aunts were plotting something, but she quickly dismissed the idea. What could they possibly be up to anyway? They were on a cruise ship in Ft. Lauderdale, about to sail to the Caribbean for seven days. They certainly couldn't involve her in their matchmaking activities again. Their last attempt three months ago had been such a failure, they hadn't even tried to attempt another match.

It hadn't been their fault, not really. The plan might have met with success if it had been anybody but Reverend Devin Tanner, their new pastor.

As a pastor's daughter, Maggie endured a childhood that had been anything but happy. Her father was a dedicated, loving pastor to his congregation—so much so, that he had little time to spend with his own family. He'd loved them, Maggie knew, but he just never realized how he neglected them. He still didn't. All her life, she'd craved his attention and was disappointed time and time again when he put church over her. She knew it was hard on her mother, too.

That's why she'd quit going to her home church the moment the church voted in Devin Tanner as their pastor.

She was attracted to him. She wouldn't be surprised if half the females in the congregation were attracted to the gorgeous man. Devin was movie-star handsome. He had short, dark brown hair and light hazel eyes. What made him even more attractive was that he didn't even seem to realize it. In the pulpit, he seemed confident but not full of himself. There was no boastfulness laced in his sermons, only sincerity.

He was a nice man—that was obvious; but when Maggie went up to shake his hand, she'd known that she was in trouble. Their gazes clashed, and for a brief moment, Maggie had been unable to look away. She'd felt an emotion so strong, she'd dropped his hand like a hot potato and run from the building.

No way was she going to be involved with a preacher. That was the only promise she'd ever made herself—and one she was going to keep!

That was why she'd acted so badly when the aunts had arranged a matchmaking dinner at their house, surprising her by adding the new pastor on the guest list. She'd been distant and cool. When he'd asked her why she hadn't been to the church in awhile, she'd retorted that it was because of him. She didn't think the church should have brought a Northerner from Indiana to pastor a Southern church. She'd told him that Cottonridge, Louisiana, was a Southern town and only another Southerner could reach the people and help the church grow.

Later, as she reflected on the evening, she'd cringed at her inane comments. He probably thought she'd been slightly nuts as she attacked him on something so ridiculous as being a Northerner! But it was all she could think of, and it had done the job she'd wanted.

He never tried to call her. In fact, when she saw him once in the grocery store, he only said a quick hello before turning the other direction. From then on, she made a point of staying away from him.

Why did such a nice man have to be involved in the ministry? Even if he was a nice person, he'd always put the church first and his family second. That was the way it worked, she'd observed.

But that was all in the past, thankfully! Since her outburst had gotten her aunts to stop their matchmaking, the embarrassing episode had been worth it. It was probably just her imagination that they were up to something.

Whom would they fix her up with, anyway? They didn't even know any men on this ship, so she felt confident nothing would happen.

The trio arrived at their cabin and, just as Maggie knew they would, her aunts began to complain about the smallness of the quarters. Maggie had tried to warn them, but all they'd seen in the brochure was probably the most expensive suite the cruise line sold. Their budget allowed for only one upgrade, and that hadn't meant a whole lot.

While they were in the midst of unpacking, a knock sounded at the door. Isabel opened it. Several of her friends from church waited on the other side. "You girls unpack later. Let's go up for lunch. You should see the buffet!" an excited voice invited from the doorway.

"Sounds like a plan!" Isabel told her, then turned to look at Maggie and Amelia. "You girls hungry?"

Amelia, who had an obsession with neatness, started to protest, but Maggie took her by the arm. "Come on, Aunt Amelia. This can wait for at least an hour. I've heard your stomach growling, so I know you're hungry."

Amelia looked at Maggie pertly. "I beg your pardon, Missy. My stomach does not growl. That must have been Isabel!"

The two aunts squabbled back and forth as they gathered their purses. Maggie finally ushered them out of the small cabin. Waiting for them were eight elderly ladies who were all dressed up for their summer holiday. One of them even had some sort of tropical straw hat with grapes wrapped around the brim. All of them were beaming with anticipation.

"Isn't this glorious? Why, I know we're going to have

such a marvelous time," Thelma Greenbaum declared. "And we're glad that you were able to join us, Maggie."

Maggie smiled. "Thanks, Miss Thelma. I have to admit, though, that I feel like I'm crashing your party."

Bertha Johnson waved her bejeweled hand, dismissing Maggie's statement. "Don't worry about that, Dear. We brought someone along so you won't feel so out of place."

Surprised, Maggie looked at her aunts, who smiled back at her innocently. "You did? Who?"

"Thelma, why don't you knock on his cabin door and see if he's ready to go to lunch?" Bertha directed, ignoring her question.

He? Wait a minute! Maggie continued to stare at her aunts and realized their faces didn't look quite so innocent as she'd thought. She was just about to ask whom they were talking about when a cabin door down the way opened. Out walked a tall, dark-haired man.

Maggie was no longer surprised. She was stunned. "You brought your pastor?" she managed to whisper in an anxious voice.

"Didn't we mention that?" Isabel asked her while Amelia pretended to be thinking about it.

Maggie put her hands on her hips and glared at them. "You know you didn't," she hissed.

She looked back up as Reverend Devin Tanner came toward them. She wondered just what part he had to play in all this. Was this his idea? That thought was quickly dismissed the moment he looked up and into her eyes.

Devin Tanner, the too-handsome bachelor preacher who had been in Maggie's thoughts more than he should have, actually scowled at her. "What are you doing here?" he demanded as the ladies all gasped at his reaction.

Yes, this certainly was going to be a long cruise.

Chapter 2

As soon as those incredulous words left Devin's mouth, he immediately wished he could take them back. He hadn't meant to blurt out the first thing that popped into his mind, but he'd been so stunned to see Maggie Weston standing there in front of him. What was she doing on the ship?

In the midst of all his confusing thoughts, he suddenly noticed the shocked gazes of the women as they stared at him with open mouths.

"Uh. . .I mean. . ." He began trying to explain himself out of the weird situation. When he saw Maggie, who had insulted him on more than one occasion, standing there with a frown on her face as if she were displeased with seeing him, he stopped stammering.

"What I meant to say was, Maggie, I'm surprised to see you on board. Are you here to see your aunts off?" he asked, not able to disguise the hope in his voice.

"No, I'm going on the cruise." She didn't look happy about it.

Neither was he. "Oh. . .I mean, oh! That's just great." *So much for having a good time.*

"Maggie, we know you work so hard and rarely get out, and we've also noticed the same with our dear pastor, so we put our heads together and. . ." Aunt Isabel's sentence drifted away as she shrugged her shoulders.

"So you thought you'd 'help' us. Is that it, ladies?" Maggie asked, her eyes narrowed. She crossed her arms and tapped her fingertips on her arm.

She really was a beautiful woman. Light brown hair framed her small features, and her remarkable pale blue eyes seemed to flash like silver but hinted at hidden depths. She wore a green sleeveless blouse with white walking shorts, and he couldn't help but notice how the clothes showed off her tanned arms and legs.

As he admired her, Devin wondered again what it was that made her dislike him so much. He'd gotten along with women all his life—sometimes too much! He'd avoided more than one marriage-minded lady simply because he'd never met anyone he knew he could spend the rest of his life with. He knew God would lead him to that person. He just had to be patient.

But any kind of patience was hard to have with this lady! She'd never even given him a chance to like her. To make matters worse, he had the feeling that he could have come to like her—very much. It wasn't just her good looks that attracted him. No, there was something else. . . a connection that seemed to spark between them when they'd first met. A recognition he'd never felt with another woman.

Obviously, it was one-sided.

Well, he wasn't about to have his company pushed on her, no matter how well meaning the ladies were.

"Uh, ladies. . .I don't think—" he began but was interrupted.

"Now, we ain't on this here cruise to think," Bertha declared, her long, rhinestone earrings making a clinking noise as she shook her head. "Didn't you ever watch *The Love Boat?* Love could be waiting around the corner for all of us!"

"Oh, for goodness' sakes, Bertha! You aren't talking about yourself, are ya?" Shirley Banks piped in, her face drawn in her usual disapproving frown. Shirley generally disapproved of everything, but nobody paid her opinions much attention. They knew deep down inside, she had a good heart. It just took awhile, sometimes, to see it.

Bertha merely looked at her friend in an I-know-something-you-don't sort of way. "Love can happen at eighty-two as well as twenty-two."

Amelia sighed loudly. "Well, at the moment, I'm more concerned about hunger than love. Are we going to eat or begin writing love sonnets?"

Apparently hunger was more important, because the ladies all started moving down the hallway so quickly, Devin and Maggie suddenly found themselves standing in the hallway alone.

Determined to be a gentleman even if it killed him, Devin smiled at her. "They're a lively group, aren't they?" he commented, picking a neutral subject.

She looked at him nervously. "That's a nice way to put it, I guess. I would call them sneaky!"

Was she always this uptight, or was it just when she was in his presence? He was sure that under normal cir-cumstances, he would know the answer to that question, but at the moment, he wasn't thinking straight about any-thing. He shook his head. "Did they do something to get you upset?"

She rolled her eyes. "They are trying to fix us up."

Now he understood. It wasn't anything to be upset over. They were just well-meaning ladies who were trying to help them out. . .no matter how misdirected they were. "And this upsets you?"

She pursed her lips and raised a knowing brow. "I don't mean to hurt your feelings and I'm sure you're a nice per-son and all, but we just wouldn't suit."

He looked at the color blooming in her cheeks and noticed her growing agitation. "You don't think so?" he asked, playing along just to see what else she'd reveal.

Maggie pushed her hair behind her ears. "Uh. . .no. So you see, I'm just going to see if I can get some of my money back and let you all go on this cruise without me," she told him as she began backing up in the hallway. "Since you're here, they really don't need me."

He stood there as she gave him a cheerful smile and started to turn. "Oh, I see," he commented in a noncha-lant tone.

She whirled back around. "What does that mean?"

He shrugged. "You're worried that the ladies might succeed in their matchmaking."

Her eyes widened with indignation, and he wondered again what it was about him that stressed her out so much. "That's ridiculous!" Maggie sputtered. "That would never cross my mind, much less worry me."

It crossed my mind, Devin thought as he tried not to be offended by her outburst. "Why don't we get something to eat, then I promise you won't have to talk to me for the rest of the trip. It's a big ship. We won't even have to see one another."

The expression that fell over her pretty features made Devin suddenly rethink how he perceived her. It was a look that said that she was sorry for having made him think she didn't like him. In fact, she looked like she was going to cry.

"I'm so sorry, Reverend Tanner. I didn't mean for you to think I—I mean, I didn't. . . ," she stammered, trying to explain herself.

"Want to be seen in my presence?" he finished for her with a gentle grin.

She bit her lip with a worried expression. "I've made a mess of this," she mumbled, more to herself than to him.

He didn't really understand exactly what she meant, but he promised himself that he'd get the whole story later. Right now, he wanted to smooth over the situation and start all over with her.

"Listen—why don't we begin again?" He smiled warmly at her and held out his hand. "Hello, Miss Weston. It's good to see you."

She laughed softly, the worry lines falling from her face. "Hello, Reverend Tanner," she returned his greeting and put her hand in his. "It's good to see you, too."

The feel of her hand made his heart race and for a moment, he could do nothing but stare at her with wonder.

"Reverend?"

Her soft voice shook him out of his stupor. His grip tightened slightly on her small hand. "May I escort you to the lunch buffet?" It was the first thing that popped into his mind.

She seemed just as flustered as he, because she pulled her hand from his and backed up a couple of steps. "Uh. . . sure." She looked everywhere but at him. Then, ignoring the offer of his arm, she whirled around and headed down the passageway.

Thinking for the umpteenth time that he wished he could figure her out, he ran to catch up with her.

Magnolia knew the minute she touched his hand she was in trouble. Then, when he'd looked at her, she knew she was in double trouble because he had felt it, too. It was there in his beautiful hazel eyes and in the small smile that lingered around his mouth.

This was why she had made it a point to stay away from him. This was why she had tried to make him dislike her at the dinner get-together at her aunts' house.

He was special and kind and handsome and all of the things she looked for in a man, but he was wrong for her. His occupation made those good qualities worthless.

She would not—could not—get involved with a preacher.

God surely must be disappointed in her. She had been raised with the knowledge that God had her future in His control as long as she let Him lead and guide her decisions. But just as sure as she knew it, she knew she wouldn't pray about her budding feelings for the Reverend Devin Tanner.

She was afraid of what He would tell her in her heart. She was afraid He wanted her future to include this handsome man with the compassionate eyes.

She couldn't take that chance.

She'd ignored the feelings that squeezed at her heart

when she'd first met him, and she'd go on ignoring them. It was just going to a be lot harder to do with both of them on the ship. . .no matter how many decks the ship boasted.

What could she do? Assuming he held any romantic interest in her was silly. The poor man had only smiled at her, not asked her out on a date!

Maggie felt better and decided to slow down and let him walk beside her. She would be his friend. Why not? He seemed like a nice guy, and she didn't have a lot of friends. That way, she could go back to her church since she had not found one she liked as well and have little chats with him every now and then.

She looked over at him and gave a breezy, approachable smile that any friend would give another. He looked momentarily stunned, then gave her a grin that made her heart drop to her stomach.

She stopped smiling and sped up, leaving him behind once again. It wasn't going to work. No way could she be "just friends" with Devin Tanner. He was just too—too manly or. . .something.

When Maggie entered a companionway she knew they'd already gone down, she realized she hadn't even thought to ask where the dining room was. She stopped suddenly and Devin walked up beside her.

"If you're tired of touring the ship, I can show you where the buffet is."

She glanced to see if he was being sarcastic, but he was just standing there with his hands on his hips, smiling his usual good-natured smile.

He probably thought she was nuts. Well, if she was nuts, he was making her that way! She was normally a rational, practical human being.

Maggie sighed as she watched him take a map of the ship from the back pocket of his khaki shorts. He glanced around to get his bearings, then pointed to the companionway to the right of him.

She was just about to dart ahead of him when he caught her hand. "I think I'd better lead," he said evenly as he pulled her after him.

"Hey, wait a minute!" she huffed. "I don't need you to hold my hand." She tried to pull it away, but he held fast.

"I don't want you to get lost."

She opened her mouth to protest, but then shut it. She actually did need help finding the buffet, after all.

If she really was being honest with herself, she would have to admit that holding his hand felt. . .nice. Well, she might as well enjoy it right now, because after lunch, she planned on avoiding him like the plague for the rest of the cruise.

For her own self-preservation, she couldn't spend any more time in the too-handsome pastor's presence!

Chapter 3

Now if she could only make her aunts and the rest of the crafty ladies believe that!

They'd saved them seats in the dining area. Of course, the seats were beside each other. She sat down and Devin followed. Everything was going well for about ten minutes, and then the matchmaking started. Maggie should have known the old ladies wouldn't give them a break, not even for lunch.

"Pastor Devin, have you been to Maggie's bookstore? Why, it's the best place to pick up a cup of coffee and the latest best-seller!" Aunt Amelia asked, then threw an obvious wink to Aunt Isabel.

It was so obvious what they were about to do, Maggie wanted to hide under the table. Devin threw a humored glance her way and looked back at Amelia. "I'm sorry to say that I haven't, but I've heard it's a great bookstore."

"Oh, it is, and she has a good selection of religious books and Bibles, too," Thelma chimed in.

Devin nodded his head politely while wiping his mouth. "That's good to know."

"I'm sure he's already got a good bookstore he likes to

go to, Miss Thelma," Maggie said quickly, then tried to change the subject. "Tell me what you ladies have planned this afternoon."

"Actually, I don't really like driving an hour to Shreveport just to get a few books. I just didn't realize you sold Christian books, Maggie. That would be a big help to me."

Maggie saw genuine interest in his eyes. "I can also order books, too, if you don't see what you need. Several pastors in town order books from my store, and I always try to keep the latest ones available."

Sitting this close to him, she noticed his eyes had beautiful gold flecks. What was she thinking? Who cared what his eyes looked like?

She started to look away, but he smiled at her again, and she found herself responding. His grin could stop traffic during rush hour! She couldn't even remember what they'd been talking about.

"I'll definitely stop by, then, when we get back."

"Huh?" She suddenly realized he'd said something and she hadn't heard a word. "Uh, I'm sorry. What did you say?"

She heard a sound coming from the ladies. When she glanced at them, she realized they were actually giggling. Giggling! Even Devin appeared to be trying to keep a straight face. Was she doomed to be constantly embarrassed on this trip?

"He said he'd come to see you at your store when y'all got back," Bertha supplied helpfully.

Maggie took a deep breath. "Thank you, Miss Bertha."

"Did you know, Maggie, Pastor Devin loves historical things like you do," Isabel informed her, throwing her sister another wink.

Devin cleared his throat for a moment, but Maggie could swear he was trying to cough back a laugh.

Despite her discomfort, she was also intrigued. Not many people were interested in history. She was an avid reader and researcher of all kinds of history, including Bible history. Every time she attempted to discuss this with others, they would get a glazed look in their eyes, and the subject would quickly come to a close. If he liked history as much as she did, what fun it would be to get into a discussion about the past with him!

"What kind of history are you interested in?" she asked, curiously.

He looked intrigued, himself. He thought for a minute. "I read a lot of Bible history, of course, but I'm also fascinated with English history. I lived in England for a bit, helping out a small church outside of Manchester. I spent all the spare time I had touring old ruins and hearing folktales from the locals."

Her eyes lit up. "No way! I love English history! I've always wanted to go to England."

"You'd love it. I remember this one abbey that—"

"Well, I guess we'll just leave y'all to your discussion," Isabel interrupted. "We've got things to do, decks to tour!" All the other ladies murmured various agreements as they got up from the table.

"Oh! Wait! I'll go with you," Maggie said as she rose.

Two sets of hands from Isabel, sitting beside her, and Bertha, standing behind Devin, pushed her back down. They certainly were a lot stronger than they looked!

"No, no! I'm sure we're not doing anything that would be any fun to young folks like you!" Bertha declared, putting on her rhinestone-studded sunglasses.

Maggie looked around nervously. "But. . ."

"See you after awhile, Dear!"

"Yes, we'll catch up with y'all later."

"Why don't you two take a tour of your own?"

"Bye now!"

Leaving only a trail of Cinnabar perfume behind them, they disappeared into the crowd.

"They never have seemed that much in a hurry at church," he marveled. "It usually takes them forever to clear out of the sanctuary on Sunday mornings. I think they wait all week to talk to each other and save it all for after the sermon!"

"Ah, but when they're on a mission, there's no stopping them. They're about as subtle as bulldozers! Did you see that wink Aunt Isabel and Aunt Amelia were passing each other?"

They both laughed.

"I think you're right about them trying to fix us up," he admitted after awhile.

Her eyes widened as she looked at him. "You didn't believe it?"

He shrugged. "I wanted to give them the benefit of the doubt."

She shook her head. "You just haven't known them very long. Give it time, and you'll find out all their devious ways, too."

He grinned. "Well, I'm sure I will. I plan to be at Cottonridge Baptist for a long time."

They were silent for awhile as they ate their lunch. Maggie kept glancing at him from the corner of her eye, and she caught him doing the same thing.

Why was this man so fascinating? Why did he have to be so handsome and nice?

After she took the last bite of dessert, she sat back and took a cooling sip of her iced tea. She tried to appear calm, but she was desperately trying to think of an excuse to leave his company. She knew they were both feeling the pressure from the ladies, and she didn't want him to think he had to hang around her.

"Well, I guess I'll finish unpacking. It was nice talking to you." She jumped up from the table.

He stood also, throwing his napkin down over his plate. "Aw, you can do that later, can't you? Why don't we take a walk and see what's on this big ship?"

Maggie's hand sought her necklace, and she toyed with the charm. "Uh, that's not necessary. The aunts read me the brochure many times, so I know what's on it." She backed up. "Besides, I don't want to monopolize your time."

He nodded but was looking at her with those golden-green eyes that seemed to see right through her. "Maggie, I don't know a soul on this ship, aside from the ladies. From whom would you be monopolizing my time?"

"Spending quality time with yourself, after spending so much time with your congregation?" she asked hopefully.

He chuckled and continued to look at her. "Are you running scared again, Maggie?"

He was too insightful for his own good, but she wasn't about to admit it. "Now what would I be afraid of?" she asked with as much bravado as she could muster.

"Now that's a question I would love to have the answer to." He pushed his chair back under the table. "Is it the same reason you left the church?"

She did not want to get into that particular discussion. "Feeling insecure, Reverend Tanner?" she shot back quickly, her chin lifting in a defensive gesture.

He didn't seem to take it offensively. "I'm just concerned. I have a feeling that with you, Maggie Weston, there is more than meets the eye."

Feeling way out of her league, she blurted out the first thing that popped into her mind. "Aren't we supposed to be walking?"

From the way his eyes widened, she suspected she'd surprised him. Well, that was good, because she'd surprised herself!

"I thought you didn't want to go walking," he answered, perplexed.

"Well, I changed my mind."

He shook his head and chuckled. "Okay." He held out his hand to her. "Ready to go?"

She picked the map of the ship off of the table where he'd set it and slapped it in his waiting palm. "Lead the way."

He laughed again and together they walked from the dining room.

↙

From an upper deck, the Cottonridge ladies watched the couple as they walked around the deck below.

Amelia, the one holding the binoculars, was reporting the details while the rest leaned as far as they could over the railing. "There they are! I told you this was going to work. Look how they keep glancing at one another."

"Oh, fiddlesticks!" Shirley chimed in as she squinted to get a better look. "He's looking at some paper, and she's just nodding her head at something he's saying. That don't mean nothing!"

"Well, that's because you ain't seeing what I'm seeing since I've got the binoculars!" Amelia scoffed as she adjusted the dial to focus them better. "Oh my! Look at that!"

"What? What did they do?" Bertha asked, looking over Amelia's shoulder.

"I'll bet he's giving her a kiss!" Dolly cried with a sigh, being the hopeless romantic that she was.

Isabel rolled her eyes and tried to pull the binoculars out of Amelia's hands. "Are you going to hog these all afternoon?"

Amelia nudged her sister out of the way, ignoring her question. "They aren't kissing, not yet, Dolly—but they have gotten a lot closer. He just patted the side of her arm."

Isabel shook her head. "And that's something to get excited over?"

"Well, it's something! She wouldn't even talk about him before today. Remember how we would keep trying to bring him up in the conversation and she would always ignore it?"

"Her father, our nephew, did that to her. She thinks all preachers are going to be like he is. I should have paid more attention to that boy when he was growing up. Our brother, may he rest in peace, spoiled him rotten and didn't teach him about the importance of family," Isabel commented.

"Well, we're just going to have to find some way of proving to her that he's not like that. But how?" Thelma strummed her fingers on the railing.

"I know, I know." Bertha shoved her glittery sunglasses

on top of her permed hairdo and waved her hands about excitedly.

All that sparkling blinded Amelia for a moment since she'd turned and was now looking at Bertha through the binoculars. "Gracious, Bertha! Can't you tone down the jewels for the cruise? There is just too much for the sun to reflect on. I can't see nothing but spots now!" Amelia cried, while rapidly blinking her eyes.

"If you'd have handed over the binoculars when I asked for them, you'd have been all right," Isabel told her righteously with a sniff.

"Could y'all be quiet for a moment and let Bertha tell us what's on her mind," Shirley ordered sternly.

"Yes, Bertha, tell us!" they all called out.

Bertha, who loved to be the center of attention, paused a bit just to bask in it for a moment. "Weeelll, it's like this. . . ."

All the ladies huddled together in a circle as Bertha unfolded her plan. When she was finished, everyone seemed thoughtful.

"That doesn't sound like a very good plan to me," Shirley commented negatively to no one's surprise.

"Do you have a better one?" Bertha asked with hands on hips.

Shirley, as well as the rest of the group, couldn't seem to top Bertha's plan, so they all agreed.

"We'll put our plan in motion tonight. We'll start out subtle, then work up to heavy duty as the cruise progresses," Bertha instructed.

Everyone nodded in agreement, then seeing motion off the balcony, Amelia whipped out her binoculars again.

"Oh, no! The couple just headed starboard! Come on, ladies, before they're out of our range!"

Shirley looked confused. "What in the world is 'starboard'?"

Isabel shook her head. "Amelia has been staying up late at night watching those old navy movies again on the classics movie channel. You don't have to know what she's talking about. Just follow her."

"Humpf!" Shirley snorted. "Silliest thing I ever heard. Hey wait up for me!" She walked quickly after the group, which was already on the move.

Chapter 4

D evin had just taken a seat at the dinner table with the ladies when he noticed that Maggie was not among them. For a moment, he was angry. He'd been so sure she'd gotten over whatever hang-up she had about him after the fun afternoon they'd shared together. Although they'd not really talked about personal things, they'd kept up a light, easy banter as they toured the ship.

He'd gotten the feeling that Maggie actually liked him, just a little. He knew he was beginning to like her a lot! He took a few deep breaths to bring his temper under control. He was jumping to conclusions. Maybe she was just late.

Suddenly, Devin became aware of all the whispering going on around him. The ladies seemed anxious about something, and since they kept taking peeks at him, he assumed that he was the topic of their conversation.

"Is something the matter, ladies?"

Ten pairs of eyes suddenly blinked at him with studied innocence, their faces as unreadable as blank pages.

"Whatever do you mean, Pastor?" Thelma spoke first.

Devin had to work hard not to smile. "I just wondered what the whispering was about. All of you seem upset."

"It's my niece!" Amelia blurted out. "She's not feeling very well."

From the worried looks of the faces around him, he got the impression that she must have come down with something serious—but how did she get so sick so fast? He just left her a couple of hours ago. She'd been fine then. He became worried, too. "Where is she? Is she with the ship's doctor?"

"She ain't—" Isabel started to say but was interrupted by her sister.

"She's lying down on a deck chair right outside the cabin. The doctor said that fresh air would help."

"So, she did see the doctor?" Devin wanted to clarify.

"Just to get some—"

"Oh, yes!" Amelia interrupted her sister again, ignoring the frown Isabel was throwing her way.

Devin was really worried about Maggie. Without thinking, he scraped his chair back and stood up. "Maybe I'll go check on her."

"Oh, that's a good idea, Pastor. She'd appreciate it. I know she would," Bertha told him, waving her bejeweled hand at him.

Just as he was walking away from the table, he heard Bertha whisper louder than he imagined she wanted to, "This is even better than my original plan!"

Devin had a sneaking suspicion the ladies were up to something, but he was too worried about Maggie to dwell on it.

This afternoon had been one of the more enjoyable times he'd spent with a woman. Sure, he'd dated every now and then, but not since he'd been at Cottonridge, and he'd always made a point of not dating women of his congregation simply because it could become too complicated if it didn't work out.

He'd been so busy at the church lately, he'd not even thought about dating. Okay, maybe he'd thought about it a little when he'd met Maggie Weston, and he might have even bent his rules for her had she stayed at his church. But her attitude toward him and blatant dislike quickly made him change his mind.

This afternoon, however, she'd been nice and friendly. She still seemed a little nervous around him, but that seemed to ease as the afternoon wore on. He even imagined that she might be interested in him. Many times, he caught her glancing at him, but she'd quickly look away.

He knew because he'd been doing the same thing!

He prayed as he raced down the steps to the lower deck that God would touch her and make her better. He prayed that it was nothing serious.

Devin found Maggie tucked away in a quiet corner of the deck. A book was lying open against her chest, her eyes closed. For a moment, he slowed his steps and simply looked at her. The wind was ruffling through her layered tresses and the setting sun was putting a soft glow on her pretty features.

Devin smiled to himself and thought for the umpteenth time since the cruise began that he was quickly becoming besotted with this Southern belle.

Shaking himself out of his thoughts, he walked up to her and called her name. When she didn't respond, he put a hand to her forehead. She felt cool. In fact, she wasn't pale or sickly looking at all.

He frowned. Was this all a charade?

She stirred and slowly opened her eyes. After a moment of getting her bearings, she focused on him. A look of pure pleasure was her first reaction as a smile curved her lips. It totally took his breath away. Then, a guarded expression clouded her features.

So, she was still building walls against him, he thought with a sigh. But the first look told him what she wanted to feel. It told him that she wanted to like him. He had six whole days of the cruise to convince her. He was going to make sure none of that time was wasted.

"Hi, Devin. What are you doing down here?" she asked while pushing her hair back from her face.

"I heard you weren't feeling well. I thought I'd come down and check on you." He pulled another chair closer and sat down beside her.

She laughed self-consciously. "I'm afraid I'm simply seasick. I had read in one of my travel books that it doesn't normally occur on cruise ships, but obviously they were wrong. As soon as I shut myself up in the cabin, I felt sick. It doesn't seem to bother me as long as I'm outdoors, though."

Devin instantly felt relieved. "That's good. . .I mean. . . it's not good that you feel bad, but good that it's nothing serious."

"I had worried that I'd gotten food poisoning or something. The doctor gave me some medicine, and now I feel fine."

"That's great!" He suddenly got an idea. "Hey, why don't I call up for a tray of food to be sent down here? We can have a picnic on the deck."

She smiled, her eyes sparkling. "That sounds wonderful!"

He was about to go to his cabin and call when Bertha came scurrying over to them. "Oh, Pastor, I was wondering when you were coming back up to the dining room?"

"Hi, Bertha. I won't be coming back up tonight. Maggie and I are going to eat down here."

Bertha frowned for a moment. "But we want you to eat with us!"

Devin looked at her with surprise. Hadn't they wanted him to spend time with Maggie? "Well, Bertha, aren't you ladies about through eating anyway?"

"Join us for dessert, then!"

Bertha had him baffled. He gave Maggie a questioning look, wondering if she knew what was going on.

She smiled at him. "Oh, go ahead, Devin. I'll be fine."

He shrugged, regretting that he was going to miss their picnic. "Will you take a walk with me afterward?"

Maggie shook her head. "I'm going to make it an early night tonight."

He looked back at Bertha. "Let's go eat dessert, Miss Bertha." He held out his arm to her.

Instead of taking it, she slapped it away. "I understand if you can't come, Pastor. I'll just tell the ladies!" she said loudly.

Now he was really confused. "But I just said I would come."

"Of course I realize you need to be with Maggie, as ill as she is!" she declared even louder.

"But she's not—"

Bertha grabbed him by the arm and pulled him closer

to her. "Would you just go along with the plan? I didn't think you'd make this so difficult!"

He shook his head. "What plan?"

Bertha sighed with exaggerated exasperation. "We're trying to get you two together, so just go along!"

"Then why did you ask me to go and eat with you?" he asked, perplexed.

"You were supposed to say that you'd rather stay with Maggie!" she whispered.

"I would have rather stayed with Maggie, but you insisted!" he whispered back.

"What are you two talking about?" Maggie asked from her chair.

Bertha looked around Devin and smiled brilliantly at her. "Oh, nothing, Dear! Go back to resting!"

She turned back to Devin. "Whoever asks you to do something, just say no, all right?"

For the life of him, Devin couldn't figure out what Bertha meant, but he wasn't going to argue. His picnic with Maggie would take place after all. He wasn't going to complain!

"All right, Miss Bertha," he said aloud and watched as she walked away.

"You're not going?" Maggie asked.

He turned back to her. "No, she decided she didn't need me."

It was Maggie's turn to look confused. "Then why did she come down here?"

He shrugged. "I have no idea." He walked back toward her. "I'll go and call the dining room. I guess we're going to have a picnic after all."

Before they'd even taken their first bite of food, another of the ladies appeared. Dolly, with her fruit-decked hat bobbing about on her head, came running up to them.

"Hi, Maggie." She then looked at Devin. "Pastor, I need your help with something. Oh my! Y'all are having a picnic! How romantic."

Devin paused a minute trying to remember what she'd said first. "Dolly, what's the matter?"

Dolly smiled at Maggie, then focused b..ck on Devin. "We need you to show us where the musical is playing. The theater is supposed to be on the Bahamas Deck, but we can't seem to locate it. Could you help us?"

Maggie was a little confused as to why Dolly and the ladies needed Devin's help and couldn't ask one of the crew. But, he was, after all, their pastor. They felt comfortable asking him.

She watched Devin start to stand up, but then he suddenly changed his mind and sat back down. Maggie looked at Dolly and saw her expression change.

"I'm sorry, Dolly. I'm having dinner with Maggie, so I can't help you," Devin told her almost hesitantly.

"That's fi—I mean, that's too bad." She shrugged her thin shoulders. "I guess we'll have to make do."

When she'd gone, Maggie turned to Devin. "What was that all about?"

Devin shook his head. "I don't know. I guess they feel dependent on me."

Maggie frowned. "Couldn't you have just helped them find the theater?"

"But I'm having dinner with you."

"Yeah, but—"

She was interrupted as Amelia came walking along the deck. She, too, made a request of Devin, which he declined. It didn't stop there. Every one of the ladies in the Cottonridge Baptist senior ladies group came to Devin, asking him to help them with one thing or another. Each time he told them no! In fact he didn't even hesitate after awhile! He was brisk with his answer and kept on eating.

Maggie had never seen such blatant lack of concern in all her life. These ladies were his responsibility! Couldn't he just pause from his precious meal to help them?

What a snob!

By the time the last lady was refused, Maggie had had enough. She threw down her napkin and stood up, glaring at Devin. "Are all Northern preachers this unconcerned about the people of their church, or do you just fit into that category?" she charged with hands on hips.

Devin looked surprised by her attack. "They didn't really need my help. In fact, I have no idea what's going on with them tonight."

"Maybe if you took the time to go help them, you might find out! Those poor women only needed a little of your time, but you were just too selfish to give it to them!"

With a huff, she grabbed her book from her lounging chair and started off to her cabin.

"But they told me to—"

"I'm through talking to you, Reverend Tanner. Good night!"

"But you don't understand. . ." His voice faded as she entered the companionway, and she was unable to hear his explanation. What did it matter anyway? She saw his true nature tonight and congratulated herself on being right about him in the first place.

To think that she was starting to like him! What in the world was she thinking?

Around the corner, the ladies were standing behind Bertha, who was in charge of the binoculars now, bursting to know what was going on.

"Oh, dear!" Bertha cried softly. "Maggie looks like she's fussing at him about something!"

Amelia crept forward and sneaked a peek. "What could she be mad about? He kept eating with her instead of seeing about us! Isn't that what she wanted?"

Isabel pulled Amelia back. "I knew we were laying it on too thick, sending all of us out there!"

Shirley made a snorting noise. "I didn't think it would work at all!"

"What is she doing now?"

Bertha adjusted the focus a little better. "Pastor Devin is looking really confused, and Maggie just stormed off. This doesn't look good."

The ladies groaned softly. They'd all pinned their hopes on Bertha's scheme.

"Uh oh! Pastor Devin's looking this way. I think he saw me!" Bertha cried while pushing all the ladies behind her back.

Shirley commented, "It's because you're wearing more jewels than what's in the Tower of London! With all those sparkles flying everywhere, it's like the Fourth of July."

"You're just jealous because you can't carry off wearing

jewels like these," Bertha told her, thrusting her chin in the air.

Shirley nodded. "Carry off? I don't have the strength to even carry them! They would weigh me clean down to the floor!"

Thelma quickly intervened. "Now let's not forget to act like the Christian ladies that we are!" She motioned for them all to gather closely. "That plan didn't work. We'll just have to put our heads together and think of another."

Chapter 5

Maggie managed to avoid Devin all day. It hadn't been an easy task, that was for sure! When she'd told her aunts she was going to tour the ship on her own, they'd tried to get her to come with them. Apparently they were involved in a shuffleboard contest, then they were going to tour the art museum.

Maggie felt badly about turning them down, but she also knew her aunts had ulterior motives in asking her to come. They'd talked nonstop last night about how wonderful their pastor was and that he would make any woman a terrific husband. Any woman who had even a morsel of good sense would want him as her beau.

Maggie had kept silent. She didn't want to get into her feelings for the man. She didn't even tell them they'd had a disagreement. No, Maggie just wanted to forget the whole thing and get on with enjoying her cruise. . .alone!

Now, she was doing just what she'd wanted to do in the first place: read her new devotional book in peace. She reclined in a lounging chair on a deck that was filled with sunbathers and those swimming in the crystal blue pool.

She had taken a quick swim, then tied a red sarong

that matched her bathing suit around her waist. Dark glasses protected her eyes from the glare of the sun and her hair was stuffed in a small cap that she used more for disguise than anything else. She hoped she blended in with the other people so much that Devin wouldn't notice her if he came looking for her.

Feeling smug that she'd successfully eluded him for the better part of the day, she breathed deeply, taking in the crisp smell of the ocean air. Sighing with a smile, she turned her attention back to her book. She had just come to the most important point of the chapter when a shadow fell over her pages. She looked up to find Devin Tanner looming over her.

He didn't look very happy.

She tried to pretend that his presence didn't affect her, so with a lift of her chin and a look of pure defiance, she asked, "Can I help you with something?"

He folded his arms over his chest and narrowed his eyes. "I'd like for you to listen to me explain what happened last night."

She turned her attention back to her book. "I think I understand quite enough, so you can save your breath!"

He dragged a chair over to her and sat down. "Maggie, I don't know why you dislike me, but I've accepted it. I'm just going to tell you what happened, and that will be it. You won't have to hide from me anymore."

She lowered her book and was startled to see a resigned sadness in his hazel eyes. She mentally chastised herself. Never had she been this rude to anyone. "I'm sorry, Devin. I didn't mean to speak so hatefully. Tell me what you wanted to say."

He regarded her for a moment. His look seemed to see deep inside her and made her heart beat a little faster.

"They told me to say no to them."

Maggie blinked. "Say no to what?"

"The ladies told me to say no to whatever they asked of me. I think it was another scheme to try to get us together."

Suddenly, Maggie understood. "They wanted me to think that you would keep all your attention on me, no matter how many people pulled at you."

Devin nodded. "Yes, but I don't know why they would think it would help their cause."

Maggie knew. Her aunts must have told the ladies of her fear of dating someone in the ministry, but she couldn't tell Devin that.

Maggie shrugged. "I don't suppose they'll give up trying to pair us off, do you?" she asked, changing the subject.

Devin smiled ruefully and shook his head. "I wouldn't count on it. They seem pretty determined."

Maggie grimaced. "What can we do? There's no telling what they'll come up with next! I can't keep avoiding them the entire cruise!"

Devin looked thoughtful for a moment. "Well, there is one thing that we can do, but I'm not sure you'll like it."

"At this point, I'll do anything."

"We can pretend we're interested in each other."

Maggie was sure she didn't hear him right. "Come again?"

He gave her a knowing smile. "You heard me the first time."

Maggie avoided his eyes by smoothing down the pages

of her book. "But I was sure you must be kidding."

He folded his arms and leaned back in his chair. "All right, let's hear your idea."

"Well, I. . ." She cleared her throat and pursed her lips. "I, uh. . .don't have one."

He didn't say a word but just waited on what she had to say next.

He really didn't have to be so smug about it! What else could they do? Saying yes to his crazy scheme would mean she would be in his presence for more time than she wanted to! That wasn't smart. He was too charming, too nice, too handsome. . . . No, it wasn't smart at all.

She was just about to tell him so, when he suddenly grabbed her hand and kissed it. Her first thought was not to pull her hand away and fuss at him, as it should have been. Instead, she thought that kiss was the nicest she'd ever received, even if it was just on her hand. It gave her a warm, cuddly feeling all the way down to her toes.

"Oh, good! I see you found Magnolia, Pastor!" her aunt Amelia observed as she led the ladies to where they were sitting.

"Why, I didn't know there were gentlemen in the world who still kissed hands," Dolly said with a girlish giggle, causing the bright blue birds on her hat to bob back and forth.

"Oh, I've known from the beginning Pastor Devin was a gentleman! I've told Amelia so several times, haven't I, Sister? I've said Pastor Devin could even be called Southern, he's such a genteel man!" Isabel patted his back and added, "Meaning no disrespect for your Northern roots, of course!"

As the ladies exchanged comments about how much a gentleman their pastor was, the "gentleman" was holding fast to Maggie's hand, despite all her efforts to pull it away.

Worse than that, however, she was upset that the hand-kissing scene had not been for her but for the benefit of the ladies. Apparently, he had decided to implement his harebrained scheme without her permission!

She would set the matter straight!

"Maggie and I have decided to go into Puerto Rico together when the ship docks tomorrow. You ladies won't mind if we tour around without you, will you?" Devin announced before she could utter a single word.

"Wait a minute...." She tried to undo the damage that he was about to do, but nobody seemed to be listening.

"Oh, that's just grand, isn't it, Sister?" Amelia crowed as she clapped her hands together.

"Marvelous, just marvelous, Sister."

"Why don't we go on and leave these two young'uns alone! I think we're cramping their style," Thelma said with a wink to Maggie and Devin.

Maggie frowned. "You don't have to—"

"You ladies could never do that, but we appreciate the time alone just the same. You know how it is when you're trying to get to know one another," Devin said smoothly, casting her a warm loving glance.

He's only pretending. Remember that, Maggie! she told herself.

The ladies made "oohing" and "aahing" sounds as they walked away, their faces all smiles and eyes twinkling. Maggie just knew they were congratulating themselves on a job well done.

What a mess!

Devin knew he was about to be fussed at royally, and Maggie didn't disappoint him. She yanked her hand from his and glared at him over her shades. "I didn't agree to this! Now they think we like each other!"

Devin studied the blush rising on her cheeks and thought that, even angry, she was pretty. "But it's the wisest course of action," he said with a shrug. "I knew you'd eventually agree."

She looked incensed. "I would event—" she sputtered. Then, the hilarity of the situation must have hit her, because she began to laugh. "You are something else, Devin Tanner, do you know that?"

"I don't know if that is a compliment or a cut-down, but I'll just take your word for it, as long as you agree to my plan," he countered with a smile.

Maggie looked down at his hand where it still held her arm gently and then back to him. "Let me just go on record to state that I don't think this is a good idea, but I will do it." She sighed and leaned back in the lounge, pulling her arm from his grasp.

Devin felt elated that she wanted to go along with him. It meant he'd get to spend more time with her. Maybe, just maybe, she'd see that he wasn't a bad guy to get to know. If nothing else, they could come away from this cruise being friends.

"So what do we do now?" he asked as he settled back in his chair beside her.

She put her sunglasses pertly on her nose and lifted her book from her lap. "What I'm going to do right now is finish reading my book. Then you can take me to dinner."

He looked at her as she began reading her book and grinned to himself. "Are you asking me out on a date, Miss Magnolia?"

An eyebrow lifted above the dark sunglasses. "A pretend date. This is all make-believe, remember."

He leaned back in the lounging chair, propping his legs up in a relaxed pose, and closed his eyes. "Of course, it's only pretend," he told her smoothly. But in his heart, he wished the word "pretend" would eventually fade from their vocabulary so he could begin a relationship with this lady who was real. . . .

And possibly make it permanent.

As the ladies made their way to a shuffleboard tournament, Isabel looked at her sister and commented, "Did you buy any of that lovey-dovey talk the pastor was spouting off back there?"

Amelia snorted. "Please, Sister. I may be old and slow, but I'm not senile."

Thelma, who'd been listening to their conversation, decided to put in her opinion. "I think our pastor's interest is real, though. Did you see the way he kept looking at her?"

Shirley frowned. "Did you see the way Magnolia was glaring back at him? It wasn't the look of love, I can assure you of that!"

"Oh, don't be such a naysayer, Shirley. She's just going to take a little convincing, is all!" Isabel contradicted. "Maybe all this 'pretending' to like him will make her realize she really fancies him!"

"Well, they won't pretend as long as we leave them

alone," Amelia commented thoughtfully. "If we stick close to them, they'll have to act like a couple."

Thelma patted Amelia on the back. "I like the way you think, Amelia." She looked to the rest of the group and gathered them around her. "Ladies, our work is not done. Now, Magnolia and Pastor Devin think they'll be alone tomorrow as they tour the island, but I have something else in mind. Now, here's what we're going to do. . . ."

Chapter 6

Maggie stood in front of her mirror and retouched her lipstick for the fifth time. She didn't even wear that much makeup! It was just nerves.

What was it about Devin Tanner that made her this way? With a sigh, she looked down at her outfit and decided her white sundress just wasn't going to do. Maybe she needed something more colorful. Maybe she should go try to buy something new in one of the ship's stores. Maybe...

"My goodness, Magnolia! How long are you going to stay in that bathroom? My bladder isn't what it used to be, you know."

Maggie sighed and opened the bathroom door. Isabel and Amelia both stood there looking at her as she stepped out.

"Uh, Dear? How many outfits did you try on this morning? I surely thought you were wearing Capri pants earlier!" Amelia commented curiously.

Isabel smiled. "It must be love, Sister. Remember the way we were when a new beau came calling? We were simply beside ourselves."

Maggie rolled her eyes. "I'm not in love, and I'm not beside myself. I simply couldn't make up my mind! Didn't you have to go to the bathroom?" she asked pointedly, changing the subject.

"It seems to have passed," Amelia said with a shrug. "Talking about your love life is much more pressing. Are you going to change clothes again, Dear?"

"Of course not," Maggie answered as if that were a silly question to ask. She put on a serene smile and stepped around them to her side of the room. No way was she going to change her dress now.

"Well, you've already changed about fifty times today, and it's not even nine in the morning," Isabel pointed out.

Subtlety was not a strong point where her family was concerned, but Maggie chose to ignore them. Instead, she focused on finding out where they'd be today so she and Devin could be somewhere else!

"What do you ladies have planned today?"

Amelia shrugged her shoulders. "We aren't sure, Dear. We might go into San Juan for a little bit, but I'm not sure all the gals are up for a long walk."

Maggie hid a smile. "Oh, well, that's what Devin and I planned to do—walk, walk, walk! So you definitely wouldn't want to come with us!"

The two aunts looked at one another, then back to Maggie. "I'm sure you're right, Dear. You two lovebirds need time alone anyway," Isabel agreed.

They were being way too accommodating, but Maggie wasn't going to argue. She looked at her watch and realized she was running late.

"I'd better go meet Devin. You both have a good time

and," she looked sternly at them, "stay out of trouble!"

They laughed and assured her they planned to have the time of their lives.

Maggie wondered about that statement as she ran out the door, but not for too long. As always, her thoughts came back to the man she was hurrying to meet.

For one thing, she couldn't believe she had agreed to pretend to be interested in him. What a laugh. She really was interested in him, and that was the problem. This whole plan was about as smart as someone who was afraid of water jumping into roaring rapids and hoping to come out alive.

How was she going to survive being with him for five more days and not fall in love with him? Or was it too late? Had she already started having feelings for him?

Ruminating over and over about it was giving her a headache, so she stopped and took a cleansing breath before she stepped out onto the deck where she knew he was waiting. She could do this—she could! She'd just keep telling herself that she liked him as a friend. That was all!

Then a thought popped into her mind. What if God wanted her to like Devin Tanner? What if he was the man who God wanted for her?

Surely not. But for good measure, she stopped, closed her eyes, and said a little prayer for guidance.

"Are you okay?"

Her eyes flew open and there stood Devin, peering at her curiously. Her cheeks immediately went hot with embarrassment.

"What were you doing?" he asked, his eyes roaming her face.

"Uh. . .why do you ask?" she stammered as she adjusted the strap of her purse on her shoulder.

He shrugged. "It looked like you were praying."

She raised her eyebrows. "Well. . .maybe I need to pray—for my sanity during this silly charade we're trying to play."

"Hey, I'm not saying there's anything wrong with praying. I encourage people to do it regularly. In fact, I would have a lot less counseling to do if folks would talk to God more."

As she listened to him talk, the embarrassment slowly seeped out of her. "You know, you're sure different from a lot of pastors I know," she mused aloud.

He cocked his head to one side. "In what way?"

"You seem—I don't know, more relaxed, I guess. My father would have never taken a week off from his church to cruise the Caribbean."

Devin looked at her with surprise. "Are you saying your father is a minister?"

The minute the words left her mouth, she wanted to drag them back in. What had possessed her to blab about personal stuff like that? She never, ever talked about her father. To anyone.

"Yes," she answered briskly. "Are you ready to go?"

He opened his mouth to say something, but after studying her closed expression, he seemed to change his mind. Instead, he held out his hand. "Sure. There's a boat that takes us to shore every fifteen minutes, so one should be ready to go about now."

For a moment, Maggie nervously stared at Devin's out-stretched hand, but against her better judgment, she found herself reaching out and taking it. A warmth seemed to spread right to her heart as his fingers enclosed her small hand. A rightness and a feeling of being well cared for swirled around in her head as he led her along.

"Do you see them anywhere?" Maggie asked as soon as they disembarked from the boat. Though the ladies hadn't decided whether they wanted to go ashore or not, Maggie wanted to make sure she and Devin wouldn't "accidentally" run into them.

Devin gave the area a brief, unconcerned glance, then turned back to Maggie. "I don't see them," he answered as he looked at her, admiring the sun-kissed glow on her face as it lifted up to look back at him. He hated to admit it, but he was becoming more and more attracted to this mysterious woman. He still couldn't figure out what made her act so distant, but he was bound and determined to find out.

"Where would you like to go first?"

Maggie lowered her gaze and seemed to grow uncomfortable. "Well, I. . .I thought we could just go our separate ways from here. I mean, since my aunts and their friends aren't around us. . . ."

Devin studied her for a long moment, wondering what exactly was going through her mind and why her rejection of him hurt so much. However, he wasn't one to give up easily. He looked away from her, pretending to study the area. "It would make more sense to stick together, wouldn't it? It's always more fun to tour a city when you have someone to share it with."

Maggie took a visible breath. "I don't want to impose on your time. I'm sure you wouldn't want to spend time with me in the market and. . ."

Devin reached over, took her hand, and put it into the crook of his arm. "I need to buy some souvenirs for my niece and nephew, and you could never impose on my time," he said smoothly as he began to pull her toward the open-air market.

"But. . ." She began to say something, but when he continued to pull her along, he heard her sigh. "Devin Tanner, do you always get your way?"

He gave her a big smile. "With you, it's been tougher than usual," he admitted.

For a long moment, they stared at one another. Devin caught his breath at the feeling that swept through him as he gazed deep into her eyes. He didn't miss the vulnerable look that crossed Maggie's face, either. Could she be feeling the strong attraction as well as he?

Suddenly she pulled away from him. It was then Devin noticed they were no longer walking but standing right in the middle of the street. The loud honk from a motor scooter seemed to send Maggie into action, for she whirled away from him and walked briskly to the curb. Devin ran to catch up with her as her bright white sundress drifted in and out of his view, then disappeared among the throng of tourists.

She was nearly to the market by the time he was at her side once again. He was prepared for her to argue again about their touring together, but it never happened. She looked up at him and, with a rueful smile, asked innocently, "I'm sorry. Was I walking too fast?"

Devin laughed, although he wasn't sure it was from the humor of her statement or from outright shock. He decided to play along. "Were you afraid they were going to sell out of goods before you could get to them?"

"Something like that," she commented, daring him to say otherwise.

Devin took her hand again. "Well then, we'd better hurry!" He was prepared for her to try to jerk away, but she didn't and that tiny victory filled his heart with more joy than it should have.

Shopping only took about an hour of their time. Maggie had bought silver necklaces for herself and her mother, and Devin purchased several handmade trinkets for his niece and nephew.

Devin suggested that they take a look at the historic El Morro fort and was pleased when she agreed. The fort was a huge six-level structure with 140-foot walls that looked out over the ocean and beyond. They walked all the way up to the top level and stared out at the crashing waves below them.

Devin looked over at Maggie as the wind brushed her hair away from her face. Her pale blue eyes looked like shimmering diamonds, and her cheeks were pink from the sun. More and more, he found himself drawn to her. She was unlike any woman he'd ever known. If she hadn't been so uptight about being around him, he knew he would have felt like God had sent her into his life.

He would have courted her, and they would have fallen in love in the ways most couples did. But she'd been uncooperative from the moment they'd met.

The question that still nagged him was, why?

He looked back out to the ocean and asked as nonchalantly as possible, "So where do your parents live now?"

She didn't answer at first. When she did, it was brief. "They live in Fort Worth, Texas." She suddenly turned toward him. "So what about your family? Where do they live?"

Her resistance to talk about her family had to be the key to finding out answers. Maybe talking about his own would help. "My family lives in Monticello, Indiana. My dad is a pastor there."

She looked at him with surprise. "You're a preacher's kid, and you still wanted to go into the ministry?"

"I'm probably a pastor today because of what my father is. He was a great example of how a Christian should be and how a pastor should lead a congregation. I wanted to be just like him." He smiled reminiscently. "I guess I still do."

Maggie was looking at him like she didn't believe him. "Didn't you sometimes feel jealous of his involvement with the church?"

He could tell he was treading on thin ground here with Maggie. This subject was obviously very important to her. "He never gave us cause to feel jealous, Maggie. Of course there were times when he had to cancel an outing or two because of an emergency, but we understood because when he was with us, he gave us his full attention. We knew he loved us."

"You were lucky, then," she said quietly as she turned away from him.

He put his hands on her shoulders and pulled her back toward him. "No, we were blessed, but I know that not everybody's that fortunate." He hesitated a moment, then spoke. "What about your father, Maggie? Did he give you cause to be jealous of his work?"

"Yes, he did, Devin. I don't want to talk about my father. It's been too nice of a day to ruin it," she replied, her voice strained.

"Okay." He let her go and turned back toward the ocean again. He leaned his arms against the rough stone railing. "Why don't we talk about you?"

She shook her head, smiling ruefully. "There's nothing to tell. I lead a boring life, I'm afraid."

"I don't know about that. You own a successful bookstore and seem to be well liked by everyone in town. Do you have any hobbies? Like to play any sports?"

She shrugged. "I like to play tennis, although I'm not very good at it. For exercise, I walk a lot. And I love to shop for antiques." She looked at him with a teasing smile. "See? Boring."

"If that's what you call boring, then I'm just as guilty. Only I like to jog rather than walk. Where do you walk, by the way? I usually go to the city park trail."

The glance she threw him was a guilty one. "I know," she admitted to his surprise. "I go there, too, but I've made sure we're not out there at the same time."

For a moment Devin just stared at her in confusion. She'd been intentionally avoiding him, even at home? "Why?" he asked, his voice slightly strained.

She shook her head, turning away from. "Devin, please. Let's just drop this subject."

Devin was tired of dropping subjects she deemed too personal. This had to do with him, and he had to know the answer. He took her shoulders and pulled her around to face him. He held an uncompromising stance as he stared at her, challenging her. "No. I will not let this drop, Maggie. I think we need to clear the air here and now. You've been avoiding me since the moment you laid eyes on me, and I want to know why." He swallowed hard and took a deep breath. "I need to know."

Maggie stared at him for a moment, then briefly closed her eyes with a sigh. She opened them again, and for the first time, Devin saw real emotion shining in her eyes. Emotion that had everything to do with him.

"I can't get involved with you, Devin. I was reared in a minister's home, and it wasn't a pleasant place to be. My father, as good-hearted as he is, has always felt he had to give all his time to his congregation. Devin, he missed half of my birthday parties because something came up or he had a board or building meeting."

She looked at him searchingly and sincerely. "If you were anything but a minister, I wouldn't be trying to push you away. I promised myself I wouldn't get involved with a minister, and it's been a pretty easy promise to keep." She paused, obviously not knowing that her feelings for him were clearly written on her face. "Until now," she whispered, her voice shaking with emotion.

For one breathless moment, Devin stared at the beautiful woman who had managed, in just three days, to turn his feelings inside out. "Maggie," he murmured as he bent toward her and brushed his lips against hers. He was stunned when she shyly kissed him back.

Pulling back, he brought his hands up to cup the sides of her face. "Maggie, I—"

Devin was suddenly interrupted when a torrent of guitar music sounded behind them. They broke apart and whirled around to see at least ten musicians, smiling big and wearing sombreros. The leader of the group bowed, stepped closer to them, and began to croon a love song just for them.

At least Devin thought it was a love song. It was sung entirely in Spanish. He looked at Maggie, and she turned to him. All embarrassment fled when she started giggling and shaking her head.

Together they said the one thing that popped into their minds. "The ladies!"

Chapter 7

After unsuccessfully trying to ditch the guitar serenade, Maggie and Devin decided to go back on the boat and find something to do there. They never did see the ladies, but both had a feeling that they were never far behind!

"Apparently, the old gals are not buying our ruse as a couple," Maggie said with a grin when she and Devin stepped back on the cruise ship. "I have a feeling that no matter what we do, they are going to keep trying to bring us together."

Devin didn't say anything as he steered her off to the side and toward an empty deck. He set their purchases down on a table, then took her hand and led her to the railing that looked out over the island. "Maggie, maybe they have the right idea."

Maggie's heart started beating furiously as she stared at his serious face. "Devin, I told you. . . ," she began.

He put his hands up in surrender. "I know, I know. You don't want to get involved with me romantically."

She took a deep, shaky breath. "That's right."

He nodded. "Because I'm a minister."

"Yep." She was relieved that he seemed to understand. . .wasn't she?

He looked casually back out over the railing. "And the fact that you kissed me just means you want to be friends, right?"

She felt her cheeks go hot and bent forward to hide her face with her hair. "Uh, about that. . . I believe you were the one doing the kissing."

He laughed and picked up the curtain of her hair, peering underneath. "And you kissing me back was just a. . . friendly gesture."

She refused to look at him. Instead, she pretended to pick a piece of lint from her skirt. "I don't think it's very gentlemanly of you to even bring that. . .point up." She lifted her head and looked at him with growing determination.

He gave her a look of regret. "I'm sorry. I won't bring it up again."

She breathed a sigh of relief. "Good."

It was then that she looked over Devin's shoulder and noticed her aunts and the rest of the ladies staring at them through binoculars. She couldn't believe it! Every one of them had her own pair!

"Oh, no! They're spying on us again," she cried softly.

"What?" Devin asked as he started to turn around, but she stopped him.

"No! Don't look!" She thought a moment. "We've got to convince them that we no longer need their matchmaking help."

Devin lifted an eyebrow. "How?"

She closed her eyes for a moment, racking her brain

trying to come up with another solution besides the one that had popped into her mind; but there were no other ideas coming forth, so she had to go with what she had. Without putting too much more thought into it, she threw her arms around his neck and kissed him.

Devin seemed to hesitate, but not for long.

It was when he began to kiss her back that Maggie knew she'd made a whopper of a mistake. She wanted to kiss him. She needed his arms around her. She longed for him to say he loved her and they'd live happily forever. That was the problem. There could be no happily ever after for them because. . .

The reason seemed to elude Maggie as he kissed her softly and put his strong arms around her. All she could think of was that this was the most wonderful man she'd ever met and she wanted to go on kissing him forever.

In the distance, she heard a cheer sound, and Devin pulled back. Stunned, they gaped at one another, then turned to where the ladies were clapping, cheering, and whistling. . .and looking straight at them.

A wary expression marred Devin's brow. "Am I going to get blamed for that one, too?"

Maggie's face went hot again, but she was determined to stare him in the eye. "I'm just trying to make them believe that we don't need their help."

"Uh huh," he grunted, as if he didn't believe her.

She didn't blame him. She didn't even believe herself.

Overhead, the notes of the "Wedding March" began to be played on the ship's intercom.

She thrust her chin up. "See? They bought it."

He merely shook his head. "What is that saying you

Southerners quote? Something about not counting your chickens before they hatch?"

They looked back up, and sure enough, the ladies were in what resembled a football huddle, whispering among themselves.

"Oh, boy!" Maggie sighed. "You may be right."

He put a friendly arm around her and grinned. "You could always kiss me again. Maybe that would help."

She nudged him with her elbow. "Forget it, Pal. No more kissing!"

"Hmmm. That chicken quote could be applied in this situation, too, you know."

"I believe the appropriate Southern saying would have something to do with donkeys flying," she told him with a serene smile.

↳⁺

The ladies were giddy with delight. Amelia corralled the women together. "This is perfect!" she crowed. "I can't believe she kissed him just because she saw us up here looking at them."

Shirley snorted. "Well, what else did you expect her to do?"

Isabel shook her head. "You don't know our Magnolia if you think kissing a man would normally be the first thing she'd do!" She smiled. "I believe she really likes him!"

Dolly nodded her head, the colorful peacock feathers in her hat flowing with the motion. "I do, too! But how can we be sure?"

Amelia smiled. "I have it all under control." She whipped out a writing tablet. "We have four days left, and

I've come up with a schedule. On each of these papers is an hour-by-hour agenda we all must follow if we are to be successful!"

As she began to pass the papers around, Shirley scowled. "I thought this was supposed to be a fun vacation."

"Oh, hush, Shirley! We all know you subscribe to the spy magazine that has stories about intrigues and spy missions. You're enjoying this as much as the rest of us are," Thelma admonished.

"I agree! The last time we had this much fun was when Ronald Dean's pigs escaped and went running down Main Street! Remember? He said if we helped him catch them, we'd all get a free ham!" Bertha chimed in.

For a moment the ladies paused and looked at Bertha like she'd lost her mind, causing her to speak in defense. "Well? I managed to catch three of them! I still have some of that ham in my freezer."

Amelia rolled her eyes and shook her head. "Forget the pigs! We've got our schedule, ladies. Let's get to work!"

↙

The ladies had more gumption and creativity than Maggie or Devin had ever imagined. For the next three days they were serenaded in every conceivable way in about four or five different languages. Some musicians had guitars, others had horns, and a couple had violins. Some could actually sing, others. . .well, others tried to sing.

But that wasn't all! The ladies would always make sure that they were present for every event or dinner Maggie and Devin attended, forcing them to act like a loving couple. Only, most of the time, they weren't acting!

What the ladies would do next actually came to be a joke between them. They both had to admit that the old gals had come up with some ingenious ideas!

At the moment, Maggie and Devin were on the ship, trying to run from the latest singer who had been sent their way. They had just begun to eat their dessert, when the man walked right up to their table and, at the top of his lungs, started singing "That's Amore!" They'd quickly left the restaurant, but this one wasn't giving up easily.

Maggie peered around the corner to see if the coast was clear. "Well, I don't see him," she whispered to Devin.

Devin leaned against the bulkhead, putting his hands over his ears. "Well, he's close by, because I can still hear him!"

Maggie laughed as she turned back to him and pulled his hands down. "Can you believe someone could be that tone deaf?"

He smiled as he linked fingers with hers. "Ah, see? If you'd been coming to the church, you'd know that there was such a person."

Maggie looked at Devin with disbelief. "Don't tell me you let Lena Reeder sing!"

"I'm afraid I was misled about her singing abilities. I guess I should have auditioned her before she sang on Sunday morning."

"You let her sing on Sunday morning?"

Devin sighed. "I'm afraid so."

Maggie was laughing so hard, she had tears in her eyes. "Oh, Dev. You should have asked someone about her."

He reached up with his free hand and gently wiped the

moisture from under her eyes. "Now, see, that's one of the disadvantages of being a pastor who's a bachelor. Normally, a minister would ask his wife's opinion."

She smiled sadly at him. "Not all of them do."

"Haven't you figured out by now that I'm nothing like your father?" he chided.

She gazed at him somberly. "I know you're not, Devin."

Her words seemed to take him off guard for a second. Then, he brought her hand up to his lips and kissed her knuckles tenderly. "You don't know how relieved I am to hear that," he told her, his voice husky with emotion.

Maggie gave him a shaky smile. "You are?"

He nodded, his tender gaze touching on each part of her upturned face. She watched as he seemed to hesitate on speaking his next words, and she wondered what he was trying to say. She didn't have to wait long.

"I'm in love with you, Maggie."

Maggie froze at his words, her mind racing at what those words actually meant to her. She had wondered if he was falling for her. She had wondered how she would feel when and if he said those three little words.

Now she knew.

She felt exactly the same way about him.

New tears were starting to pool in her eyes. "Oh, Devin. I—I mean, I. . . ," she stammered as she tried to come up with the right words to say to him.

Devin took her tears to mean something else. He suddenly looked defeated as his shoulders slumped. He tried to smile but failed at the attempt as he reached in his pocket, then handed her his hankie. "It's. . . .it's okay,

Maggie. You don't have to worry about saying anything. I know how you feel about my profession."

She lightly put a hand over his mouth, stilling his speech. "You don't understand, Devin. I'm in love with you, too."

She expected him to be overjoyed and hug her or something! Instead, he stood stock-still and looked at her warily. "Is that a happy 'I'm in love with you' or a sad 'I'm in love with you, but we could never be together' kind of declaration?"

She decided to throw her arms around him. "That is a very, very happy declaration!"

He held her close as he gazed down at her face in wonderment. "And it doesn't matter that I'm a pastor?"

She shook her head, her expression serious. "No, but I may have some rough spots every once in awhile you may have to help me through. I know you're not like my father, Devin. You're such a good and generous man. I feel very blessed to have you in my life."

"Ah, Magnolia Weston, I'm the blessed one." He brushed her lips with a gentle kiss. "Did you know that I've prayed day and night that God would work this out between us? I knew from the moment I met you that you were someone special, and when I found myself falling in love with you, I prayed for His guidance and direction." He gave her such a loving look, she wanted to cry again. "I know God sent you to me, Maggie. I'm so blessed."

At that, she did start crying, but it was quickly smothered as he held her to him and pressed her head into his shoulder. A chuckle rumbled in his chest then, and she asked him what was so funny.

He bent his head and said softly, "You know, I think I just saw a donkey fly by!"

A laugh broke through her tears and she hugged him close. "Don't rub it in!" she teased.

Suddenly, what seemed like a lightning storm exploded around them. They quickly sprang apart, and Maggie had to squint to see past all the flashing lights.

"Oh, that was just beautiful, Pastor! I don't believe any of my three late husbands ever made such an eloquent proclamation!" Bertha's rings glittered as she clasped her hands together.

Maggie, still blinking from the flashes, frowned at the group. "You were spying on us?" she asked, embarrassed.

Amelia smiled brightly. "Of course we were! We've worked very hard to see this moment!"

Dolly sighed, her hands to her heart. "And it looks like our hard work paid off!"

Devin, who was looking quite embarrassed himself, spoke up then. "Uh, ladies? Do you mind giving us a few minutes here?"

Thelma smiled broadly. "Okay—only if you promise to fill us in later!"

Devin exchanged a grin with Maggie, then looked back at the ladies. "We promise."

Thelma nodded and started to lead the ladies away, but the strains of a familiar song suddenly grew closer. Stepping from around the corner, smiling big and singing loudly, was their love song crooner. "That's amore!" he sang as he finished the song on a high note that didn't quite meet its mark, his arms thrown wide, knocking Dolly's pinecone chapeau from her head.

The ladies giggled at the outrageous display, while Devin put his arm around Maggie and winked. "It certainly is!" he exclaimed in agreement.

The next morning, as the ship headed back to their Florida port, Maggie sat by the Ping-Pong tables watching Devin and Amelia playing doubles with Isabel and Bertha. *He is such an unbelievable man,* Maggie thought for the umpteenth time since he'd made his declaration last night. It still didn't seem real that they were about to embark on a real relationship.

Part of her was still scared inside. Part of her kept hearing her mother's voice as she made Maggie promise never to get involved with a minister, to never go through the lonely, miserable life that she had had. Then, the other part of her wanted to forget her promise. She recognized that she loved Devin and knew he was a strong, compassionate, Christian man. He wasn't one to neglect those he loved. He wasn't one to get so involved in helping others that he forgot his family.

Was he?

Of course not! she told herself firmly.

Raising her face to the sky, she whispered a quick, silent prayer. *God, please help me deal with this. Please lead me and guide me. I don't want to make a mistake, and I pray I'll know what to do when situations arise that frighten me or make me doubt.*

A tap on her shoulder broke her from her prayer, and she turned to see a ship's officer standing by her.

"Are you Maggie Weston?" he asked, and she nodded.

"You have a phone call. If you'll follow me, I'll show you where to take it."

After telling Devin about the call, she hurriedly followed the officer.

Chapter 8

A half an hour later, Maggie still hadn't returned, so Devin went to look for her. He still couldn't believe Maggie had told him that she loved him. He knew she had feelings for him, but he never thought she'd admit it.

Thank God, she did. Already, he was making plans for them. Already, he could visualize the day he would ask her to marry him.

Whether she believed it or not, she would make a wonderful pastor's wife. She was so thoughtful, and he knew she watched after many of the elderly ladies in his church, doing their shopping for them, giving them books and coffee when they couldn't afford them. He'd also noticed that she smiled and greeted everyone she passed by.

Last night, he'd returned to his cabin and spent an hour on his knees, thanking God for sending Maggie into his life. He prayed for guidance and direction. He knew that together, with God's help, they'd make such a great team. He was looking forward to each moment to come.

When he'd reached her room, he knocked but got no answer. Sighing, he realized he must have just missed her.

She was probably waiting for him by the Ping-Pong tables!

Shaking his head and grinning happily, he trotted up the hall and out onto the open deck. He was just about to run up the stairs when he spotted her. He started to call out her name, but something stopped him.

She was leaning against the railing, just staring out into the ocean. Her countenance seemed pensive; her hands clutched the railing tightly.

Something was very wrong.

Whispering a prayer for her, he slowly walked to where she stood. When he reached her, she didn't look in his direction. There were tears falling down her cheeks.

"Maggie?" he asked hesitantly as he put a comforting hand on her back. "Has something happened?"

For a moment, she looked down at her hands, and then she lifted her head, still looking away from him. "That was my aunt. My mother was rushed to the hospital, suffering from kidney stones," she said, her voice strangely flat and devoid of emotion.

"Is she going to be all right?"

"Yes, no thanks to my father. She called him at the church to tell him she was feeling ill and thought she needed to go to the hospital. Dad told her he was about to go into a board meeting and would come get her as soon as it was over." Maggie reached up and harshly wiped the tears from her eyes, finally betraying the emotions she was really feeling. "Mom waited nearly an hour, but the pain became worse and worse. Finally, she called an ambulance. The doctors told my aunt that she was lucky. Waiting that long could have caused her to lose a kidney."

An uneasiness fell over Devin as he heard her words

and felt the wall she'd erected around herself. He wanted to put his arms around her and tell her everything was all right, that he loved her and would help her get through this.

But he knew that she wouldn't allow that. He was standing right next to her, but there might as well have been fifty miles between them.

However, he wasn't going to give up so easily. He continued to rub her back and forced himself to sound cheerful. "Well, why don't we fly over there as soon as we dock in Florida? I'm sure your mother will feel better with you there, and it would be a great time to—"

"No," she interrupted softly but firmly as she turned to face him, backing a few steps away from him. "I can't do this, Devin."

Panic spread like a cold rain through his body as he stared at her. "Maggie, I love you. You love me. We can get through anything with God's help," he reasoned as he fought to keep his voice from breaking.

She started crying again. Putting her hands up and backing away from him, she argued, "I'm sorry, Devin. I really am. I don't want to hurt you. But I just can't. . ." Her voice broke and she turned to run away, but he caught her arm.

Turning her toward him, he forced her to look at him. "You're hurting us both, Maggie, and it doesn't have to be this way." He felt his eyes tear up, but he blinked them back. "I am not your father, Maggie. I promise you, I'd never neglect you like he's done your mother. Never. You've got to trust in me." He paused. "No. Trust in God that He has His hands on us and this relationship."

Maggie shook her head frantically. "Don't you see, Devin? This was a sign from God. He's reminding me of the promise that I made to myself and my mother!" she cried.

"Maggie, it was not a sign! A test, maybe, but not a sign!" Then suddenly he froze as he recalled her other words. "You made a promise to your mother? I thought it was something you'd only promised yourself."

Maggie shook off his hands and backed away. "What does that matter?" she charged, her motions agitated.

"Maggie, did you tell your mother about us?" he asked, everything suddenly starting to make sense.

She closed her eyes wearily and rubbed a hand over her forehead. "Devin, please. . ."

"Did you tell your mother about us?" he asked again, enunciating each word clearly.

She looked at him for a moment and answered simply, "Yes, I did."

He nodded his head, his eyes understanding. "And she reminded you of your promise."

She turned away, and it seemed as though she was trying to bring her emotions under control. "She reminded me of what's important," she countered, her voice calmer now.

Devin stepped up to her and framed her face with his hands, gazing deeply into her eyes, praying she'd see just how much he loved her. "We're what's important, Maggie. Not some promise you made long ago. We were meant to be. Please don't throw that away."

For a moment, he thought he'd gotten through to her, but that moment was quickly gone. She reached up and took his hands from her face and backed away for one last time. "I'm sorry, Devin. I just can't," she whispered brokenly.

Devin raked his hands through his hair with despair as he watched her run away. His mind balked at the thought of her being out of his life forever.

What do I do now, Lord? he prayed. *Please, show me what to do.*

He heard a noise behind him and realized he wasn't alone. The ladies were all there, looking at him solemnly and contritely. "We didn't mean for you to get hurt, Pastor. We'd have never tried to play matchmakers if we knew this would happen," Amelia told him, her wrinkled face filled with concern.

Bertha patted him on his arm. "It's all our fault. We're just a group of meddling old women who should have known better."

Isabel nodded, patting him on the other arm. "Bertha's right. I wouldn't blame you if you just washed your hands of all of us! We deserve it."

Devin smiled at them and put his arms around both ladies. "Blame you for what? For bringing the most wonderful woman into my life?"

The ladies all looked shocked. "But, Pastor, we ruined your whole trip and quite possibly your life!" Dolly added dramatically, earning her a nudge and a frown from Shirley.

"Dolly, I promise you that this was the best vacation I've ever had, and my life is not quite ruined, yet."

Amelia peered at him shrewdly. "Are you saying you haven't given up?"

He shook his head. "Nope, but I've got an idea that's

going to need your assistance. Can you help?"

Isabel smiled, nodding to the others in agreement. "We're at your service, Pastor! What do you want us to do?"

He motioned for them to come closer. "Here is what I need. . . ."

A week later, Maggie was back to her normal routine and feeling more miserable than she'd ever felt in her life. Everywhere she went, she seemed to run into Devin. Twice, he'd actually come into the bookstore, smiling at her and acting like nothing was wrong. He didn't seem bothered or heartbroken or. . .anything! He just seemed like his normal self.

Why couldn't she? Why couldn't she go back to being the same person she'd been before the cruise? Maybe because she wasn't that person anymore. She was tired of holding resentment against her father and building walls to keep from getting hurt. It hadn't worked, had it? She'd fallen in love with Devin, wall or no.

She still loved him.

That was what propelled her to call her father and have a long talk with him. She told him that she forgave him for all he'd done and she no longer wanted to resent him or have bad feelings for him. Maggie talked to her mother and told her that she was going to have to let Maggie lead her own life. If Maggie got hurt from a bad relationship, then so be it—but it would be her choice.

If she wanted to date a minister and fall in love with him, it didn't mean it had to end up like her father and mother's relationship.

It was still hard to think differently about that, but

Maggie could sense God working in her, healing old wounds, and giving her wisdom about what to believe.

But did that mean she was ready to give Devin a call and tell him she'd been wrong? What if he didn't want to try again? What if he was ready to move on? What if he kept on being polite and friendly?

Maggie didn't know if she could stand just being his friend when she wanted so much more. Late Saturday night, she had just come home from the bookstore and was fixing a sandwich when her doorbell rang. She ran to open it and found her aunts, along with Bertha and Dolly, standing at her door. She smiled curiously at them. "Well, hello! Come on in, and I'll make you all a cup of tea."

She started to open the door wider when Amelia waved her hand for her stop. "Oh, no, Magnolia! There's no time for that. We need you to come down to the church for a minute."

Maggie looked at the ladies, who were all nodding eagerly. "Why?"

Isabel stepped up. "Just because! Now are you going to make us stand out here all night, or are you going to get in the car with us?"

Maggie gave a surprised laugh as she stared at them and waited for a better explanation. When there didn't seem to be one coming, she sighed and shrugged. "Let me get my purse."

As Maggie walked out to the car with them, she couldn't help being beside herself with curiosity. Could this be another matchmaking attempt? Surely not. Her aunts hadn't so much as mentioned Devin the whole week! She even thought they felt badly for trying to fix them up in the first place.

So what were they up to?

What greeted her in the fellowship hall of the church was not what she expected. There were about thirty people who Maggie was sure she'd never seen in her life, all standing around the room. In the center of them was Devin.

She turned to her aunt Amelia. "What's going on?"

Amelia winked at her and gave her a little push. "You'll see! Now, get in there and don't forget to tell me all about it later on!" With that, the ladies left, closing the door behind them.

Uneasy about standing in a room with a bunch of strangers, Maggie decided to latch on to the only person she knew, and that was Devin. When she reached him, she smiled tentatively. "Hi. Uh, what's going on?"

He surprised her by leaning forward and kissing her softly on the cheek. "Hi, Maggie. I just wanted to introduce you to my family and a few of my friends."

Maggie scanned the room and swallowed nervously. "A few?"

He laughed and steered her toward an attractive middle-aged couple. "Let me introduce you to Mom and Dad first."

For the next hour, Maggie met and talked with all thirty of his friends, relatives, and even a couple of his teachers who had all come down to Louisiana to meet her. They had story after story to tell about Devin, what a nice, dependable person he was, and what a good friend he was when you needed him, and on and on.

After about the fourth person, Maggie started to get the picture. Devin hadn't given up on her after all. He'd just felt she needed some convincing about what kind of person he was, so he brought references. Thirty live references.

Maggie loved him even more for going to so much trouble.

When she'd met them all, he told them good-bye and led her outside. "You mind going for a walk?" he asked her while holding out his hand.

She smiled at him and placed her hand in his. "Sounds good."

They were quiet for a little while, and Maggie's stomach was churning, wondering what he was going to say.

Finally he spoke. "Maggie, I thought maybe you needed to know more about me, so I got the ladies to help me round up some of my family and friends to talk with you. I had no idea most of them would want to come! I'm sorry if you felt like it was a little too much."

She glanced up at him and grinned. "They were a little overwhelming, but it was nice getting to know them and hearing them talk about you." She tugged on his hand teasingly. "They sure think highly of you."

He stopped walking and turned her to face him, putting his hands on her shoulders. "The important thing is, Maggie, what do you think about me—about us?" he asked, his voice serious, his expression hopeful.

She reached up and laid her hands on his chest, feeling the strong beat of his heart under her palms. "I think you are a wonderful, special man, and I love you with all my heart."

Maggie watched a stillness come over him, and he took a deep breath. "You didn't need me to bring my entourage tonight, did you? You'd figured it out," he guessed, his voice filled with wonderment.

She nodded. "I've done a lot of praying this week. I even talked to my parents," she explained, going into detail about what she and her father and mother spoke about. "I've still got a ways to go, Devin, but I don't want to go it alone. God brought you to me, and I'm not going to give you back! Not this time."

He laughed and hugged her. "Ah, Maggie, I love you, Sweetheart. Don't worry. I would have gathered more friends and relatives if these didn't work! I wasn't going to let you walk away that easily!"

She snuggled in his arms. "I'm glad."

He moved back, then, and kissed her softly. A feeling of love and wonderment was wrapped up in that little kiss. And more than that, a feeling of coming home.

After a moment, Devin rubbed his nose with hers. "I love you, Maggie, and I want it all—marriage, kids, the whole works. I want you with me forever."

She kissed him lightly, smiling as she did so. "Is that a proposal, Reverend Tanner?"

He looked at her with mock seriousness. "Give me more credit than that! I can't introduce you to my family, make up with you, and propose all in one night! These things take time!"

She raised her eyebrows and he began to chuckle. "I plan to propose tomorrow night!" he announced happily.

"Oh, why can't you do it now? We're all waiting with baited breath!" a loud voice sounded from the bushes beside them.

To their surprise the whole Cottonridge Baptist ladies group popped up from behind the bushes, holding video cameras and tape recorders. Dolly even dressed for the occasion in a hat that sported shrubbery sticking out everywhere.

Devin shook his head, looking first at the ladies, then at Maggie. With a grin, he shrugged. "Well, if you can't beat them. . ." He bent down on one knee, and taking her hand in his, he made his proposal. "Maggie, I love you with all my heart. Will you marry me?"

Maggie's heart seemed to skip a beat as his love radiated out to her and filled her with joy. "Oh, yes, I will marry you, Devin."

He started to stand up, but someone yelled, "What? We didn't hear Maggie's answer!"

Maggie laughed and started to yell her answer to them when Devin beat her to it. "She said yes!"

A cheer went up, and Devin hugged Maggie. In that moment, Maggie sent up a prayer of thanks for all God had done for her and especially for sending them their own group of crafty matchmakers!

KIMBERLEY COMEAUX

Kim is married to Brian, who is a music minister, a songwriter, and formerly the lead singer for The Imperials. They have a son named Tyler and live in Louisiana. Kim turned her attention toward writing Christian fiction when she discovered songwriting wasn't for her, because she loves to read, especially romance. "I started out with an idea and before I knew it, I'd written a book-length story." Kim has two full novels published with **Heartsong Presents**.

Troubled Waters

by Linda Goodnight

Dedication

Dedicated to Frank Case, who has been there for me
through all my "troubled waters."
Love you, Daddy.

Chapter 1

Why on earth had she agreed to this?

Carrie Bridges folded her arms and tilted her head toward the morning sun as a small plane lifted off into the incredibly blue sky. A soft breeze whispered through her hair, and the sweet fragrance of honeysuckle tickled her nose. Carrie hardly noticed.

Neither the beauty of a cloudless June day nor the promise of a week in Bermuda could lift the heavy load of despair that weighed her down. The hurt, the betrayal were too great. It would take more than an exotic vacation to mend what was wrong between her and Greg. It would take a miracle.

While she stood in the breezeway of the small private airport, wishing she'd refused to come, Greg made a routine check of his sleek, single-engine airplane. He was a good pilot, she'd grant him that. Bitterly, she realized he should be good. He'd spent far more time in that fancy plane than he'd spent with his own family. The familiar ache of rejection throbbed at her temples. She jabbed a finger against the nosepiece of her designer sunglasses, angry with herself for still caring.

"Great day for flying," Greg called, coming toward her across the sunlit tarmac, his smile wide in a tanned, handsome face. A peach golf shirt curved over his athletic chest and tapered neatly into khaki slacks that he wore with casual elegance. All those hours at the health club had served him well, just as they had her. People considered them the perfect couple—fit, tanned, good-looking, and successful. If only they knew she no longer measured success by good looks or the size of Greg's bank account. She'd learned the hard way that a handsome face and fine-tuned body didn't make the man.

Greg went on talking, the tiny bronzed lines around his blue eyes crinkling. "Couldn't be more perfect."

When she didn't reply, his smile faded. He touched her arm. "Come on, Carrie," he urged in his quiet voice, a rich, warm baritone that once had made her heart hammer in anticipation. "You have to try."

"No, I don't, Greg." She retracted her arm and stepped away. "I only said I'd come. I never said I'd try."

Greg looked beyond her to the waiting plane and sighed heavily, raking a hand through his sun-kissed hair. Then he closed his eyes and stood silently for such a long time, Carrie grew uncomfortable. She watched him with a frown. What was he doing? Praying? Well, she hoped not. That would be beyond hypocritical!

When he looked at her again, the anger was gone, replaced by a serenity that infuriated his wife even further. What right did he have to be at peace? He was the one who'd destroyed their marriage.

Greg took her arm again and gave a gentle tug. "Come on, Cutie," he said, clearly determined to pretend all was well. "The islands

Not at all duped by th
seen him use to his advan
tantly followed him to the
make this trip and she'd a
the marriage counselor th
When the divorce finally c
she hadn't tried. She could

He opened the door, ar
seater, adjusting her seat belt as Greg hopped inside and
started the engine.

The bags were loaded in back along with all the items
Greg thought necessary for a trip over the ocean. Not
that she worried. The plane was relatively new, Greg was
a safe and experienced pilot, and the weather was, as
Greg had pointed out, perfect for flying. They'd be on the
beautiful, pink beaches in no time.

Bermuda. How would she endure a week alone on a
romantic, exotic island with this man? No matter what he
said or did, he couldn't repair what was broken. She
wouldn't allow it. Pain this great could only be endured
once. She'd use this week to show him just how dead
their marriage was. By the time they returned to Raleigh,
he'd be more than happy to sign the divorce papers and
give her half of their highly successful software business.

Body stiff, arms crossed, Carrie scooted as far away
from her husband as possible and stared out at the vast,
blue horizon. Except for the hum of the engine, uncomfortable silence filled the small cabin. From the corner of
her eye, she saw Greg glance her way several times,
though he made no attempt at conversation. Why

very discussion became a battle.

...ne than seemed possible, the aircraft left the ...l terra firma and hummed smoothly above the ...ean.

...I have some snacks back there if you're hungry." Greg waved a hand toward the rear of the plane.

Carrie slowly turned to look at him. Snacks. They'd barely spoken three civil words in the last six months, and he wanted to offer her snacks. After nine years of marriage, he didn't know her at all. Indignant, she shook her head.

"No, thanks."

At her chilly tone, dismay flashed through Greg's blue eyes. Carrie refused to feel guilty. Everything that happened was Greg's fault. Everything. He'd destroyed their happiness. She'd once loved him so much, she'd have jumped from this plane without a parachute if he'd asked her to. He'd destroyed her love, squeezed it out of her bit by bit over the last few years with his neglect. The most recent episode had been the proverbial straw that broke the camel's back. She would never be that vulnerable—or stupid—again.

"Remember the last trip we took together?" Greg's voice was hopeful. He seemed determined to make jolly conversation.

"Do you mean the time Dylan broke his arm while you and I were snorkeling in the Cayman Islands?"

Greg sighed. "We had a wonderful time, Carrie."

"Yes, at the expense of our son." Even now, the shame and guilt threatened to cripple her. She'd been laughing and cavorting with Greg, unreachable by phone, while her baby lay in surgery to repair a compound fracture.

Greg sent her a weary look. "Can't you get over that? He fell out of the swing. Three-year-old boys do that. It would have happened even if you'd been standing there, watching."

"We'll never know that for sure." The old nagging fear started up inside her. "Now we're taking that same chance again." What if something happened to Kristen or Dylan while she was gone? What if they needed her? Did they feel abandoned and afraid, the way she had felt as a child?

Greg reached across the seat and squeezed her hand. "They'll be fine, Carrie. My parents know how protective you are. Don't you think they'll watch them every minute?"

Carrie slid her hand from beneath Greg's, but the warmth of his reassurance eased her tension the slightest bit. They would be fine. Unlike the time Dylan had been hurt, she had a cell phone with her. They could call, or she could call them, anytime.

She reached inside the oversized straw purse at her feet and extracted the phone.

"We've only been gone a couple of hours, Carrie," Greg said gently. "Why don't you call them when we get there?"

"They might need me." She punched in the numbers.

He bounced a fist against his muscled thigh. "You're smothering them."

Carrie gasped and jabbed a finger at the off button, disconnecting the call before it could ring. She turned on him in a fury.

"Smothering? Smothering?" Her voice rose an octave. "At least I've been there. At least I show up for their ballgames and birthday parties. At least I don't let them down time and time again by making promises I don't keep."

"Exactly what is that supposed to mean?" The vein below his left eye throbbed, an indication that she'd finally ruffled his well-composed feathers. Good. He'd ruffled hers enough lately.

"You know what I'm talking about."

"I have a business to run, Carrie. Even though I work long hours, I've been there for you and the kids. Don't try to lay that guilt on me."

"You've been there for me? What a laugh!" All the pent-up rage and frustration of the last six months pushed to the surface.

Greg took a deep breath and exhaled slowly. "All right. I've made mistakes. The business has demanded too much of my time during the last few years, but software is changing and growing so fast right now. You may not like the time I spend working, but you sure like to spend the money I make."

"The money you make? That business is half mine. I worked just as hard to get it off the ground as you did. Remember?"

Greg was silent for a moment. He scanned the instrument panel and then the cloudless sky, checking and rechecking. Carrie knew he was making a concerted effort to regain his calm. His expression softened and when he spoke again, he did so without anger. "Yes, I do remember. You're the best partner a man could ever have. You know more about the marketing end of the software business than I ever will. That's why I've had to work twice as hard since you quit to stay home with the kids."

"You have good people working for you."

"None as good as you."

"You don't need me anymore." Why did that sound so pathetic, like a plea for reassurance? Was she still that needy little girl who'd cried for comfort that never came?

"No, Carrie, you're wrong." His gaze locked on hers and held. "I'll always need you."

Some of Carrie's bitterness eased. Greg had needed her once. She'd felt so accomplished, so worthwhile as director of marketing for Sunshine Software; but as the company had grown, so had their family. She'd turned more and more work over to other employees until she'd trained her way out of a job. Now Kristen and Dylan took up every minute of her day.

She glanced over at her pilot husband, his hands firmly on the controls. She hardly knew him anymore. What had happened to the struggling, young college student she'd fallen in love with? They'd been so poor, starting the company on a loan and a prayer. There had been lots of prayer back then, but prayer, like so many other things, slowly gave way to the relentless pace of a burgeoning business. Now, they supposedly had it all, but she felt so terribly, terribly empty.

She lifted the telephone again and punched in the numbers, then waited until she heard the familiar sound of Kristen's seven-year-old voice.

"Hi, Sweetheart. I just called to see if you and Dylan are all right."

Greg frowned, then clenched his jaw and returned his concentration to the vast blue panorama outside the cockpit window. She didn't care if he thought her overprotective. She had to check on her babies and let them know she'd always be there for them.

After a few minutes of excited chatter from both children, Carrie spoke to her mother-in-law and was assured that the kids were fine and having a grand time. She should have felt better, but as she returned the phone to her purse, the nagging sense that something was amiss continued to plague her.

Greg quirked an eyebrow. "Satisfied?"

A loud popping sound froze the angry retort on Carrie's lips. "What was that?" she gasped.

Greg frowned and scanned the instrument panel. "I don't know, but something's not right."

The plane's warning system suddenly shrieked through the cabin.

Carrie clutched her throat to keep from crying out. Greg was a good pilot. He could handle any problem that arose. They would be fine. They had to be fine for Kristen and Dylan.

Greg reached out to push the throttle up, and his fingers trembled. The plane did not respond. Fear rose in Carrie like morning sickness. If the ever-self-confident Greg was nervous, something was very wrong.

"Greg?"

"Stay calm, Sweetheart."

Her gaze searched the instrument panel. Carrie felt helpless and stupid for not understanding what she saw there. "What is it? What's happening?"

The plane popped again and the engine sputtered to silence.

Greg's answer, spoken through pale lips, sent shock waves down her spine.

"Buckle up, Honey." His voice was amazingly calm.

"Grab that pillow back there, lay it in your lap, and put your face down on it." He swallowed. "Don't look up until we hit the water."

Chapter 2

The next few moments became a haze of frantic activity and mind-numbing fear as Carrie fumbled for the pillow in the backseat. Her fingers shook so hard, she could barely buckle the seat belt again. Eyes wide and throat dry with terror, she watched Greg battle the disabled aircraft. His own gaze alternated between the instruments flashing bizarre, unfathomable warnings and the rapidly approaching sea.

A frenzied cascade of questions tumbled through Carrie's head, but she knew better than to ask them. All Greg's concentration must remain focused on bringing the plane down into the water as gently as possible.

"God, help us," he muttered softly.

No! Carrie thought, gripping the pillow fiercely as the plane rocked from side to side. *I need more time. My babies need me. They'll think I've left them, abandoned them.*

Thoughts whirled through her mind, thousands of them, spinning out of control like the wounded plane. Foolish thoughts of next week's hair appointment. Vicious thoughts that Greg's lover would never see him again. Agonized thoughts of Kristen and Dylan and of the broken marriage that would end forever in the Atlantic Ocean.

Helplessly watching her husband scramble to right the crippled plane, the dark curtain of despair inside Carrie suddenly parted so that she saw her life very clearly. She was about to die, angry and estranged from the only person who had ever made her feel worthwhile. Why had they done this to each other? How had they grown so far apart?

She wished she could pray, but she couldn't—all she could do was feel the regret. . . .

Beside her, Greg fumbled for the radio with one hand while the other fought the controls. Leaning forward, Carrie yanked the transmitter from its holder and thrust it against her husband's grim mouth. Gratitude flickered briefly in his eyes before he barked their coordinates into the mouthpiece.

"Mayday! Mayday! Mayday!" Greg shouted, and Carrie's pulse reverberated with the cry.

Static crackled, but no answering voice came to reassure them that the distress call had been heard.

"Greg?" Terror choked her.

"Pray, Sweetheart. Only God can help us now."

Every nerve ending prickled in fear. They were going to die. And she was as estranged from God as she was from her husband.

As if trapped in a strange time warp, everything moved in slow motion; but at the same time, it all happened too fast. The azure sky blended with the matching ocean, then the two became one vast expanse of rapidly approaching, glistening water. The eerie silence of the dead engine served as a reminder of just how helpless they were.

"Get your head down, Carrie!"

This time, Carrie followed his command.

"The Lord is my shepherd, I shall not want. Though I walk through the valley of death, I will fear no evil, for You are with me. . . ." Greg's quiet paraphrase of the Twenty-third Psalm rose above the sound of rushing wind to penetrate Carrie's fog of terror. For some reason, the words made her immeasurably sad. Regret, deep and yearning, pulled at her.

Prayer. When had that ever made any difference? As a little girl, she'd prayed for her mother to come home. As a lonely wife, she'd prayed for her husband to come home. She'd always wanted to believe God was with her. She'd longed for that with all her heart—yet somehow, He seemed so far away. Would God help them? She'd never felt Him helping her before, but she had to try. Kristen and Dylan were worth everything.

"Please, God. Please," she choked through lips stiff with fear. "Take care of my babies. Don't let them be afraid and alone. Tell them I love them. Let them know that I'd never leave them on purpose. Please, God. Not for me—for them. Take care of my babies."

Carrie felt Greg's strong hand clutch her cold one, and she raised her head just enough to meet his gaze. Tears glistened in her husband's eyes.

"God will make a way," he said fiercely. "I'll get you back to your babies."

In the next instant, a powerful jolt shook the plane. The sound of splintering metal and violently spraying water created a deafening roar. Somewhere in the cacophonous insanity that followed, Carrie was sure she heard Greg cry out, "I love you."

Then darkness swallowed her.

When she opened her eyes, an eerie quiet vibrated all around. The stench of fuel burned her nose and a dull pain throbbed in her head. Where was she? Where was Greg?

With a sudden horror of being alone at sea, she jerked upright, twisting to the left toward the pilot's seat. To her immense relief, Greg was there, struggling to release his seat belt, though crumpled fiberglass and dangling wires slowed his efforts.

"You all right?" His tense gaze searched her for injuries.

Carrie nodded, not at all certain. "Are you?" Her words croaked out, shaky and weak.

Greg grunted in reply and moved toward her. His expression was a study in control, but she didn't feel the same sense of calm. They were down and still alive. That was something, but they must keep their wits about them if they hoped to survive, and hysteria threatened to overwhelm her. Locking her gaze onto Greg, she drew strength from his composure. Though clearly shaken, he was still Greg, the man who was always in control. He would know what to do.

The plane rocked, listing to one side. The stench of oil and fuel grew stronger. Water gurgled and pooled on the floorboard, chilling her feet.

"Greg?" Carrie grappled for something to hold on to as the nauseating motion continued. Panic rose in her like bile. "We're sinking!"

"Stay calm." He extended a palm, blue eyes telegraphing confidence as he made rapid-fire decisions.

"Get out of the plane. Grab a piece of anything floating and hold on until I find the life raft."

With a quick squeeze of her shoulders, he brushed his lips across her cold, trembling ones, kicked at the ruptured plane door. . .and pushed her into the ocean.

Icy water shocked her warm body. Salt water filled her mouth and she spat, remembering all the stories of dehydration caused by swallowing seawater. Wreckage from the plane lay scattered in concentric circles all around. Carrie grabbed for the largest piece, wrapping her arms around the unrecognizable bit of fiberglass. Behind her, an ominous sizzling sound crackled and spewed. Kicking, Carrie pushed away from the aircraft, frightened anew at the devastation. How had they survived when so little of the plane was still intact?

Something bumped against her now bare feet and she screamed, kicking more wildly, imagining sharks and deadly sea snakes. Her loose, silk slacks billowed up around her thighs, exposing her legs to whatever horror lay beneath the waves. She screamed again, panicked.

"Carrie?" Greg's concerned voice reached her, though he was nowhere in sight.

Before Carrie had a chance to plead for help, a pair of blue jeans bobbed to the surface beside her. Blue jeans, probably Greg's, had been her stalker. Carrie slumped against the debris, almost sobbing with relief.

"I'm okay." Her words were breathless, shaky. "Where are you?"

During the last five years, she'd asked that same question every time he missed a social function or one of the children's activities. Now the words held more than anger and the fear of rejection. They were a matter of life and death.

He swam toward her across the littered sea, towing a bright orange rubber dinghy. The square four-foot craft had already inflated, popping a tentlike canopy into the air. Though the three-sided cover couldn't have been more than a couple of feet high, it trapped the wind and made Greg's swim slow and laborious. Behind him, flames began to sputter from the downed plane, sending spirals of black smoke skyward.

Throat tight, heart pounding, a rush of adrenaline surged through numb legs and arms, propelling Carrie farther away from the crash site.

"Fire!" she cried.

Greg looked over his shoulder and fear flared in his face. Though the fire was just beginning, it could erupt into an inferno in a matter of seconds. All it had to do was reach the spilling fuel. Paddling desperately with his one free arm, he made his way toward Carrie.

When he drew near enough, he shoved the raft toward her. Carrie lunged for the handholds, scrambling on board. She reached back to offer Greg a hand up, only to discover him swimming away.

"Greg. Get back here. It's burning!" With the oil and fuel seeping from the ruptured plane, the whole ocean could catch fire in moments. What was he doing? Had the crash disoriented him?

"Greg, no! Come back!"

On he swam, directly toward the billows of black smoke. Carrie coughed as the slight breeze drifted the stench closer. Helplessly, on hands and knees, she clung to the edge of the vinyl raft and watched, shivering with cold and shock. Greg was a strong swimmer, but the powerful current created by the downed plane kept pushing him back. He looked to be tiring, but was either too confused or too stubborn to turn back.

With all the energy left in her trembling, exhausted body, Carrie grabbed the bale bucket and tried to maneuver the dinghy back in Greg's direction. Already, their chances of survival were slim. If they became separated, the situation would be hopeless.

At least one hundred yards from her now, Greg lifted something black high into the air and shouted, though his words were lost in the crackle of fire and the rush of current. He turned and paddled rapidly in her direction, shoving aside chunks of wreckage as he came. Behind him, flames licked up the sides of the shattered fuselage and an ominous glow hovered above the oil-slicked ocean. The caustic stench of melting aircraft filled the air.

Arms aching, Carrie struggled to maintain position, too afraid to move nearer and determined not to drift farther away. Her eyes watered from the thick, acrid smoke, and as she paused to wipe them, she lost sight of Greg. Alarmed, she peered across the debris-littered gray green sea.

"Where are you?" She turned all of the way around inside the dinghy, searching wildly in every direction. Where could he be? "Greg," she called again.

No answer. How could he have disappeared like that? Had exhaustion overtaken him? A cramp? A shark? Was Greg dead? Her Greg? The father of her children, her first love. Tears gathered, but she refused to let them fall.

There was simply no time for weeping. If Greg was anywhere near, she had to find him. Urgently, she tried to row the raft toward the last place she'd seen her husband.

The current pushed against her, straining her already cramping, trembling muscles. She'd moved only two or three feet when the sky suddenly flared a deep orange. Carrie froze as an explosion ripped the air.

Throwing her arms protectively over her head, she fell to the bottom of the raft and curled into a ball. The small lifeboat rocked crazily. Water splashed on board. Shards of metal, fiberglass, and burning debris showered down around her.

When she'd last seen Greg, he was still too close to the plane. There was no way he could have survived such a blast. One prayer kept rumbling through her head: "Oh, God, please don't let Greg die."

Chapter 3

During Carrie's childhood, her troubled, alcoholic mother had disappeared more times than Carrie could remember. Her father, a highly respected physician, buried his own distress in longer hours at the hospital, leaving a frightened little girl alone for days at a time. Carrie had considered childhood the worst time of her life. She'd been wrong. Nothing compared to the terrifying abandonment she suffered now.

At the mercy of the current and the blast, the tiny raft pitched wildly about; but Carrie remained in the bottom, head down, too stunned to cry. Her thoughts vacillated between grief that Greg was dead and fury that he'd insisted on making this trip in the first place.

"Oh, Greg. Oh, what am I going to do?" she moaned, gripping her tangled, drenched hair with both hands.

"Carrie!" Greg's voice shocked her.

"You're alive!" she screamed, jubilant. Relief shuddered through her. Scrambling onto her knees, she leaned over the slick, vinyl edge of the raft, hands outstretched.

Holding to a section of the plane's wing, Greg propelled himself toward the raft. When he was within a few feet, Carrie grabbed the wing and drew it alongside the dinghy.

With clearly ebbing strength, Greg tossed a soggy backpack into the raft, climbed aboard, and collapsed, panting, on the floor. His usually glowing complexion was pasty. Bits of an unknown gray and silver material speckled his sopping blond hair. Blood oozed from a small wound just above his wrist.

"You're hurt." Battling the constant dip and sway of the raft, Carrie balanced on all fours at her husband's side. Tentatively, she reached toward the bloody arm.

Greg pulled away and sat up, gazing down at the small cut. "It's all right." Attempting to flex his wrist, he winced and cradled the arm against his chest. "Something must have bruised it in the blast."

"I thought you were dead. What on earth possessed you to go back?" Carrie wanted to be angry, but the attempt fell flat. She was too relieved to have him sitting safely in front of her.

"Water." He closed his eyes and lay back again, clearly spent.

"Water?" she laughed in disbelief. "We're surrounded by the stuff, in case you haven't noticed."

Raising his good arm, he gestured at the backpack. "Fresh water. There's a bottle in that bag. When I saw the bag floating so close to us, I had to get it. I wanted to salvage more, but this was the only thing I could reach in time. Without water, we won't survive more than a couple of days."

"Days?" Carrie's heart tripped in renewed fear. "Do you think it will take that long before we're rescued?"

"This corridor of the Atlantic is teeming with traffic." Greg's voice was soothing, reassuring. "We could be spotted in minutes, especially after that blast."

Carrie suspected he was intentionally downplaying the situation but knew too little about the region to be certain. Then he gently stroked her cheekbone, turning the subject away from rescue, she was sure.

"You're going to have a shiner. Sorry, Sweetheart." Even sopping wet in the chilly breeze, Greg's fingers felt warm against her skin. "More sorry than I can ever say."

For a moment, their glances met and held, and Carrie wondered if he was talking about the black eye or the plane crash or their marital problems. She edged away from his touch, sharply reminded that an apology wouldn't change any of them.

"What are we to do until help arrives?" Worriedly, she searched the vast ocean. Except for a demolished airplane, a tiny rubber raft, and the two of them, there was nothing.

With a slight shrug and a ghost of a grin, Greg said, "Enjoy the scenery. Pretend we're on a whale watch. Get a tan."

Carrie jerked upright, sending the dinghy careening crazily. The floor, made of heavy, rubberized canvas, was strong, but not very supportive. Every movement dumped them toward the center. Sinking down again, Carrie gripped the overhead canopy to steady herself. "How dare you be so cavalier? This is my life you've played Russian roulette with. Because of your selfishness, my babies may lose both of their parents. If you hadn't insisted we come on this stupid trip. . ."

Greg closed his eyes and lay back in the dinghy, swallowing convulsively. When he spoke, his voice was patient, solicitous—the voice he used with reluctant vendors and eccentric software designers. "If we have any chance of surviving this, we have to work together. Teamwork, Carrie. We have to lay aside our personal problems if we ever hope to see our kids again."

Acknowledging the truth in his words, Carrie softened the slightest bit. Nothing mattered at this point except survival.

Greg was smart and resourceful. If anyone could find a way to hang on until help arrived, Greg could. Carrie stiffened her spine, determined to do her part.

Taking a deep breath, she said quietly, "Okay. Teamwork."

His eyes flew open in surprise. A smug smile pulled at Carrie's lips. *How odd,* she thought, *to be able to smile in a situation so dire.*

Using his good arm for leverage, Greg sat up and surveyed the scene around them. In the distance, the fire still burned. "If we're lucky, someone will have heard our call for help and dispatched a rescue team. If they arrive before the smoke is gone, we'll be easier to spot."

"What if they don't?"

Greg looked at her sharply. "We use everything we've got to keep fighting until someone does find us. We'll stay near the wreckage as long as possible, but if all else fails, we'll sail this little rubber boat toward land." He paused. "Praying wouldn't hurt anything, either."

Carrie rolled her eyes. "If God gave one fig about us, we wouldn't be stranded in the middle of the Bermuda

Triangle in a life raft."

"We survived the crash, didn't we?"

Humbled, Carrie relented. "Yes, we did, at that."

Greg smiled at her bemused expression. "Remember what we used to say? That as long as we're together, nothing can defeat us?"

Of course, she remembered. That had been their motto—the two of them against the world, invincible.

"Things have changed—"

"Not that," Greg interrupted, his handsome face tense with determination. "We can do this, Sweetheart. I'm going to get you back home to those kids. I promise." He glanced back toward the crash site. "And we'd better get started now."

Adrenaline surged through Carrie as she followed the direction of his gaze. The plane wreckage was scattering rapidly on the waves and the fire was dying down, leaving only a thin trail of smoke. Already, their dinghy had drifted a considerable distance from the crash site.

Gesturing at the raft's side, Greg scooted toward her. "We'll toss that anchor overboard. That should help hold us close to the plane for awhile, anyway."

Greg winced as he stretched his arm out and grabbed the small, metal sea anchor.

"I think your arm is more than bruised."

"It's all right." He looked down at the oozing wound.

"You've said that before, but I don't believe it. Here." She untied the expensive scarf from around her neck. In the near-tropical heat, the thin silk had already dried, and the gritty feel of crystallized salt roughened the texture. "We can use this to make a sling."

"No. I can't use my arm if it's all trussed up."

"You can't use it, anyway. Now let me do this." When he offered no further resistance, Carrie fashioned an efficient sling around his forearm. On her knees in front of him, she reached behind his head to secure the scarf. His tanned skin was warm beneath her touch and their bodies so close she could feel his breath against her cheek. A sudden memory arose of Greg holding her in his arms, warming her against the December chill as they waited for the attendant to pound a base on their first scraggly Christmas tree. Even the pungent scent of pine rushed back as Carrie recalled a time when she'd felt so secure, so loved. For a moment, she longed to lean against his chest and let him banish the fear raging inside her.

"Pretty fancy," Greg cracked, oblivious to her sentimental musings. "A designer sling."

Slowly, Carrie dropped her arms but remained within inches of her husband. "Only the best for Raleigh's up-and-coming businessman of the year," she quipped. Then, disturbed at how easily she could be charmed by Greg's nearness, she tilted away and looked up into the cloudless, blue sky. Though the sun was already moving down toward the horizon, the heat remained intense. What had been much-needed warmth when they first clambered aboard the raft was now scorching her skin and sealing the salt against her tender flesh.

Suddenly alert, Greg also turned his attention to the sky. "Do you hear something?"

Squinting, Carrie listened hard. Waves clapped against the dinghy, but above that she heard a faint sound, too indistinct to identify.

"Is it a bird?"

"I hope it's a plane."

"No, wait." Greg met her gaze with a wry grin. "It's . . . Superman."

Carrie laughed in spite of herself. "How can you joke?"

"How can I not?" He pointed. There, in the distance, a silver speck moved toward them and the droning increased.

Carrie jumped to her feet. "It is a plane!"

The boat teetered precariously, and she slipped back to the wet, slick floor. "We're rescued. Thank God."

Greg wasn't so quick to rejoice. He squinted at the plane's approach, then removed Carrie's scarf from his arm, gripped the canopy top for support and stood, waving the tiny piece of silk. "Wave your arms, Honey, and anything else you can find. They're more likely to see movement."

Quickly, Carrie scanned the raft and, finding nothing with which to signal, slung her arms into the air and yelled at the top of her lungs. The plane looked so small, she feared the two of them appeared like inconsequential specks of nothing. How would they ever be seen?

In a fluid motion that belied his injured condition, Greg thrust the scarf toward her, then ripped off his golf shirt and swung it overhead. The peach garment made a bright spot against the azure sky while Carrie's puny bit of blue print silk blended with the heavens.

Blue. Why had she worn blue? Red would have shown up so much better, but Greg loved her in red, so she'd ignored the dozen or so crimson outfits in favor of the cool blue. Her spitefulness may have cost them their only chance at rescue.

Hope withered as the plane slowly vanished into the sunlight, and the droning faded to silence until only the harsh, disappointed breathing of two castaways remained.

Tears gathered in Carrie's eyes and clogged her throat. She slumped forward over her knees. "Now what?"

Greg eased down beside her. "Hey," he said, stroking her tangled hair. "Don't give up. I don't even think that plane was searching for us. It was flying too high. Another one could be on the way right now, following the signal from our emergency locator."

"It will be dark soon." Her voice trembled. She raised her face and shamelessly allowed the tears to fall. "I'm so scared."

"Oh, Baby." Before Carrie could resist, Greg gathered her in his arms and drew them both beneath the canopy. "Don't be scared. I'll take care of you, no matter what happens."

As foolish as the promise was, a wonderful feeling of protection and security enveloped Carrie when Greg cradled her against his warm, sturdy chest. His heart beat against her ear. He smelled of salt and sea, but she didn't mind. Part of her love for him had always been his strength and confidence, and she absorbed it from him now.

The sun inched closer to the west and dusky light filled the air. With the loss of the sun came a sudden drop in temperature. Constant sea spray misted the couple and even with the protection of the canopy, Carrie shivered. Greg drew her closer, warming her body with his.

When his lips grazed her forehead, she tensed. She hadn't allowed Greg to kiss her since. . . An image of her husband holding another woman rose in Carrie's mind.

Though it took all her willpower, Carrie pulled away. "Don't, Greg."

She felt his disappointment, but he released her. Goosebumps prickled her arms as the chilly wind rushed in to take Greg's place. Shivering, she rubbed at them.

"Carrie." Greg spoke without anger. The timbre of his voice warmed her from the inside out. "No matter what you think of me, we have to share body heat. It's a matter of survival."

Survive. All she'd done for months was survive, and she wasn't about to stop now. With an almost grim determination, she returned to Greg's side and, without a word, snuggled into his arms. He'd replaced his shirt, but she could still feel his warmth and the strong beating of his heart against her cheek. The longing to really hold him was intense, but she blocked the emotion. Her children needed her, and she'd do whatever it took to get home to them, even if it meant snuggling against Greg's body once again. But she would not allow herself to enjoy it.

Chapter 4

Greg wrapped his arms around Carrie and thought of all the other times he'd held her. He'd missed this—this touch of her tall, slender body against his. The softness of her skin. The special scent of her hair that even a dunk in the ocean couldn't erase.

Drawing in a deep breath, he listened to the water lapping against the raft. His heart felt like a fist clenched inside his chest, tight and squeezing. This was a fine predicament he'd gotten them into, and he had to find a way out. Carrie and their children were his life. Protecting them was his job. After a childhood of barely getting by, he had worked so hard to be successful, but as trite as it sounded, without his family—without his Carrie—money meant nothing at all.

Carrie stirred, and he lightly stroked her back, murmuring loving promises as he pulled her closer. "Oh, Carrie, I love you." He swallowed and clamped his eyes shut against the torrent of emotion pressing behind them. "I love you so much. I promise not to let you down this time. No matter what I have to do, I'll get you back home to your babies."

Placing a kiss against her temple, he sealed his promise, knowing she must be asleep because she'd never consciously allow him such liberty. He was determined to change that, to make up for his stupid, stupid error in judgment. What ever had possessed him to look at another woman when he had Carrie?

Darkness descended, pure and absolute, in a way that never happened in the city. The stars above dimpled in silver splendor, and a matching moon reflected on the endless ocean. In another situation, the view would have been awe-inspiring. Greg looked up, imagining God in His heaven, ever awake and ready to hear the call of His children. That's what Pastor Simms had said anyway, and Greg could feel the pull and the reassurance of Someone greater than himself, even in this seemingly impossible situation.

In the hours of counseling over the last few months, Greg had learned a great deal about God as well as about himself and his floundering marriage. He'd been more lost than he was now the first time he'd stumbled into the pastor's study, confused, angry, and terrified. The reverend had wisely pointed him to God first, saying he had to get that relationship in order before the other would ever come right. When he'd prayed with the minister, primarily as a means to get his wife back, he'd gotten much more in the process. Pastor had been right. Now, he had Someone much wiser than he to help him win Carrie's love and trust again.

"Go back to those early days of marriage, Greg," Pastor Simms had said. "Remind her of why she married you. Woo her. Win her all over again by doing the things that charmed her in the past."

And he would. He'd do anything. Anything. . .though he hadn't counted on trying to renew his marriage while stranded in a lifeboat. Now, more than ever, he had to find a way back into her heart before it was too late. There was no way to know how much time they had left.

"Lord," he whispered to the inky sky. "You can see how desperate we are down here, how much we need Your help. I don't know what to do, and as much as I hate to admit it, I'm scared. Scared of not being man enough to handle dying. Scared of my kids growing up without me. Scared of letting something happen to Carrie."

Resting his head back against the taut cushion of the vinyl raft, Greg closed his eyes, a raw and primitive grief welling up inside him. "I promised to get her back home to her babies, Lord, and I know what it may take to do that. Help me be man enough to see it through."

As Greg drifted off to sleep, his last thoughts were of his children. . .and Carrie.

⚓

The first light of dawn, pink and stunning, shot rays into the heavens and across the quiet ocean. Gently untangling himself from Carrie's long slender limbs, Greg edged from beneath the orange canopy to stretch his cramped, aching muscles. As expected, the night had been long and miserable.

His wrist throbbed, reminding him of the injury, so he peeked under the makeshift sling. The bone was broken. He was certain of that much, and the redness and swelling indicated the first signs of infection. He didn't know a lot about sea survival, but he did know that injuries exacerbate rapidly in the unrelenting water and salt. He adjusted Carrie's scarf to better support the wrist and cover the oozing sore. No sense in worrying Carrie about it. There was nothing either of them could do except pray, and all through the long night he'd prayed.

He'd led Carrie to believe they could sail the dinghy toward Bermuda if all else failed, but he hadn't told her how far they were from land. If he calculated correctly, a good two hundred miles lay between them and the pink shores of Bermuda. Along the way was the dead calm and the violent storms of the Sargasso Sea deep inside the mysterious and deadly area known as the Bermuda Triangle. The chances of maneuvering this tiny vinyl craft that far in those conditions were extremely small, but he'd try it if all else failed.

He glanced back at his wife's sleeping form, the familiar feelings of guilt and failure rising up to torture him. Even lost at sea, he couldn't stop thinking about his crippled marriage. He was a man who had built a huge business from the ground up on a shoestring. He was a doer, a mover and shaker. He loved taking control and making things happen. So how had he allowed their relationship to crumble?

He knew the answer. He'd been Carrie's everything, and that had made his failure even more unbearable.

After the kids came and the business skyrocketed, their marriage had spun out of control. He loved his job and never minded the long hours, but Carrie wanted him by her side constantly. She couldn't understand that he had to work so hard to provide the kind of life she and the kids deserved. Unlike his working-class family, she'd never done without a single material thing in her life.

When they married, he'd promised that she never would, and yet she expected him to be at her beck and call and still earn enough money to keep her happy.

Carrie stirred again, and Greg smiled. Even in this unthinkable situation, she was the most beautiful woman he'd ever seen. Her rare combination of grace and elegance reminded him of Jacqueline Kennedy, and he'd always felt like a king with her on his arm. Somehow, some way, if they survived this disaster, he'd find a way to make her his again.

Sighing, his gaze fell to the small backpack rescued in the aftermath of the crash. The bag contained a single bottle of fresh water. Only one—a small one at that. Removing it from the pack, he solemnly studied the words printed in blue. These few ounces were hardly enough for one of them to last a day in this heat.

The talk he'd had with God last night drifted across his consciousness and for the first time since the crash, he felt encouraged. Stooping, he moved under the canopy to Carrie.

"Hey, Sleepyhead. Time for coffee."

As Carrie stretched and groaned, Greg knelt beside her, offering the water.

"Coffee," Carrie mumbled in a sleep-scratched voice, eyes still closed. A tiny smile lifted her full, generous mouth.

Heartened by that reception, Greg continued in a teasing manner. "Yep. The finest imported coffee in the world. I ground these beans myself." He removed the lid and touched the bottle to her lips. "Smell that fresh, mountain-grown aroma?"

"Mmm." Carrie sat up straighter and pushed her long, dark hair away from her face. Taking the water, she shrank against the side of the raft, the now fully awakened Carrie less welcoming than the drowsy one. "I really am thirsty." As she tilted the bottle, she paused. "How much should I drink? We have to conserve, don't we?"

"Take what you want for now. We'll worry about rationing if help doesn't come soon."

"What about you?"

"Oh, don't worry about me. There's another bottle." Somewhere.

Carrie took several sips. "Ah, that's good. I don't suppose you could rustle up an omelet to go with this delicious espresso, could you?"

Greg shook his head. "Wish I could say yes, but I'm afraid we'll have to fish for our dinner."

Carrie frowned, unconvinced. "With what?"

"Never question the ingenuity of a computer geek." With more enthusiasm than he felt, Greg winked and began removing his belt.

Even though the chances of catching any fish were slim, he had to make the effort. If he could manage to shape the buckle into a hook, at least they'd have a fishing line. As he struggled to brace the belt against one knee and work it with his good hand, Carrie quietly took one side and pulled. In no time, they'd transformed the belt into a leather fishing line, complete with a gold-plated hook.

"Teamwork," Greg said, pleased that she'd helped him, though the effort had set his arm to throbbing again. Absently, he rubbed at it.

Carrie frowned. "Is your arm worse this morning?"

He drew the wounded limb to one side. "It's fine."

"Let me see. I didn't grow up a doctor's daughter for nothing." With gentle hands, Carrie supported his wrist while sliding the scarf out of the way. "Oooh." She drew the word out, worrying over him. "This looks a lot more swollen than yesterday, and the cut is redder, too. We need to clean it." She reached back for the container of water.

"No," Greg answered quickly. Taking the bottle, he stowed it in the backpack. "Seawater will do fine."

Actually, he had no idea if seawater was a good idea or not, but he saw little choice. They were going to need every drop of drinking water they had.

Though Carrie looked doubtful, she didn't argue.

As Greg knelt and swished the wound in the sea, Carrie joined him at the raft's edge. His chest tightened with the unspoken support. For some reason that he would not question, she had softened toward him this morning. He wanted to believe she still cared, no matter what their problems. Having her beside him was worth the injury, even if it meant getting his arm ripped off by a shark.

Sharks! Greg yanked his arm into the boat. He hadn't considered the danger of sharks. With a worried survey of the water, he prayed there were none in the area. Tranquil, green blue waves lapped at the side of the raft, though what lay beneath them remained a troublesome mystery.

"What shall we use for bait?" Carrie's voice interrupted his worries.

Not my arm, he thought wryly, shaking off the latest

concern as he refocused on the need for food. With Carrie looking at him with confidence in her clear green eyes, waiting for him to come up with a solution, he couldn't let her down. He'd wanted to see that expression on her face again for so long, he'd do anything to keep it there. Retying the makeshift sling gave him a moment to think, and he was glad when Carrie reached up to help. As she leaned forward, her silver earrings dangled, brushing against his cheek. He smiled inwardly. He had found a fishing lure.

"Are you willing to sacrifice one of those earrings?" he asked.

A momentary look of puzzlement was replaced by admiration. A quick study, Carrie immediately grasped his intent. Nodding, she reached up to remove the quarter-sized, silver disk from her earlobe. "You're a genius, Mr. Bridges."

"Hardly." Shaking his head, Greg took the offered earring. A genius wouldn't have crashed his wife in the middle of the Atlantic. Nor would he have hurt her by looking at another woman. "I've been an idiot, Carrie. A fool and an idiot."

At the reminder of his indiscretion, the admiration disappeared and she turned away, retreating beneath the awning while he fashioned a serviceable lure from the expensive silver, then cast it into the sea at the end of his makeshift line.

The next few hours passed without success. Occasionally, Carrie slipped out to join him, offering to take over the fishing chore. Each time he refused, determined to accomplish this one thing for her. His belly gnawed with hunger. Though she hadn't complained, Greg was certain that Carrie, with her smaller physique and delicate skin, must be suffering the effects of no food and so much sun.

"I've always heard there are plenty of fish in the sea, but I'll never believe that again," Carrie quipped, coming up beside Greg once again. "You're getting sunburned. Why don't you go into the shade and let me try for awhile?"

Though his arm throbbed and his knees were growing weak, Greg shook his head. "I'm okay, but thanks for caring."

Instantly Greg regretted his choice of words. Carrie tensed. "I never said I cared. I just offered to help. Right now, survival is the issue, not caring."

Heaving a sigh, Greg drew the belt into the boat and fiddled absently with the makeshift lure. So much for thinking she'd softened. This is what his marriage had come down to. Even if they were somehow rescued, Carrie was never going to forgive him.

Once, she'd sparkled whenever he entered a room. He remembered her first pregnancy, how she glowed then with an inner radiance that took his breath away. That had been such an incredible time, so rich with uncharted territory for them to explore together. One particular night stood out in his memory—the night he'd first felt his child move inside Carrie's body.

She'd been propped up in bed, reading some book about raising the perfect child, her slightly rounded stomach poking up beneath the thin sheet. She wasn't very big yet, though she'd been proudly wearing maternity tops for more than two months. Greg flopped across the bed sideways, bringing his face in line with the mound that harbored his child. Since the day he'd discovered his wife was pregnant, Greg had looked forward to nightly conversations with his offspring. Someone had told him babies could hear inside the womb, and Greg wanted to be sure his baby knew its daddy's voice.

"Hey, Kid." He tapped his knuckles softly on Carrie's belly. "You awake? This is your daddy out here. How's it going in there?" He cocked his head at an angle and pretended to listen. "What? Again? Oh, you poor kid. Sure, I'll tell her."

Carrie lay her book on her chest. "Tell me what?"

"He says to stop with the fried jalepeno peppers and orange sherbet." Greg gave a shiver of disgust. "Gives him heartburn."

Carrie giggled. "Heartburn, huh?"

"Yeah." Greg nodded knowingly. "But he's all over that lasagna you made tonight. Great stuff."

"His daddy likes that, too," she mused. "Imagine that."

"Must be in the genes."

Stifling a laugh, Carrie arched an eyebrow knowingly. "Bet he loves pizza."

Greg brightened. "I don't know, but that's important. I'd better ask." Placing both hands around his wife's belly, he stared down as though gazing into a crystal ball. "Hey, little buddy, do you like pizza? You do? Uh-huh, I see. None of those sissy veggie pizzas. I got ya, Pal. I'll tell your mom. She'll understand."

"He's a pepperoni man all the way," Greg reported to Carrie's smiling face.

"Like father, like son." Arching her back, Carrie stretched and settled farther into the pillows with a serene smile. "How do you get him to tell you all these things? He never says a word to me."

"That's because you're too far away from the microphone." He tapped her belly button. "I speak into this and the little man hears every word. Besides, it's a guy thing. Male bonding. He'll talk to you later."

"What if he's a girl?"

Greg wrinkled his brow, thinking. A girl. A sweet little girl who looked like Carrie and smelled like Carrie and laughed like Carrie. Two of them. He sighed blissfully. Talk about paradise.

"Hey, Bud," he said into the "microphone" as he winked at his wife, "it's okay if you're a girl—as long as you like pizza."

Carrie laughed and swatted him with her book. "Greg Bridges, you are so—" She froze, a transfixed expression on her face.

"Carrie? What's wrong?" Automatically, his hands encircled her belly, this time protectively. "Is it the baby? Is she okay?"

Carrie pressed her fingers over his. "He's moving again. Hold your hand right there. Just wait."

Heart hammering in anticipation, Greg held his breath and waited, greedy to feel the child he'd made with this woman he loved so much. She'd felt movement for weeks, but Greg had yet to share the experience. They waited, silent and tense, hungering for the magic moment that only the two of them could ever share. Then it came, a flutter like the wings of a caged butterfly, a rippling of the tiny swimmer, stirring the waters inside his mother.

Greg held fast to Carrie's gaze, knowing the wonder in her face was reflected on his own. He rejoiced to see it there, to know that she, too, was moved beyond words by this event. His throat had grown thick with myriad emotions—awe, joy, responsibility, fear, pride, and a love so enormous he'd thought his chest would explode.

The sound of yelling broke through his poignant memories, mentally jerking him back into the little four-by-four lifeboat. "Greg, help me. Hurry!"

Greg's adrenaline kicked in. Carrie needed him.

Chapter 5

Carrie squealed and grabbed for the small fish flopping wildly at her feet.

"Come on, Greg. Don't just stand there. Help me catch him before he jumps out." Greg had a strange expression on his face, but Carrie had no time to think about it. She made another slap at the slick flying fish that had the misfortune of landing in the raft during one of his leaps.

Her abrupt motions set the tiny boat to wobbling crazily, and she lost her balance, falling onto her side. Greg sprang into action, scrambling after the hapless fish on both knees and one good hand. The swaying boat unbalanced him as well, and when he lunged for the silvery fish, he fell across Carrie, pinning her to the floor of the raft.

The fish gave one final lurch, careened into Carrie's knee, and rested momentarily on the floor of the boat beneath her thigh. With Greg's body across her, Carrie couldn't use her hands to capture the prize. Seeing their only hope of food about to escape, she snapped her knees together, trapping the fish.

"I've got him. I've got him. Hurry. Get up." The fish's tail pounded wildly against her skin. She could feel him slipping away.

Greg whipped around and clamped a hand over the squirming creature. "Got ya!" he shouted, exultant.

A breathless, tangled mass of arms and legs, they lay on the wet deck with their wiggling catch between them. Despite her determination to remain distant, Carrie couldn't help laughing at the ridiculous situation.

"We finally caught one."

"I think he caught us," Greg answered, eyeing the small fish with a grin completely out of proportion to the accomplishment. Carefully, he eased their catch out of Carrie's knee grasp and into his own firm grip.

"Now what do we do? Rub two sticks together and make a fire to roast him over?"

"Hmm, good point," Greg answered. "All I have left is a soggy wallet and my house key." Brightening, he handed her the fish, dug in his pants pocket, and produced the key. Reclaiming their catch, he braced it against his knee with his wounded arm and used the key to crudely gut the fish. "My dear, you are about to eat the finest sushi this side of Tokyo."

During the early years of their marriage, when they'd had little money for nights out, Greg's imagination had turned tuna into lobster and their tiny apartment into romantic locales. With his teasing charm and creative bent, he'd more than made up for what they lacked.

Carrie opened her mouth to tell him just how ridiculous his idea was, but common sense stopped her. She was thirsty, hungry, scared, and going stir-crazy from hours of nothing but aimless drifting. Greg was valiantly trying to make an impossible predicament more tolerable and help them both forget, if only for awhile, how desperate their situation was. What harm would there be in playing along? Pretense was better than reality.

Curling to a sitting position, she took the crudely cleaned fish and began rolling the flesh into pinwheels. "Sushi sounds delightful." She lifted an eyebrow. "Shall we dress for dinner? I just bought the most fabulous outfit."

Greg's look of pleased surprise told her that he remembered those imaginary dates, too. "Absolutely. I'll call ahead for reservations."

"I do hope we get a table overlooking the ocean."

Carrie's deadpan quip drew a bark of laughter from Greg. "I think that can be arranged. With a woman as beautiful as you on my arm, we'll have the best seat in the place."

Her skin felt raw and irritated from the salt and sun, her hair was a tangled mess, and her beautiful silk outfit ruined, but Greg's words and glances still had the power to make her believe she was beautiful—even when they were pretending. When the "sushi" was ready, Greg took her hand and helped her to her feet. Silly as it was, Carrie's heart did a strange somersault. For some reason, the crazy adventure of capturing the fish eased the strain between them, and Carrie had to admit she was glad.

"Why, thank you, Sir." She curtsied, careful not to rock the boat and send them both sprawling. "I must say you look particularly roguish in that designer sling."

Greg lifted her hand and brushed his lips over her

fingertips. "You, my darling, are stunning in that red gown."

Carrie glanced down at her rumpled blue blouse and salt-crusted white slacks, allowing herself a giggle.

"I believe our table is ready." With a grand, sweeping gesture, Greg motioned inside the pitiful shelter. "Shall we go in to dinner?"

Carrie entered first, carrying the handful of "sushi." Crossing her ankles, she slid down into the corner of the raft, leaning back against the puffy vinyl sides. Greg followed suit, settling beside her, a bit too close for comfort, but Carrie didn't protest. She'd promised a truce and would keep that promise until they were safely back on dry land. For now, staying alive was far more important than their marital problems.

"Is this table acceptable?" Greg asked.

"The view of the ocean is exceptional."

Greg took in the endless, watery sight and laughed. "You're right as always, my darling. Now, shall we dine?" Taking the sushi from her hand, he held a tiny roll against her lips.

Warmth crept into Carrie's stomach at the very idea of Greg feeding her. Shrinking back, she shook her head. "Greg, no."

"Old Japanese custom," he teased. "Bad luck comes to those who reject honorable intentions."

"That sounds more like a Chinese fortune cookie."

"Hmm. You could be right, at that." With a jaunty grin, he tapped her lips. "Whatever nationality, it's good advice. Now, eat."

Hunger overcame her resistance. This was a game,

nothing more. Parting her lips and ignoring the strong fishy scent, she took the proffered bite and quickly gulped it down.

"My turn." Greg's mouth opened expectantly.

Carrie wanted to refuse, but she didn't. Heart beating a little faster, her fingers trembled when she brushed Greg's warm, dry lips. After only a nibble, Greg grimaced and offered the remaining fish to Carrie. "You eat it. You're a bigger fan of sushi than I."

"You need to eat, too," Carrie protested.

Greg patted his flat belly. "I could stand to loose a few pounds. You can't."

Pretending insult, Carrie rested a hand on one hip. "Are you saying I'm too skinny?"

"Not at all." Greg waggled his eyebrows. "There is nothing wrong with your body. Fact is," he slipped one arm around her narrow waist, "it's absolutely perfect."

Though Carrie sidled away from his embrace, she flushed with pleasure. Since the night she'd walked into Greg's office and seen him embracing another woman, Carrie's self-esteem had taken a beating. When Greg tapped her lips again, she took the remaining fish without protest. All the while, he teased and flattered, making outlandish comments about her beauty and intelligence. He made her laugh and, for awhile, forget all the heartache and trouble that lay between them.

Here on the sea, they were simply two castaways with no future and no past. Nothing mattered except this moment. Who knew how many more they might have?

"Waiter," Greg snapped his fingers, then held the plastic water bottle up to the invisible maitre d'. "Haven't you any finer crystal than this? Only the best will do for my wife." In the full force of silliness, he set down the bottle and withdrew his damp, swollen wallet, extracted a thick wad of hundred dollar bills and waved them in the air. "While you're at it bring her diamonds and furs, a mansion in Maui, a. . ."

Suddenly, Greg's voice dwindled away. His smile became a pensive look of regret and longing. Gazing from Carrie's bedraggled appearance to the money in his hand, he swallowed hard. "When we get home, I'm going to buy you all those things, Sweetheart. Whatever it is you want, whatever it takes to prove how sorry I am, I'll get it for you. No matter what the cost."

Icy disappointment cut through Carrie. The game of pretend turned as sour as their marriage. She glared at the cash, repulsed. "Is that what you think? That I only want things? That I only care about money?"

Carrie yanked the bills from his hand, holding them aloft. "Don't you understand I was a thousand times happier when all we had were dreams? I hate this." Voice rising, she shook the money at him. "I hate what it's done to you, what it's done to us. I hate it, hate it, hate it!"

In a fury, she flung their vacation cash into the air. The sea breeze caught the lightweight paper, and before either of them could react, several thousand dollars fluttered away and drifted down onto the sparkling ocean. In stunned silence, they both stared as the bills wafted like tiny green canoes farther and farther out to sea.

Carrie clapped a horrified hand over her mouth. "Greg, I'm so sorry. What a stupid thing to do."

His face held no anger, only surprise at her revelation. "I never knew you felt that way. I thought. . ." He shook his head like a prizefighter who'd taken too many blows. "What a mess."

"I'll get the bail bucket. Perhaps we can maneuver close enough to grab some of them."

Greg stopped her with a touch on the arm. "Forget about it. All the money on Wall Street won't help us out here."

Gripping the slick vinyl sides, Carrie knelt at the raft's edge and stared out to sea. Once there had been more between them than a bank account and material possessions—so much more, that her heart grieved at the loss. The raft listed slightly as Greg knelt, too, facing her profile.

"What's happened to us, Carrie?" The ache in Greg's whisper tore at Carrie's defenses. "Where did we go wrong?"

"There!" Carrie jerked upright, sending the raft into wild gyrations. Water splashed on board. "Look, Greg." Hardly able to contain her excitement, she grabbed her bewildered partner by the arms. "Land! I see land."

Beside her, Greg stiffened and carefully extracted his injured wrist from her grip. His pained expression quickly changed to amazement as he followed her pointing finger. Cradling his wound against his chest, he scrambled for the bail bucket and started paddling toward the distant speck of land.

"Maybe we can make it before sundown."

Carrie lunged for the backpack, a pitiful oar, but all she had. They breathlessly paddled in anticipatory silence. Soon, soon, they would reach the distant shore and safety, where she could call her children and hear their precious voices once again. The nightmare would be over. Maybe Greg's prayers had worked.

After more than an hour of desperate effort, the land disappeared as suddenly as it had come. Greg stopped paddling and lay back, exhausted.

"Greg, we have to keep on. We have to. Please, don't stop now. You can do it."

"It's no use."

"What are you talking about? We have to be very near land by now. It was so close."

"There is no land, Carrie." Dejection filled his voice.

"But, I saw it. . . ." As realization washed over her, Carrie sagged onto the damp, rubber floor. "No land?" She looked at Greg, expression pleading.

"A mirage, Sweetheart." Eyes closed, chest heaving, he lay against the side, spent. "Only a mirage."

All the fight went out of Carrie. Reality set in as she accepted the truth. They might never be rescued. She might never see her children again. Her worst fear would be realized. Kristen and Dylan would grow up thinking their mother and father had abandoned them.

Though she couldn't imagine having a drop of spare fluid in her body, salty tears burned her eyelids as she began to weep—softly, at first, then louder as the torrent of hurt and loss gushed forth.

In the next instant, Greg's strong arms came around her, drawing her against his chest. Though the sling made for an awkward embrace, the ever-resourceful Greg managed to hold her as if he had two good arms.

"Shh." His murmured words ruffled her damp hair.

"Don't cry. Please don't cry."

Taking the only comfort available, Carrie returned his embrace, burying her face in the warm curve of his neck. When the great wave of grief subsided, Carrie felt as limp and empty as an old pair of pantyhose.

When Greg unwound her arms from around his neck and moved away beneath the canopy, Carrie buried her face in her hands, humiliated. She'd thrown herself on him and he was clearly disgusted, unable to deal with her hysteria. When the little four-by-four boat listed, heralding Greg's return, Carrie peeked through her fingers. Instead of the disgust she had expected, all she saw on Greg's face was tender concern.

"Drink this." As he'd done several times that day, he pressed the water bottle against her raw, swollen lips. Gratefully, she sipped, savoring the precious liquid, moistening her lips and mouth before swallowing.

"You'd better drink some, too. We seem to be conserving it pretty well, don't you think?"

Greg's odd reaction piqued her concern. Hesitating, he stared down at the water and rubbed a hand over his lips, the sound grating like sandpaper. Though he had to be thirsty after two days in this heat and salt, he seemed reluctant to drink. True, the supply in this bottle was low, right at the bottom edge of the label, but there was yet another full bottle in the backpack.

Finally he complied, lifting the bottle quickly to his lips. Then he capped the container and stashed it back inside the bag tied firmly to the side of the boat.

When he returned to her side and gathered her into his arms once again, she went gratefully, needing the solace of his touch. She was too disheartened at that moment to hold a grudge or to worry about his odd behavior toward the water.

They drifted awhile in silence, holding each other close, the incessant slap of surf against the frail raft the only sound. Another day had come and gone, and there was still no sign of rescue.

Chapter 6

With the third day came an increasing sense of lethargy, and Carrie noticed that Greg looked dazed and weary. He continued to ply her with morning "coffee"—her ration of water—and to make bad jokes about their situation, but now the effort grew increasingly forced. After a half-hearted, unsuccessful attempt to catch fish, heat, hunger, and thirst drove them beneath the canopy to conserve what little energy they had left. Though Greg wouldn't admit it, Carrie knew the hope for rescue was fading with each day that passed.

They lay together beneath the orange canopy, listless and discouraged. The sun blistered down, heating the vinyl raft to a miserable temperature.

"Remember when we were newlyweds?" Greg asked, his voice husky, whether from thirst or emotion, she couldn't tell. "All those times we sat out on the fire escape and wished on that first star."

"I remember." Something about the gentle rocking of the boat and the reminiscence in Greg's voice stripped away the last vestige of Carrie's resistance. What did it matter if they talked openly now? The past was probably all the time they'd ever have. "That was the best time of our lives."

The sweet memory eased some of her fear and despair.

"What? That crowded, crummy little three-room apartment?" He shifted, turning so that she lay across his lap, gazing up. Disbelief shone in his eyes.

"I loved that place!" Carrie protested.

"You're kidding, right?" When she shook her head, he went on. "I was so ashamed of taking you from your father's elegant home to that place, but it was all I could afford."

"Oh, Greg." Carrie pressed one hand against his chest, amazed he felt that way. "We were so happy then—just the two of us with so much hope for the future, working together."

"We couldn't even afford an office." Greg's mouth twisted downward.

"That was the best part. We were together, all day, every day, building the business. You and me against the world."

She treasured that wonderful time. The lack of money hadn't bothered her at all. After growing up alone and frightened in a mansion filled with things, she'd found security in their tiny apartment. Most of all, she'd found someone who loved her enough to be with her every hour of the day. She'd give up everything they owned to go back to that time.

"Strange that we never discussed it. I was afraid if I didn't make the business succeed in a hurry, you'd pack up and go home to your father."

The confident, controlled Greg Bridges, afraid? As the

image formed in Carrie's mind, her heart softened. Greg had been afraid of losing her.

"I prayed every night for success, for a way to give you all the things you needed and deserved."

Happiness curled in Carrie's stomach, filling it in a way the meager bits of fish hadn't. "You did?"

"Sometimes I'd wake up in the night and just lie there for hours, watching you sleep, thanking God for you, and praying."

The purl of pleasure billowed higher. No matter how he'd hurt her, she loved this man with all her heart. Trust was another matter.

"We never should have left that apartment." The notion was foolish, she knew, but a part of her believed it.

Greg furrowed his brow in agreement. "We left something essential behind when the business took off and we moved on to bigger things."

"Togetherness?"

He shook his head and motioned upward with one finger. "God."

The familiar empty ache rose in Carrie's chest. What had happened to her faith? To that marvelous peace and contentment she'd experienced in those long ago days? It had dwindled away, little by little, crowded out by a busy life.

"Why did you bring that up?" she asked.

"I've wanted to discuss this with you for a long time."

"Why didn't you?"

"The time never seemed right, and I wasn't sure how you'd react."

"To God?"

"To me." He shrugged. "To my new relationship with God."

"A new relationship?" So that was it. God was the difference she'd felt and seen in Greg during this entire ordeal. "So when did you get all holy?"

The question came out wrong, crudely—when in truth, she longed to hear the answer. Greg was different.

"I'm a long way from being holy, but I have put my life back in God's hands. When I realized I was about to lose you and the kids, I had to get some help. At first, I went to the pastor, thinking he could talk some sense into you, but good old Pastor Simms thought I was the one who needed talking to. He was right. During the counseling sessions, he led me to see how I'd let Sunshine Software become my god and that the terrible gnawing need in my gut wasn't for more money, prestige, or even for my family; it was that empty spot only the Lord can fill."

Funny, they'd met at a Christian organization on campus and both had committed their lives to Christ, but Greg hadn't been to church since their business took off like a rocket. Though disappointed that her husband didn't want to spend his Sundays with her, Carrie wanted her children to grow up with Christian values; so she'd attended church, watched over the nursery, and served on committees. No one was more active or involved in the huge metropolitan church than Carrie Bridges. For all her industry, though, she found little comfort or fulfillment there. She'd done her best, worked her hardest to do what was right, and yet God, like her own parents, seemed to ignore her. Greg on the other hand, was so full of sin, he'd dishonored his marriage vows; but here he was, claiming a peace with God and himself—a peace that she didn't have. Piercing hurt and resentment stabbed through Carrie. God was there for Greg, but not for her. Where was the fairness—the love—in that?

"I know I don't deserve God's forgiveness," Greg said softly. "Or yours, for that matter."

Carrie jerked her head up. "How did you know what I was thinking?"

Greg's smile was sad. "Because it's what you should be thinking. You have a right." He reached for her hand and held it lightly. His felt dry and hot. "Fortunately for me, God doesn't give us what we deserve. I asked Him for forgiveness and mercy, and He gave it to me, along with a peace that I can't begin to explain." His voice lowered, almost pleading. "God's forgiven me, Carrie. I hope you will, too. I'm not the same selfish fool who hurt you by getting involved with someone else. You have to believe that I love you. I don't want to lose you. Melanie was a mistake I would never make again."

"Melanie Warner." Carrie's mouth twisted bitterly. Just saying the name left a bad taste.

"If I had it to do all over again—"

"Well, you don't. Nothing can erase what you did to us." Carrie pushed his hand away. "Not even God. Please. Let's not talk about this anymore."

Carrie scooted out from under the raft's canopy as far as possible, but even at that, she and Greg were separated by less than four feet of space. Even if they were stuck here forever, she couldn't bear to listen to Greg's confession. More than that, she didn't want to feel the powerful tug of his personality, charming his way back into her good graces. Once he'd been her best friend, her lover, her protector. He was her hero, and she was the princess he'd rescued from the lonely ivory tower. Now, they'd probably die out here, hurt and disillusioned.

The wet rubber tube groaned as Greg scooted out beside her. "I never meant to hurt you."

Cynical anger bubbled to the surface as Carrie faced him, arms crossed. "Really?" She curled her lip. "Did you expect I'd be pleased to discover my husband had taken a mistress?"

"Melanie was never my mistress." His one good arm came up in supplication. "Why can't you believe that?"

"I know what I saw." She spat the ugly words. The vision of Greg holding Melanie in his arms was indelibly imprinted on her memory.

"You saw a lonely, confused, stupid man about to make the worst mistake of his life. Thanks to you, nothing happened." Greg thrust an agitated hand through his salt-encrusted hair. "As hard as this is for you to believe, I am thankful every day that you walked into that office. I promise you, Carrie, nothing physical happened between Melanie and me."

Carrie wanted to believe him, but she knew what she'd seen. "You were holding her. . ." The words choked her to say them aloud, but she finally managed. "Kissing her."

The memory of that moment, when she'd seen Greg embracing another woman, still made her tremble with rage and hurt. She couldn't even remember why she'd gone to Greg's office that evening. Perhaps some wifely instinct had kicked into gear, but she'd gone there secure—and left shattered.

Zipping past security with a wave, she'd sashayed into the elevator, absently humming along to the violin music coming from the overhead speakers. Disembarking on the top floor that housed the executive offices, she tapped across plush carpeting toward the door marked President and CEO. Taking a moment, she traced the words, knowing how proud Greg was of his success. She was proud for him. They'd worked so hard to get to this point and now all their dreams had come true.

With a satisfied smile, Carrie pushed open the door to a dimly lit room. A familiar scent filled her nostrils. Candles? Puzzled, she reached for the light switch. Shock froze the cheerful greeting on her lips as light illuminated the office. Greg's jacket was draped on a chair, his silk tie carelessly crumpled on the desktop. As though she'd been struck in the stomach by a torpedo, all the air whooshed out of her. Greg and Melanie stood near the sofa, arms wrapped around one another. They'd been kissing. Carrie could tell by the crimson flush of guilt suffusing both of their faces. Melanie gazed in bemused adoration at Carrie's husband. Greg, looking shocked and horrified, stood frozen in place, his body still pressed close to his employee's.

Mustering all her dignity, Carrie turned and left without a word. The sound of Greg calling out, running after her, pounding on the elevator barely penetrated her devastated fog. She hurried away, unable, unwilling to listen. As she drove off into the night, she saw him in the mirror, running across the dimly lit parking garage. Barely three blocks later, she pulled the car off the road to vomit.

Shaking, mind numb, she drove on home, collected her children, and moved to a hotel.

She'd learned a painful lesson that night. Words, even vows, meant nothing. The proof of love was in the action, and nothing Greg could buy or say would ever erase distrust, no matter how badly she wanted to believe in him again. Even lost on the ocean, with little hope of rescue, she couldn't risk trusting him again.

Heart aching, Carrie twisted around in the lifeboat, her back to her husband as she stared out across the never-ending green water. In a quiet, faraway voice, she said, "Even if I could believe she wasn't your mistress, I can't forget what happened. You're my husband, but you didn't want me. You wanted another woman."

The raft creaked again as Greg shifted in the crowded space. "I'm not trying to downplay what happened. It was wrong, pure and simple. I had convinced myself Melanie was a friend, someone to talk to, someone who under-stood the pressures of my job. You'd always been my sounding board, but you'd become so distant, so preoccu-pied with Kristen and Dylan—"

Carrie's hackles rose. She spun her head around to snap, "You're blaming me? For your. . .sin?"

"No, that's not what I mean. I tried to talk to you about things, but we seemed to be going in different directions. I needed someone. . ." In frustration, Greg gripped the inflated side with his one good hand. The vinyl had to burn, but he paid no mind as he pleaded for her understanding.

Carrie wanted to say she'd been lonely, too. She'd needed someone to talk to just as badly. Someone to help with the kids. A shoulder to lean on. But something stopped the ugly words from forming as she remembered the times Greg had asked her to go with him on business trips, to parties, or just out to lunch. For Carrie, leaving the children alone for even a few hours had been too risky.

Her best friend, Lisa, had warned her more than once that a man as successful and attractive as Greg was a prime target for other women; but in her arrogance, Carrie had reasoned that Greg was as loyal as a cocker spaniel. Lisa had even suggested that Greg showed signs of neglect. Foolishly, Carrie chalked it up to job stress and overwork. Looking back on one particular night, she saw that she'd been wrong.

A party, one of Greg's functions created to solidify old business friendships and create new ones, was in full swing in the ballroom of Raleigh's finest hotel. With his charming wit and electric energy, Greg was in his glory as the host.

Catching Carrie's I-need-to-talk-to-you look, Greg broke away from a circle of elegantly clad guests and came to her. Hand on her elbow, he bent low to ask, "What's up, Gorgeous?" His eyes questioned the purse and coat in her hands.

Though she wore an outrageously expensive satin gown purchased solely for this event and had spent hours getting ready, Carrie was too preoccupied to pay much attention to the admiring glow in Greg's eyes.

"It's Dylan," she said worriedly. "The sitter can't get him to sleep."

"How do you know that?"

"I called to check, of course." Actually, she'd called

four times in the hour and a half since arriving at the hotel. "When I talked to him, he started crying." Her chest filled with dread at the notion that her baby was alone and scared. Never mind that he had a perfectly competent sitter from church whom he knew and liked. He needed his mother. "I've got to go home."

"If you'll stop calling every fifteen minutes, he'll settle down." Two furrows formed in Greg's forehead.

"He's terrified!"

"No, he isn't. You're the one who's terrified. Why can't you realize that?"

"You'll never understand, will you?" she accused. "Children need a mother."

Staring off across the wide room, Greg sighed. "I need you, too. Please stay. Marvin Colbert is here." At her questioning look, he jogged her memory. "Marvin Colbert, the biggest software publisher in the country, who just happens to be very impressed with your ideas for marketing children's products through breakfast cereal manufacturers. This could be our best chance of bringing him on board."

"You can explain it to him."

"It's your idea. You'll have the details down and know the best slant to take much better than I. Come on, Carrie. I need you. Say you'll stay."

Suffocated by the pressure of wanting to please Greg, but knowing she must take care of her babies, Carrie searched for a way out. From the corner of her eye, she saw Melanie Warner, Greg's marketing coordinator, dressed in blue sequins, standing near the bandstand. With a wave of her hand, Carrie drew the woman to her side.

"I have to leave early," she told Melanie. "You wouldn't mind helping Greg reel in the Colbert account, would you?"

"Sure. I'd be happy to." The attractive blond smiled, first at Carrie, then at Greg. "I've already visited some with Mr. Colbert, and Greg's told me enough about the new ad campaign idea that I think the two of us can win him over."

Carrie turned to Greg with a too-bright smile. "You see? Wasn't that easy?"

From his expression, Greg was not as pleased with the arrangement as she had hoped, but he relented. "Sure." Without returning her smile, Greg released her elbow. "See you back at the house, then."

As she headed for the exit, Carrie felt Greg's gaze following her. At the door, she turned to find him watching, his mouth a thin line of disappointment. Beside him, Melanie Warner was saying something. Just as Carrie stepped out the door, she saw the woman lay a pink-nailed hand on Greg's arm. Though some small part of her sent up a warning flare, Carrie had ignored it. Greg loved her. Melanie was only an employee, the woman who'd replaced her as marketing director for Sunshine Software.

With sinking heart, Carrie realized Melanie had replaced her in more ways than one, all with Carrie's blessing. She hadn't taken care of Greg, so Melanie had.

With a terrible certainty, Carrie acknowledged her part in damaging their relationship. Greg had wanted her by his side, had needed her, too, and she'd neglected him time and time again because of her paranoia concerning their children. Had he loved her much more than she loved him? Was that why he'd put up with her neglect?

"Oh, Greg," she murmured, resting her head wearily on the side of the raft. "I wasn't so perfect either, was I?"

"Shh." He slipped an arm around her waist and when she didn't resist, he pulled her against him once more. "You're close enough to perfect for me. I was the failure. When we get back home, I'll be different. You can be sure of that. No more late nights. No more week-long business trips unless you're willing to go with me. I'll make every little school play, dance recital, and birthday party from now on." He kissed her temple. "If there's one thing I've learned from this it's that family is more important than success. I'll be there for you and the kids, if you'll let me."

She longed to believe him, but a part of her was so afraid of being hurt again. Perhaps he meant all these sweet words here in the middle of the ocean, but would he still feel this way when—and if—they made it back home? "I just don't know what to think anymore."

"Then don't think." With his one good hand, he pressed her head against his shoulder. "Rest. Save your energy. We have to get off this ocean before any of it matters anyway."

Rest. Save your energy. That's all she could do anymore as strength ebbed with each passing minute. Sleep. Sleep. If only she wasn't so thirsty. . . .

When Carrie opened her eyes again, darkness spread over them like a velvet cloak dotted with sequins. Beneath her ear, Greg's chest rose and fell in rapid, shallow breaths. His heart beat fast and weak. Fear skittered through her. With a worried frown, Carrie drew away from his feverish embrace.

"Greg," she said. "Are you all right?"

Whether by instinct or design, Greg reached out and pulled her back into his arms. "Fine," he murmured groggily. "Don't worry."

Heavy fatigue and weakness pulled her under again.

When the fourth morning broke upon them, Carrie was almost too exhausted and weak to care. She lay beside Greg, listening to the water lap against the side of the raft and the ragged sound of her husband's breathing. A growing sense of alarm forced her to move. Something was very wrong with Greg. His body was hot and, except for an occasional moan, he hadn't stirred.

Rousing herself, Carrie gently removed the now badly frayed silk scarf to check his arm. Swollen twice the normal size, the wound had widened and now oozed alarmingly. The entire arm was hard and red. At her touch, Greg hissed in pain. Glazed eyes shot open.

"May as well leave it wrapped up," he grunted. "Nothing we can do for it." He slumped back against the raft, eyes closing. Tight lines of pain etched his mouth and brow.

Taking the ragged scarf, Carrie dipped it into the sea over and over again to gently cleanse the wound. That done, she repositioned the makeshift sling, hoping to relieve the terrible stress she saw on Greg's face.

She'd thought it was impossible to be any more afraid than she'd been during the crash, but now she knew better. Greg was in charge then, vowing to take care of her.

Now, he was too weak and ill to keep his promises, and she was forced to take control. Her life—and Greg's—depended on her actions.

She knew they had to be terribly low on water, but Greg's skin was so hot and his lips cracked and dry. Her own parched body screamed for a drink, but because of the fever, Greg needed fluids even more than she.

Careful not to tilt the raft any more than necessary, she crawled to the small backpack, still securely tied to the side. Peering into the bag, she frowned, puzzled at what she saw—one bottle, containing only a swallow of precious drinking water. The same bottle she'd drunk from last night. Where was the other one? Greg's supply. A frightening suspicion sprouted in her mind.

Wetting her hand in the ocean, Carrie passed it across Greg's hot face, rousing him. "Where's the other bottle of water?"

"What other—" Confusion fogged Greg's blue eyes, then cleared momentarily. With an almost imperceptible shake of his head, he murmured, "There is no more."

The magnitude of his confession slammed into her. "If there is no more, what have you been drinking?" She knew the answer before the words were out. "Oh, Greg, what have you done?"

Six months of keeping an emotional distance drained away as she contemplated the enormity of Greg's sacrifice. Sick and injured, he'd ignored the pressing needs of his own body to make sure she survived. "You dear, sweet, foolish man."

Eyes closed, Greg managed a wan smile. "Promised to get you back to your babies. You gotta hang on. . .for them."

"Don't you talk like that, Greg Bridges. We're in this boat together, and we're leaving it together. You and me against the world, remember?"

When he didn't reply, the knot of fear and anxiety inside Carrie grew until she was shaking. Though she tried to force the remaining water between Greg's lips, he somehow managed to turn away. "You. Drink."

Then he fell silent. Time after time throughout the morning, she bathed his face in seawater, forcing herself to remain alert, determined to care for this man who'd proven in the most fundamental way possible just how much he really loved her. She'd wanted proof of his love, and now that she had it, she was going to lose him all over again—this time forever.

"Greg, I'm sorry," she murmured over and over again. "Please don't die. Please stay with me. I need. . ."

Suddenly, one side of the raft lifted high into the air. Like a rag doll, Greg flopped toward her. With all her strength, Carrie grabbed for him, throwing her body atop his and holding on to the canopy while the tiny lifeboat undulated wildly back and forth. Water sloshed on board.

The thought sprang into Carrie's head that a tidal wave had struck, but the glassy sea remained calm around them. Then, as quickly as it had begun, the motion stopped. Exhausted, Carrie struggled up, clinging to the slick, wet side. A long, dark shadow, wide as a horse, swam lazily from beneath the raft. Electric terror leaped through every nerve ending in Carrie's tortured body. Beside her, Greg roused, his body freshly soaked from the episode. "Wha. . ."

"Shark!" she blurted, then wished she hadn't. Greg was helpless to do anything but worry. Not surprisingly, he attempted to struggle upright.

"No. Be still." The strength in her voice shocked them both. "He might come back."

Too ill to argue, Greg slumped down into the bottom of the raft, cradling the battered arm to his chest.

Head propped upon the salt-encrusted lower tube of the raft, Carrie lay stiff and terrified, throat so dry her tongue felt swollen. How could they hold on much longer?

Ssshhhh. From behind her left ear came a barely perceptible hissing. Had her head not been right next to the spot, she might not have heard it. But there it was— the hiss of escaping air. A sound that could only mean one thing: The shark had ripped a hole in one of the inflated tubes.

Hopelessness replaced the hammering terror. She had no idea how long it would take for the tube to empty, but it couldn't last long. As soon as the tube deflated, the sharks would take over. With certain finality, Carrie realized that she and Greg were likely spending their last day on earth.

Her eyes burned, longing for tears, but she was far too dehydrated to produce any. Sorrow and regret welled inside her. She'd made so many mistakes, missed so much time of happiness with Greg by holding on to anger and unforgiveness.

Most of all, she regretted the awful, empty spot that should have been filled with faith. She was dying and, unlike Greg, she had no peace with God.

Squinting up into the blistering sun, she whispered,

"God, I've been so angry with You. Why didn't You help me when I was a child? Why didn't You keep Greg from straying? Why didn't You appreciate all I did for my church? I tried so hard." Painful, dry sobs rose in her parched throat. "Why didn't You love me?"

As soon as the childish words were uttered, Carrie had her answer. Deep inside came a reminder that throughout her childhood, regardless of how many times she'd been left on her own in the sprawling mansion, nothing bad had happened. She'd been miraculously protected from all the tragedies that could befall a child left alone. And God had protected her marriage from adultery. Hadn't she gone to the office that night on a whim and interrupted the tryst? Couldn't that have been God's doing?

"What about the peace, God?" she questioned. "Greg has peace. Can't I have that, too?"

"Come to me, all you who are weary and burdened, and I will give you rest." The verse from a hundred sermons sprang into her mind. *Come to me.* God was already there, reaching toward her. She only had to respond.

Gladly, with a relief she hadn't known possible in such circumstances, Carrie stretched her heart toward the Heavenly Father. "I am weary, Lord. Please give me that rest and peace and forgive all the wrong I've done."

Another wave washed over her, but this was a wave of peace and assurance, promising God's love. She could even feel His smile.

Beneath her head, she could also feel the slowly deflating tube of air. She gave up then, knowing the end would come soon. Though she suffered for her children's sake and prayed for them to grow up whole and strong and filled with God's love, dying no longer seemed so frightening.

When Greg moaned, she struggled to his side and collapsed beside him. If she had to die, she wanted to be with Greg.

"I love you, Greg. I'm so sorry."

"Don't quit." The sudden, raspy whisper was strangely forceful. "Hang on. Help is coming."

He sounded so sure, Carrie roused up enough to look out across the sea. Nothing but white-capped water loomed on the horizon. She glanced down at her husband. Wounded, weak, and helpless, his skin ravaged by sun and salt, Greg had never seemed more manly to Carrie. He truly was the hero she'd once thought him to be. How could she give up after he'd sacrificed his own drinking water to save her? Her condition couldn't be as bad as his, and yet he continued to rouse himself from time to time to encourage her. A surge of determination stiffened her trembling limbs. She could not let his sacrifice be in vain. Carrie Annette Carter Bridges was a survivor. She would fight until there was no fight left in her.

Once more, she found the water container and un-capped it. Only a few precious drops remained. Without hesitation, she tilted the opening against Greg's lax mouth. He shook his head.

Taking his face with one hand, Carrie persisted. "I won't drink another drop until you do."

The threat worked like magic. Greg's cracked lips parted. To Carrie's dismay, the liquid scarcely penetrated the swollen dryness of Greg's mucous membranes.

"You," he insisted, and she knew he meant for her to

drink, too. Obediently, she moistened her lips. Then the bottle was empty. Carrie lay back, waiting.

She was almost expecting the jolt when one side of the raft once more shot upward. The shark was back.

"Help us, Lord!"

The water container flew from her hand and out to sea. The undulations halted as the shark darted after the potential prey. Though relieved at the reprieve, Carrie had no doubt the monster would return.

At least four inches of water now filled the dinghy. Carrie debated on bailing, but a glance around told her the bucket was as lost as the water bottle.

There was nothing left to do but wait, think, and pray.

She thought about her beautiful children and was glad they were safe at home. She loved them so much, too much, she supposed because they'd become her little gods. Greg had been right when he'd called her overprotective. She understood now that her childhood fears had caused her to be obsessive, though it was too late to do a thing about it. She'd wasted so much time with her childish fears and petty anger.

Gently, she stroked the whiskered face of her beloved. If she had it all to do over again, she'd be there for this good, good man. She'd be the woman he married, the wife he deserved, and the partner he respected. She couldn't bear to lose him, to watch him die out here in the middle of the Bermuda Triangle.

"Please God, save Greg. Our children need a father, and he's a much better person than I. Please find a way to take him home again."

At the sound of her voice, Greg jerked. His blue eyes opened, glazed and unfocused.

"They're coming." He lifted a trembling hand. "See, I told you they were coming."

A chill prickled the hairs on Carrie's arms. Greg was delirious. Even in delirium, optimistic Greg was determined to have her rescued.

"Shh," she murmured and cradled his head closer to her heart.

With an uncanny strength, Greg yanked away. More water splashed into the deflating raft. "They're coming, I tell you!"

"Okay, Sweetheart," Carrie said. Hoping to appease him and keep him still, she looked toward the horizon.

"No, over there!" With his good hand, Greg grappled for the top tube and tried to pull himself around to the other side. His weak grip slipped off the slick tube. He fell exhausted into the rising tide of seawater lining the bottom of the raft.

With what little strength she had left, Carrie helped Greg to a sitting position, propping his head on the top tube, high above the encroaching water. He continued to thrash and murmur, "They're coming."

Yes, they're coming, all right. A fleet of sharks the size of battleships.

But Carrie kept her fears to herself. Without knowing why, she slowly rotated in the listing raft. A burst of energy shot through her aching body. There, on the horizon, a speck of some kind. Was it another mirage? A figment of an imagination that wanted to believe in Greg's delirious ranting? Mirage or not, it was the only hope she had.

Careful not to upset the damaged lifeboat, Carrie stood, holding the canopy for balance. Much like standing on a leaking air mattress, the vinyl beneath her feet dipped deeper into the sea.

"Here!" she shouted, waving and yelling as loud as her raw throat would allow. If only she had the bail bucket so that she could maneuver closer to the mysterious speck.

For several torturous minutes, Carrie shouted and waved. Though the speck seemed to grow larger, Carrie's strength quickly faded, and she slumped into the raft to rest.

"Help me, Jesus. I'm so tired. I can't do this alone. Help me."

She had a sudden mental image of Jesus walking on the Sea of Galilee, coming to rescue His floundering disciples. God made the water. He could even walk on it. Clinging to what seemed like a promise, Carrie forced her trembling legs to hold her up again.

The dark speck had grown again, and now she could see. Some type of boat moved directly toward them.

After what seemed an eternity, a foghorn ripped the silence. The first new sound she'd heard in days, the harsh, renting noise was beautiful. Near-delirious joy made her want to jump up and down, but she knew better than to risk upsetting the damaged raft. Just a few more minutes and they would be safe.

Wham! The horrifyingly familiar impact of a massive shark lifted the lifeboat out of the water. As it slammed down again, Carrie lost her balance and fell onto Greg's inert body. Holding fast to her husband and the thin protection of vinyl, Carrie refused to give up. Not now, not when rescue was so tantalizingly near.

Struggling once more to her feet, Carrie screamed, "Shark!" until her raspy, tortured voice became a whisper. The shark struck again and Carrie fell, tumbling into darkness.

⚓

Rapid-fire Spanish volleyed somewhere above her. Strange male voices shouted, and rough hands grappled at her aching flesh. Dully aware of ropes and body slings and of being lifted upward, Carrie battled to open her eyes.

"Greg," she managed. "Where's Greg?"

No answer came, and she wondered if she'd even spoken, so dry was her throat. With great effort, she tried again, opening her mouth, only to feel the soothing splash of fresh water flood her lips and tongue. Greedily, she drank, grasping for more when the hard hands pushed her away.

"*Un poco*, Señora. A little."

She understood and nodded. Too much, too fast would make her sick—but oh, she wanted more so badly.

"Greg?" she tried again.

"Do not worry. Only rest."

Chapter 7

W ho would have imagined that a small fishing village on the shores of Puerto Rico could look so much like paradise? Or that a boat full of rough-hewn fishermen could remind her of angels?

Carrie stared out the window of the small, rural clinic, the only medical facility for miles. Dressed in a hospital gown and dragging her IV pole, she settled into the chair beside Greg's bed. Intravenous fluids chock-full of antibiotic dripped steadily into Greg's arm as well. The broken one lay at his side, protected only by a splint. No casting could be done until the infection healed, and Carrie opted to wait until Greg was well enough to be airlifted home to Raleigh to his personal physician. If that ever happened.

Two full days had passed since their rescue. With the constant drip of fluids into her body, nourishing meals, and plenty of rest in a clean bed, Carrie was beginning to rebound. Though weak and thin, she was already presiding over Greg's care. Greg, on the other hand, remained in a stupor, sometimes crying out and thrashing. At other times, he lay still and pale as death. Only the rise and fall of his chest told her he was still alive.

She relentlessly prayed the dehydration hadn't damaged his internal organs and that the infection would subside.

Touching his forehead, Carrie was relieved to find the skin cool and dry. Perhaps his fever had broken for good this time. His breathing was regular this morning, and for the first time he appeared asleep instead of in a coma. Hope flared in Carrie's heart. They'd been through so much. She couldn't bear to lose him now.

"I called the kids again this morning." Her throat, still ravaged by thirst and screaming, was husky and deep, but she spoke in an intentionally chipper voice, hoping to penetrate her beloved's darkness. "You were right, you know. They weren't a bit worried. In fact, they didn't even know anything was wrong. Your mother, bless her, kept her worry to herself. When we didn't call, she alerted every search-and-rescue facility on the continent."

Carrie studied her skinny hands. Gone were the salon manicure and French nails, but she couldn't have cared less. "I think she even called the FBI and the president. We had hundreds of people searching for us, only to be found by a crew of Spanish-speaking fishermen who didn't even know we were missing."

"God took care of us."

Carrie's head shot up. A pair of blue eyes, deeply weary but shining with love, stared back at her.

"Greg! Oh, my precious Greg." Without considering the IVs, Carrie threw herself across his chest. "I love you."

A soft chuckle rumbled against Carrie's ear. "I'd be in a plane crash and stranded on the ocean any day to hear those words."

"You won't have to." Raising up, she kissed his chin

and stroked the side of his jaw. "This experience opened my eyes to what's really important in life—not pride or being right, but forgiveness and love and family."

"And God?"

"Oh, yes." A smile of wonder lit her face. "The Lord and I had some long talks while you were napping, and I found that peace you told me about."

Greg sighed happily and closed his eyes, though his voice remained strong. "I think He must have a sense of humor."

"Who? God?" Carrie levered back, puzzled by such a curious suggestion.

Greg lifted his brow in confirmation, the ghost of a grin twitching around his cracked lips. "I prayed for time alone with you, just the two of us. Time when nothing else—not the kids, not the business, not anything—could intrude. I wanted you completely alone with me so I could make you believe in me again. I never imagined the answer would be a life raft in the Bermuda Triangle."

Carrie pursed her lips in gentle sarcasm. "Next time be more specific."

"I hope there is no next time. From now on, sink or float, we're in this marriage boat together."

Though she groaned at the silly pun, secretly Carrie was delighted to hear him making jokes. Her Greg was back. Her hero. The man who would literally give his life for hers.

Growing serious, Carrie said, "I'll never forget what you did out there, giving up your share of the water for me."

"I'd do it again, if need be."

Carrie's throat thickened with the enormity of his

admission. Knowing such love was almost too much to contain. "I know you would. How can I ever. . ." Tears misted her eyes as she sought some way to thank this wonderful man and express just how much she loved him.

Greg, seeing her struggle, rescued her once again. Gesturing toward the pitcher at his bedside, he said, "Speaking of water, could I have a drink of the real thing?" He gave a mock scowl toward his IV. "This stuff has no taste at all."

Searching his face, Carrie saw that he wanted no accolades for his heroic action. If Greg had his way, she would be the only one to ever know what he'd done. She would know, and that was enough for him. Never again would she doubt his devotion.

Following his lead, she forced a playful reply and held the plastic water pitcher aloft. "The accommodations in this luxury hotel are exceptional, Darling. Pure spring water, never before seen or touched by humans, fresh from a remote, mountain village in Siberia."

"Are there mountains in Siberia?"

"How would I know?" She smiled through wet-lashed eyes as she pressed the water cup to Greg's mouth.

Greg sipped, then grimaced. "Tastes like the bottom of the aquarium tank."

"When was the last time you drank out of the aquarium tank?"

"Must have been the polluted creek that runs behind the sanitation plant."

Laughing, Carrie dropped a kiss on Greg's smooth, soap-scented cheek. "It's so good to laugh with you again. Thank God, you're going to be all right."

"Thank God, we're going to be all right." He paused

and frowned. "We are, aren't we?"

She knew he was discussing their marriage and not their physical conditions. "Yes. If you can forgive me for being so blind."

Hooking his good arm around her neck, Greg pulled Carrie down for a kiss. Chapped lips scraped together like sandpaper. They chuckled into each other's faces, too happy to care.

"I'll never rock the boat again," he teased. Carrie rolled her eyes in response, then burst out laughing.

They were still giggling like giddy kids when a knock sounded at the door. Following their "Come in," a middle-aged man dressed in fisherman's garb entered the room. Carrie recognized him immediately.

"Mr. Riverez." Though his face was weathered and lined, to Carrie he was beautiful, this God-sent fisherman who'd saved their lives.

"Señora." He gripped a battered hat in both hands. Glancing toward Greg, he said, "You are better, yes?"

"Much." Greg held out his good hand. "You must be the man who rescued us."

The fisherman returned the handshake with a grin. "Sí. My crew and me. We had been out for days. The fishing is bad, so we pray. We know that God speaks when we see the American dollars, many of them, floating in the sea. We follow the trail, and there you are. God must love you very much to go to such trouble."

Eyes widening in shock, Carrie clapped a hand over her mouth. Indeed. God must love them very much. Looking toward Greg, she saw the familiar glitter of humor.

"I hope you kept that money, Mr. Riverez. You certainly earned it."

The fisherman waved his hand. "God sent the money. It is His." A grin cracked the sun-bronzed face. "But He sent it to my boat, so I give some to the church and pay my crew. The rest I give to Maria." He nodded solemnly.

"The Virgin Mary?"

The man looked up in surprise. "No, Señora. Maria, my wife."

Afraid of insulting the kindly man but longing to laugh at her foolish misconception, Carrie bit her lip and wilted into the nearby chair.

"Señora, you are tiring. I will go now." Before Carrie could recover enough to protest, the fisherman donned his hat. *"Vaya con Dios."*

"Gracias, my friend," Greg said softly. "Vaya con Dios."

After the door closed, Carrie took a deep breath and leaned her head on Greg's chest. "That man saved our lives."

"You helped by tossing that money overboard."

"Strange how God used those bills to lead someone to us, isn't it?"

"Naw, it wasn't strange at all." A teasing grin quivered around Greg's mouth. "You know what they say—cast your bread upon the waters and after many days it will return to you. . . ."

Carrie gave Greg a playful whack and collapsed in hysterical laughter, safe and secure in a way she'd never been before. Perhaps everything that had happened was God's plan, after all. Snuggled against Greg's warm side, she smiled at the thought running through her mind.

By setting them adrift, God had calmed the troubled waters of their marriage.

LINDA GOODNIGHT

Linda and her husband, Gene, live on a farm in their native Oklahoma. They have a blended family of six grown children. An elementary teacher for the past sixteen years, Linda is also a licensed nurse. Readers can write to her at gnight@brightok.net.

By the
Silvery Moon

by JoAnn A. Grote

Prologue

Chrissy Bonet stared out her dorm window at the stars twinkling in the deep sapphire sky. Tomorrow was her college graduation, the day she'd worked toward for four years. She had a number of job interviews lined up, thanks to the high grades she'd earned in her double majors of English literature and education.

What she didn't have in her life was a great love. Of course, a woman didn't need a man to make her life complete, but the right man could be a nice addition. She knew just the kind of man she wanted.

She leaned closer to the window, her hands resting on the old, wooden window ledge, her gaze on the starstudded heavens. "Dearest Father God, I'd love to walk through life with a gentle man with a compassionate heart and the soul of a poet. If it's not too much trouble and if it won't disrupt Your plans irreparably, would You please bring such a man into my life? Thank You, Father God. Amen."

Ryan Windom stared out his dorm window at the stars twinkling in the deep sapphire sky. Tomorrow was his college graduation, the day he'd worked toward for four years. Thanks to the high grades he'd earned in his environmental sciences major, he had a couple of job interviews lined up.

What he didn't have was a wife or even a possible candidate for a wife, but he knew just the kind of woman he wanted.

He leaned closer to the window, his hands on the cool marble window ledge, his gaze on the star-studded heavens. "Lord, I'd sure like a wife. A woman who knows how to stick it out during life's rough patches. A woman who's strong enough for a man to lean on occasionally—not that I expect to do a lot of leaning. I expect to be there for her when she needs to lean on someone, too. From what I've seen of life, leaning needs to go both ways. So, if it's not too much to ask, could You find me a woman like that? Soon would be nice. I'm getting a mite lonesome waiting for her. Thanks. Amen."

Chapter 1

E liza Hornberg would make a great state attorney general, and you well know it, Charles Bonet." Chrissy stood toe-to-toe and chin-to-chin with her twin brother, dainty fists on her pink satin-clad hips.

Charlie folded his arms, rocked back on his heels, and plastered a superior look on his lean face. "Any man would make a better attorney general than any woman. The position demands a calm, logical approach to problem solving. Women think with their emotions."

Chrissy rolled her eyes. "That's a ridiculous argument."

Watching them, Ryan Windom knew Charlie was only egging on his sister. Charlie and Ryan had been roommates for the last nine months at the University of Minnesota. He knew well that Charlie believed women to be as intelligent and capable as men. Ryan suspected Chrissy knew it, too, and she was getting as much of a kick out of the exchange as Charlie.

Ryan didn't know Miss Eliza Hornberg, but he knew she was a friend of Charlie's parents and had just been appointed to replace the state's attorney general, who had resigned following a heart attack.

Miss Hornberg and the twins' other graduation party guests had left for the evening. Charlie, Chrissy, and Ryan had come out to the porch overlooking Lake Minnetonka to relax.

Ryan leaned back against the stone porch wall, slid his hands into the trouser pockets of his pale gray suit, and took advantage of the opportunity to get a better look at his former roommate's sister. Stars and the moon from the cloudless night sky offered only faint light. But gentle lamplight glowing through the French doors that opened onto the porch fell around Chrissy as softly as a caress and presented Ryan with a lovely image.

He'd seen pictures of Christiana Bonet, but the pictures hadn't caught the sheen in the thick, black hair curling under just below the level of that chin that looked both delicate and stubborn at the same time. Nor had they shown the dozen freckles sparsely scattered across the bridge of that small, straight nose and below eyes as blue as Minnesota's lakes. The deep pink knit top she wore added color to her cheeks. Or was the blush from her continuing confrontation with Charlie?

"It's common knowledge," Charlie was explaining with a tone of exaggerated indulgence, "that women generally do better on English tests and men do better on math tests." He arched black eyebrows and shook his head. "What does that tell us? Men are more logical."

"Hmph." Chrissy crossed her arms and impatiently tapped perfectly manicured pink nails. "I say it tells us men don't communicate well. You call that a strength?"

Ryan rubbed a hand over his mouth and swallowed a chuckle.

"Women are emotional," Charlie insisted, going back to his old argument. "They aren't problem solvers."

"Eliza is an attorney. I think handling lawsuits qualifies as problem solving."

Charlie spread his arms wide. "She's an exception."

"An example of capable womanhood, not an exception." Chrissy's pink-tinted lips tightened in apparent disgust. "Honestly, Charlie, you'd think we were living back in the days of our French fur trader ancestor, when people believed women were less intelligent than men because women's brains were smaller. It isn't size that counts—not in brains and not in brawn."

Charlie's grin grew larger.

"Okay," Chrissy blurted out, "I'll admit that men are capable of more extreme physical feats than women."

Charlie chuckled, pleasure at his success in every laugh line.

"But under normal circumstances, women are equal to men in mental or physical feats."

"Prove it." Ryan almost took back his challenge as soon as the words were out. Chalk it up to the idea that had appeared full-blown in his mind only moments earlier.

"Wha. . .what did you say?" Chrissy asked.

He met her surprised gaze with a smile. There was no chance she'd take him up on his suggestion, so why not continue with it? "Prove you're right. Charlie and I are planning a canoe trip next month. A week in the Boundary Waters should show us you're made of the same stern stuff as men."

Chrissy blinked several times. Ryan had the impression she was searching for a graceful way out. His heartbeat picked up as he awaited her answer. Charlie's bellows of laughter drowned out the lapping of the waves against the shore and the leaves' dance in the evening breeze.

Chrissy threw a venomous glance at her brother. Rosy nails hid inside dainty fists. The set of her lips showed determination when she turned back to Ryan. "I'll do it."

Ryan felt he'd lost a moment in time. He'd heard of people's hearts skipping a beat. This was more like his brain skipping a thought. He hadn't expected her to agree to the proverbial glove he'd tossed down.

Charlie's laugh broke off, then started again, louder than ever. "You, on a canoe trip," he managed between gasps and hoots, pointing at Chrissy. He sank into a cast-iron chair, bent over, and grasped his stomach in laughter.

Chrissy's cheeks turned from their lovely flush to a deep red.

Charlie wiped away a tear. "The closest you've been to a wilderness trip is swimming off our beach."

A rush of dismay washed through Ryan. Charlie's bantering had started out in fun, but it had gone past that point. His attitude was hurting Chrissy's pride. Ryan regretted his part in causing her pain.

"It was a dumb suggestion," he started.

Chrissy and Charlie appeared to not hear him. Chrissy shrugged. "It's a trip to northern Minnesota, not down a river in a South American jungle. How difficult can it be?"

"The Boundary Waters are wilderness." Smothered chuckles accented Charlie's words.

Charlie was right. No motorboats were allowed in most of the Boundary Waters. None of civilization's conveniences were allowed. Everything that was carried in had to be carried out. There were no resorts and no stores.

His gaze took in her flawless makeup, the pink skirt and top, the pampered pink nails, the delicate pearls at her ears, and the perfectly styled hair. All that and her soft voice pointed to a woman who used her wiles to snare a man, not man a canoe. *We'll end up baby-sitting her.*

Comprehension dawned like a swift blow. His dismay at Chrissy's agreement to join their trip had nothing to do with Chrissy's feelings, but with his attraction to her.

He'd been immediately captivated by her charm and the unself-conscious, warm welcome she'd given to him, not to mention her delicate beauty. All evening he'd watched her—discreetly, he fervently hoped. He'd had no intention of acting on that attraction.

It wasn't that he didn't want a woman in his life, but he knew the type of woman he wanted. He was definitely not looking for a powder puff. Chrissy was a powder puff if ever he'd seen one. Women like Chrissy might be charming at parties like this, but from his experience, they did all the leaning in a relationship and none of the supporting.

He shook his head slightly. No, in spite of his attraction to her, Chrissy was not the woman for him. He'd had no plan to play with temptation.

No conscious plan, that is. Then, he'd blurted out the suggestion that she join them on the canoe trip. Because of his big mouth, he'd be spending a week in her company. He stifled a groan. He'd been looking forward to that canoe trip. Now all he saw were rapids ahead.

Chapter 2

What was I thinking agreeing to this trip?
Chrissy dropped her pack by the river's edge.
Already this morning, she had portaged a
heavy canvas pack and a paddle downhill for a mile and a
half after driving an hour on a little, winding road. She'd
just reached water for the first time on the trip. It wasn't
yet eight in the morning and she was covered with sticky,
smelly, bug-repelling goop.

She should have backed out last night, when Ryan
had the audacity to go through her luggage and proclaim
almost everything she'd brought inappropriate or unnec-
essary. That lovely experience had been followed by a trip
to stores in Ely to buy dull khaki twill pants, ugly boots,
mosquito netting for her head and a paddle.

She suspected the entire evening had been an attempt
to get her to back out of the agreement. As much as she
was tempted to do so, she'd agreed to the challenge, and
she was going to stick it out.

Ryan lowered the canoe from his shoulders. He and
Charlie turned over the narrow, aluminum vessel and put
it in the water alongside a large, flat rock at the river's

edge. "Hold this for us, will you, Chrissy?" Ryan asked.

She squatted beside the canoe and held it where he showed her, along the top of one side near the middle. Ryan began packing, laying the large green canvas Duluth bags flat.

Chrissy watched him, aware of his athletic build. A funny-looking fishing hat covered his close-cropped blond hair. His face was broad and tanned, but both he and Charlie had given up shaving for the duration, and stubble was already apparent. Charlie had talked a lot about Ryan since they roomed together at college. Mostly, he'd raved about Ryan's athletic abilities as captain of the swim team and a medalist in track. Athletes had never impressed her. As far as she was concerned, six-pack abs only meant a guy spent way too much time in the gym. She preferred men who improved their minds, loved the written word, and were gentle and compassionate.

Ryan bent over the side of the canoe, apparently checking to see the items lashed to the sides were still secure after the downhill trip. "This is one of the least popular entry points to the Boundary Waters," he explained in a voice that showed his attention was more on what he was doing than what he was saying.

"Why?"

"The long portage to get here deters a lot of people, I expect."

"You mean there are places we can get to water without walking a mile and a half?" She didn't try to hide her disgust.

He darted a grin at her. "Sure, but the easier entry points have more people around. The Forest Service limits the number of groups who can enter at each place. Only one group a day is allowed to enter here. Charlie and I like it because it feels like true wilderness right away with only trees, wildlife, and water around."

She had to admit, at least to herself, that it was peaceful here. The river barely made a sound as it meandered past. Birds sang in the trees and from the tops of bulrushes near the shore.

She inspected the inside of the canoe with curiosity. "There are only two seats. Where does the third person sit?"

"On the bottom of the canoe." Charlie grinned at her.

Ryan tossed a green and beige square cushion into the canoe. "That's what this is for."

Chrissy studied the nearly full canoe. "Doesn't look like there's room for a person in between the packs."

"Not to worry," Charlie assured her. "You'll man the bow seat at first."

"You might as well learn at the beginning," Ryan said. "The current's not strong here. We won't run into any rapids today. It's as easy a place as any to learn a few basic strokes." Ryan squatted beside her and pointed to one end of the canoe. "That's the bow. The other end is the stern. The bow is usually pointed the direction you're headed. When the stern paddler gives an order, the bow paddler obeys immediately. Got it?"

"Yes, oh Mighty One."

He didn't grin back. "Never walk in the canoe when it's on land. When you get in, walk on the keel line as much as possible. The keel runs down the middle of the canoe."

"Got it."

"Don't stand up in the canoe unless you're holding on to the gunwales."

"Gunwales?"

"You've been clutching them. They're the rails along the top of the canoe. The pieces stretching from gunwale to gunwale are thwarts." He ran a hand lightly across the nearest gunwale. His tanned hand with its blunt nails looked large and capable next to hers.

Charlie came up to them carrying two paddles. "This is the last of it. The other paddle is lashed inside the canoe." He handed a paddle to Ryan and gave the shorter, bent-shaft paddle they'd purchased in Ely the day before to Chrissy.

Charlie held the canoe while Ryan showed Chrissy how to hold her paddle with one hand gripping the end and the other hand on the neck, where the shaft met the paddle. He demonstrated the basic forward stroke, and she imitated him as best she could.

"Put the paddle in the water about two feet in front of you," he directed. "Pull it back through the water, parallel to the keel, not in a curve. End the stroke when you reach your hips. When you move it back to the starting position, hold the paddle parallel to the water. That's called feathering. There's less wind resistance that way, and you won't tire as quickly."

They donned their lifejackets—required by law, Charlie reminded her—and climbed into the canoe. Chrissy tried to act nonchalant as she took her place at the bow, but her heart was racing in anticipation. The men might have considered the portage the beginning of the trip, but it was a canoe trip, and to Chrissy, that meant spending time in a canoe. She'd always thought it must be the most romantic of ways to travel.

Charlie took his place in the middle of the canoe, stuffed among the packs. Ryan pushed the canoe off from shore and stepped into the stern with one smooth motion. He took his seat and called to her. "We'll stay out of the main current while you practice a couple strokes. Charlie will give you pointers as we go along. We'll be heading downstream, north."

"Downstream is north?"

"Yes, the Stuart flows north. Don't worry. This is a lazy little river. You'll be able to handle it."

She bit back her retort. Of course, she'd be able to handle it. Hadn't she said so from the beginning?

Chapter 3

The Boundary Waters' legendary flies and mosquitoes weren't bothering Chrissy yet, but the sting of Charlie's pointers made up for the insects' lack.

"What are you doing with your knees to your chest like a grasshopper?" he'd started. "You'll never keep your balance that way. Tuck your knees under you."

"Vertical!" he'd yelled next. "Keep the paddle vertical." Chrissy tried.

"Vertical!" Charlie bellowed. "Don't you know the meaning of the word?"

"How am I supposed to keep it vertical when I'm pulling it through the water?"

"You don't pull it. You push it. Push it with the hand on the top of the shaft. Guide the paddle in a straight line with the hand on the neck."

Chrissy pressed her lips together firmly, determined not to tell him what she thought of his lame advice. She could feel her face flaming. She was accustomed to her brother's sarcastic manner, but she didn't appreciate it in front of Ryan. It was embarrassing enough that she couldn't master the most simple paddle stroke without

Charlie blaring her stupidity to Ryan and the local wildlife.

She pushed with the hand on top of the shaft. The paddle still didn't go vertical, but she immediately felt the difference in her muscles. It was amazing how much strength it took to push around a little water.

"Turn into it," Charlie ordered. "Pivot your shoulders as you push. It's the only way to keep the paddle vertical."

Chrissy tried. "It works!"

"Good job, Chrissy." Ryan's compliment left her heart glowing.

A couple minutes later, Ryan said, "Now that you've got the idea, we'll start changing sides every few minutes. That way, the canoe will stay in a relatively straight line, and your muscles won't get as sore. Or rather, they'll be equally sore on each side of your body. When I say 'hut,' change sides."

"Hut? Isn't that a football term?"

She heard his rich, deep chuckle and wished she was facing him.

Soon they fell into a rhythm, their paddles moving through the water in unison, changing sides at the same time. Her confidence began to return and with it a joy in the physical effort and the easy partnership she felt with Ryan.

Charlie, apparently feeling his duty toward developing her canoeing skills was over for the moment, had settled his fishing hat over his eyes and promptly fallen asleep.

Chrissy couldn't imagine napping with this exciting new world opening about her. Now that she didn't need to concentrate completely on her strokes, she watched the banks for signs of wildlife.

At times, the river seemed little more than a trickle through tall weeds. The day grew warmer and the mosquitoes began to swarm unmercifully. The guys pulled out their mosquito headnets and donned them. With a sense of surrender, Chrissy followed suit.

A blue heron stood on long legs in wild grass, watching the water for dinner. Delighted with the sight, Chrissy turned to see whether Ryan had noticed the bird. He had. His smile reflected the wonder she knew shone from her eyes.

He pointed toward shore with his paddle. Chrissy's gaze followed. A large, round-shelled turtle was sunning himself on a tree trunk that had fallen into the river. As the canoe slid past, the turtle almost soundlessly slipped into the water. The only sign he'd been there were the rings of water where he'd dropped beneath the surface.

Crack!

The sound startled her so much, she almost dropped her paddle. "What was that?"

"A beaver," Ryan answered, "slapping the water with its tail. It's a method beavers use to warn each other. One of them must have seen us coming."

Chrissy scanned the river's width eagerly, hoping to spot one of the creatures.

"Start paddling." Urgency underscored Ryan's voice. "We'll head for that point on our right, just before the bend."

The canoe started to swing to the right, and Chrissy put all her strength into paddling, feeling the pull in her shoulder muscles. She wanted to ask what was wrong, but she knew this wasn't the moment for talk. Even on the slow-moving Stuart River, a minute of talking instead of paddling might carry them past the point Ryan wanted to reach. Her short time on the river had already taught her that.

The shoreline was almost a ledge. Water had washed out land, leaving a small ledgelike top edge of wild grass and tangled tree roots holding together the black dirt and rocks.

She followed the instructions Ryan called to her as they neared the ledge. His voice must have awakened Charlie, because he grabbed for a tree trunk when they slid alongside it in the calm water near shore.

"Time for lunch already?" Charlie asked, his hands acting like an anchor about the rough bark trunk of a pine.

"Heard a beaver." Ryan climbed out of the canoe.

"Ah." Charlie nodded, looking wise.

"Ah, what?" Chrissy hated to ask.

"Where there are beaver, there's a dam," Ryan explained. "I'll check around the bend and see how far away their home is." He turned to enter the birch and aspen forest.

"Wait—can I go with you?" Chrissy called. "I've never seen a beaver dam."

Ryan hesitated and Chrissy thought he was going to refuse her, but in the end he said, "Sure." He grabbed a rope that was attached to the bow and wrapped one end around the tree Charlie was holding.

"Thanks." Charlie released his hold.

When Chrissy unfolded her legs from beneath her, they felt as if they were stuck with burning pins and needles. She'd been so engrossed in the experience of the trip, she hadn't noticed they'd fallen asleep.

Ryan was steadying the canoe while Charlie started to climb out, and they didn't notice her attempt to stand. She realized with dismay that her wobbly legs weren't obeying her brain's orders.

"Hey, what are you doing?" Charlie bellowed.

She barely noticed. She was trying to sit back down, bending over and reaching for the gunwales, but her legs wouldn't hold her with their usual grace and strength for that simple maneuver, either.

Then everything seemed to happen at once and in slow motion. Chrissy circled her arms to help regain her balance. "Oh. . .O. . .o. . .oh!"

Ryan let go of the gunwales. He lunged, reaching both arms for her. "Chrissy!"

Charlie twisted toward her as Ryan stretched past him to grab her.

Chrissy plopped down on the bow seat, knocking the air from her lungs in an "oof!"

Ryan's foot slipped on the edge of the land. He slid between the shore and the canoe, his eyes wide in surprise. He grasped the gunwale beside her. The canoe started to tip, and he let go. Water closed over his head.

Chapter 4

R yan!" Chrissy clutched the gunwale of the rocking canoe and tried not to lean too close to the
side while she looked into the water.

Ryan's head bobbed above water. He grabbed a tree
root and climbed up the muddy bank, slipping and sliding.

"You okay?" Charlie asked while trying to pull the
canoe back alongside the bank.

"Dandy." Ryan shook water from his hands. His
angry gaze bored into Chrissy. "I told you, never stand in
the canoe without holding onto the gunwales."

"I'm sorry." She was a little sorry but felt guilty for not
feeling sorrier. Her voice shook from trying to hold back
her laughter. "I tried. It was my legs. They just wouldn't
work."

Waist to toes, he was covered in muck from the river
bottom. His fisherman's hat drooped around his head like
a sunflower too heavy for its stalk. A water weed rested
on the hat's crown, a delicate, white flower bouncing
cheerfully above his head-netted face.

She was sorry about the muck, but that flower. . .

He knelt down on the bank and leaned over to wash

the mud from his hands. She carefully retrieved the flower.

Ryan took one look at it and set his lips in a firm line. Chrissy broke into peals of laughter.

Ryan stood and made a move as though to wipe his hands on his muck-caked pants. He stopped himself just in time and shook the water from his hands in one fierce movement. "I'll go check on that beaver dam." He turned and walked between trunks of birch and aspen, his shoes squishing with every step.

Chrissy wiped away tears of laughter.

"Wouldn't be so funny if you were the one who'd fallen in," Charlie reminded her.

She could hardly deny it.

"Or if he'd twisted an ankle slipping off the bank that way," Charlie added darkly.

She hadn't thought of that possibility. It would have been awful if he'd been injured trying to keep her from falling. She dropped the flower into a slot in the gunwales. She was subdued when she assured Charlie, "I'll be more careful in the future."

A couple minutes later, Ryan returned. Chrissy noticed his khakis were no longer muck-caked. He must have rinsed them out in the water on the other side of the point.

He informed them there was, indeed, a beaver dam beyond the bend. "How about if we dig out a snack since we're stopped?"

"I'll second that," Chrissy said. "I could eat a turkey dinner with all the trimmings."

Charlie dug into the food pack, pulled out two plastic bags, and handed them to Chrissy. One held gorp, a mixture of nuts, dried fruit, and M&Ms. The other held beef jerky, thin rectangles of smoked meat so withered and dry it looked like someone had left it in a desert for a century.

Chrissy dropped down on the wild grass at the riverbank and sighed in surrender. The guys sat beside her. A slight breeze caused the leaves above them to dance. Two chipmunks sat on their haunches on a moss-covered fallen log and watched the humans with greedy expressions.

A headache was threatening. Chrissy could feel the edges of it and suspected its cause was caffeine withdrawal. She was accustomed to a few glasses of diet cola each day. She'd been astounded to learn she wouldn't be allowed to take any soda pop along on the trip. "Remember," Ryan had said sternly as he took the six-pack away from her last night and set it back on the grocery store shelf, "everything you take into canoe country, you carry back out."

Ryan handed her a bottle of water.

She accepted it with raised brows. "I couldn't pack bottles of diet cola, but it's acceptable to bring bottles of water?"

"That's your only one. Charlie and I each have one, too. Once a day we purify water from a river or lake and pour some into these bottles to carry with us during the day."

Chrissy felt the blood drain from her cheeks. She held up the container, searching the contents for signs of creatures from the river.

"Don't worry. We start out the trip with mineral water from the store." Now Ryan was grinning.

"I knew that." Why did such an infuriating, superior grin have to look so good on him?

Chrissy decided she was going to make that first bottle

of water last as long as possible, but she'd forgotten how thirsty jerky and nuts made her. Two-thirds of her bottle was gone by the end of the snack.

Ryan decided it would be easier to walk the canoe past the beaver dam than carry it.

Chrissy wondered what he meant by walking the canoe. A mental image of Ryan saying sternly, "Heel, canoe," flashed through her mind.

They did walk the canoe, but not until they'd paddled around the point with Charlie taking up the bow position and Chrissy squeezed between the packs. They pulled back to shore just before the beaver dam. Here, the bottom wasn't as silty as where Ryan had slid beneath the canoe. The water was also shallower. Ryan and Charlie stepped into the water. Ryan grabbed the stern and Charlie, the bow.

Chrissy followed. "Ooooh!" The cold water took her breath away. Her stomach tensed. Both arms flew up instinctively, as though such a position would keep her warmer. She forced them down again and held onto the gunwale at midcanoe with one hand.

They literally carried the canoe around one end of the dam. She didn't see any beavers. Apparently, nature's builders were waiting for the human intruders to leave. The domed structure of mud and branches fascinated her. "It looks like a long, wooden haystack."

Ryan pointed at the opposite shoreline. "Beaver like aspen forests. There won't be any aspen left here after a few years. Then, the beaver will move on."

"I was so excited to see the dam, I didn't notice the stumps and fallen trees," she admitted.

Her gaze met Ryan's smiling eyes. "That's what I love about rivers." His voice was as deep, but as soft as the wind in the aspen leaves above them. "You never know what you'll find around the next bend. Dr. John Bigsby traveled through the Boundary Waters back in '23. Eighteen twenty three, that is. He wrote about one of the rivers, 'When once in the river, all is romantic—that is, beautiful and dangerous.' "

He turned and started walking again. Chrissy had difficulty keeping her attention on her footing. Her mind was reeling from this surprising aspect of Ryan's personality.

She'd never heard the term romantic that way, as "beautiful and dangerous." She thought of romance as peaceful, exhilarating, and deeply joy-filled. Dangerous? Perhaps that, too, for there was always a risk in giving one's heart.

Did Ryan Windom know about that risk, she wondered, or was all romance to him the beauty and danger of the wilderness?

Chapter 5

After they passed the dam, there was another portage. When the Duluths were repacked in the canoe, Ryan turned to Charlie. "Are you going to spell Chrissy for awhile, or would you like to take the stern?"

"Chrissy doesn't need anyone to spell her. She's tough. Right, Chrissy? I'll be glad to take the stern for you, though."

Ryan's gaze met Chrissy's and he raised his brows in a silent question.

"I don't mind paddling a bit longer," she assured him. "It's fun."

She's a good sport, Ryan thought, *at least so far.*

"Not too much farther, and we'll enter an area destroyed by forest fire back in '96. A lot of low growth there. Good area for spotting wildlife. If the creatures hear us before they see us, we won't see them. Paddling will be quieter if you keep the paddle underwater. Like this."

He showed her how to turn the paddle at the end of the stroke so it was parallel to the keel and form an oval back up to the beginning stroke placement.

"If you see wildlife, don't say anything. Nod in the direction you want us to look. If Charlie or I see something, we'll rock the canoe slightly."

Ryan settled among the Duluth packs midship. With no paddling duties, he was free to watch Chrissy. He could see she was struggling with the silent paddle stroke. He showed her how to shift the position of her upper hand to make the stroke easier.

His thoughts drifted back to the night before in Ely. He'd expected her to be insulted when he told her she needed fewer and different clothing for the trip. In anticipation of her resistance and anger, he'd steeled himself and been more harsh than was necessary. She hadn't been happy about the changes, but she'd gone along with them.

She'd been more distrustful than angry. He couldn't blame her. Charlie would love to see her break down and admit the trip was too rough for her. Her brother didn't want her to be given any unfair advantages, but Ryan didn't think it unreasonable to give her the same information they'd give any male traveling with them in the Boundary Waters for the first time.

If Charlie has his way, thought Ryan, *she'll want to turn back by dawn tomorrow.* Charlie couldn't seem to get it through his head that if Chrissy's trip was over early, so was theirs.

Soon, charred tree trunks stood out against the clear, blue sky like an etching, marking the path of the White Feather Fire as clearly as tombstones. As always, his stomach muscles tightened at the sight. His imagination was better than he appreciated at conjuring up pictures of terrified deer, rabbits, mice, bear, chipmunks, and other wildlife racing the flames. Too many hadn't won the race.

Low-growing bushes and short new trees crowded the land where the proud old trees had stood. New life. A new cycle. He knew such changes were necessary for the survival of the forest, but he hated the cost.

Chrissy gasped and clapped a hand over her mouth, her eyes wide.

Instantly alert, he followed her gaze to the bull moose that stood in the weeds at the river's edge. It had been grazing, its head beneath the water. Weeds and roots dangled from its mouth. More weeds were threaded through the antlers that stretched six feet across.

He'd seen many moose in the Boundary Waters through the years. Each trip, he watched for them and treasured the sightings. They never failed to send a thrill through him and spread goosebumps up and down his arms. Today, the reaction paled beside the warm joy that spread through his chest at the wonder he saw on Chrissy's face.

The moose saw them and snorted, sending riplets along the top of the water.

Caution quickened Ryan's senses. Chrissy turned her gaze to him. He saw fear had replaced the awe in her eyes. He lifted a hand slowly and placed a finger against his lips in the universal signal for silence, smiling slightly in an attempt to reassure her.

With another snort, the moose turned, plunged out of the water and into the brush, then started off at a trot.

Chrissy's shoulders dropped three inches as she sighed in obvious relief. "I thought he might charge us," she whispered. "I knew moose are large, but I never realized how large. He could have bulldozed our canoe."

Ryan and Charlie burst into laughter at her description. Ryan said, "Bull moose aren't much danger at this time of year. During mating season, they're ornery and unpredictable. If we see a cow with a calf, watch out. Mother moose have been known to trample cars to protect their young."

They soon turned onto a stream that fed into the river. "We're headed for White Feather Lake," he told Chrissy. "That's where we'll camp tonight."

The lake wasn't far. They located a campsite on the north shore. Ryan was the first to step out of the canoe. When he turned to squat beside the canoe and hold it for the others, he was surprised to see the disappointment on Chrissy's face.

"We're stopping so soon?" she asked. "I thought we'd canoe all day."

Charlie barked out a laugh. "Bet you won't be complaining about stopping early tomorrow. Your muscles will be screaming for rest by then."

"It's always best to stop before dark," Ryan said.

"Besides, this gives us time to fish before dinner," Charlie added.

Chrissy stretched her arms high over her head. "Do you realize we haven't seen another human being since we left the car this morning?"

"That's one of the reasons we chose this route—solitude." Charlie picked up the largest Duluth. "Let's make camp." He nodded toward a place not far from shore. "That spot looks pretty even and is clear of stubble that could tear the tent."

Chrissy and Ryan picked up packs and followed him. Ryan stopped so suddenly, Chrissy stumbled on his heels. "Sorry. I was looking at the tracks." He pointed them out to her. "Those huge ones are moose. Looks like a smaller moose came along, too. And over there are some deer tracks. We should have a great opportunity to see more large wildlife come dusk and dawn."

When they reached Charlie, he was withdrawing a tarp and an oblong, waterproof bag from the Duluth. "Watch closely," he ordered Chrissy, "so you'll know how to do it tomorrow." He spread the tarp on the ground, then fiberglass pieces from another bag. The pieces snapped together like a toy building set to form poles. Then Charlie shook out the green nylon tent. Ryan helped him slip the poles into channels sewn across the tent. Charlie slipped one end of the pole into a small pocket at the base of the tent, and the whole piece flexed into a rainbow shape as Ryan tucked his end into the opposing foundation pocket.

Ryan noticed with approval that Chrissy stepped forward and helped Charlie slip the other two poles in their respective pockets, though she watched Charlie closely to see what to do. It only took a couple minutes to get the tent pitched.

When they were done, Chrissy stood back, shaking her head. "I thought we'd have to cut tent poles and tie a rope between some trees to support the tent, the way we did in scout camp. This doesn't even look like a tent. It looks like a soft-sided, upturned bowl."

Ryan grinned. "Sounds like the folks you camped with were behind the times. Besides, it's against the law now to cut down live trees in the Boundary Waters for tent poles."

He pulled folding fishing rods and a rope from the food pack.

"Uh, why did you pack the fishing rods with the food?" Chrissy asked.

"Bears have an incredible sense of smell. Fishing rods tend to smell like fish. We keep everything with a food scent in the same pack, then we fly the pack."

"Fly it? Is that anything like walking the canoe?"

Charlie groaned, but Ryan chuckled. "Flying the pack means hanging it so bears and other creatures can't get to it." He fastened the rope to the straps on the food pack, tied a rock to the other end of the rope, and threw it over a strong branch. The blue pack swung into the air, jerking to a stop about ten feet off the ground. "That should do it."

"Ryan and I are going fishing," Charlie announced. "We only brought two rods, but we can switch back and forth with you, Sis."

Chrissy hesitated. "I thought I'd take a swim. Between the heat and the bug goop, I feel like a swatch of sticky, old-fashioned flypaper."

Ryan chuckled. "Best looking flypaper I ever saw."

Chrissy didn't know whether to feel flattered or insulted.

Charlie looked up from the fishing pole he was piecing together, an uncharacteristically innocent look on his face. "Course, good looking flypaper isn't usually what a guy's looking for in a woman."

Chrissy couldn't think up a worthy, scathing reply.

"Are you coming fishing or not?" Charlie asked impatiently. "If you don't catch your own, don't count on eating ours."

"I'd like to go with you, but there's something I need to do first."

"What?"

Brothers can be so dense, she thought. "You know," she said in a low voice.

"Oh, that." He dug into the supply bag.

Chrissy was relieved to see from the corner of her eye that Ryan was heading back to the canoe.

Charlie got out the necessary supplies and handed her a pronged tool.

"This looks like a garden trowel," she said.

"Yep. You dig down four to six inches. When you're done, replace the dirt."

"You have got to be kidding," she said for the tenth time since the trip began.

"Nope. And don't. . .uh, you know, until you're at least 150 feet away from shore."

Chrissy turned on her heel and marched toward the trees. She darted a look at the flying pack, and her heart quivered. At 150 feet back in the brush, the guys would never reach her in time if a bear or mother moose took offense at her presence.

"Hey, Chrissy!"

She turned just inside the tree line to find out what Ryan wanted.

"Be sure to watch carefully for a couple landmarks. It's easy to get lost in the woods."

Her gaze swept the trees. He was right, of course. There were no man-made paths here to a common out-house. Everything looked the same. Noting a three-trunk birch on her right, she stalked forward, grumbling under her breath about women who let their brothers goad them into doing stupid things, like taking canoe trips.

Chapter 6

Chrissy sat on a cushion in the bottom of the canoe, proud of herself for making it back to camp with no false turns. More than that, she felt fortunate she hadn't run into any wild creatures aside from squirrels and birds.

The guys didn't paddle far from camp. They stopped where they could cast their lines into the edge of a patch of bulrushes. Immediately, Ryan handed her his fishing rod. "You can use mine."

Charlie held out a fist. "Here. Turned over a couple rocks and found some worms. They make great bait."

Chrissy opened her palm to accept the worm, trying not to wrinkle her nose and withdraw in distaste. She was determined to prove to these two that she could do anything they could do in the wilderness. "Including putting innocent little wriggling worms on hooks," she muttered.

"What was that?" Ryan leaned near.

"Just wondering which end of this critter to stick the hook into. How do you hold onto these squirmy things?"

Ryan plucked the worm from her hand between his thumb and forefinger. "I'll show you how to do it. You can put on the next one."

"Sure." She grinned to show she wasn't afraid to bait her hook. Her grin died, and the hair stood up on her head when she saw what he did to the helpless worm.

He took the rod and showed her how to cast with a flick of the wrist, then reeled it back in. His attitude was casual, as though he was unaware a creature was struggling for life at the end of the line. He handed the pole to Chrissy. She imitated his cast as best she could.

"Good job," he congratulated when the hook dropped right between two tall bulrushes.

"Bet you can't do that well on your next cast," Charlie taunted.

Ryan's praise and Charlie's jab didn't register. For Chrissy it was sufficient that the worm was underwater where she couldn't see it suffer. She made herself change focus to what Ryan was saying.

"Start reeling it in, slow and easy. You want to get the fish's attention."

Reluctantly, she did as he said, all too aware that when the line was fully reeled in, she'd be looking at that poor worm again. The line stopped with a jerk, then started unreeling fast. "You've got a bite. Set the hook." Ryan's voice was filled with anticipation.

Chrissy looked at him blankly. The reel continued to spool out in a whir.

Ryan grabbed the middle of the rod and jerked it to one side. The rod bowed. "Start reeling it in."

It was like trying to walk against an eighty-mile-an-hour wind, but she did it, one slow turn at a time. She gritted her teeth until her jaw hurt. Then, suddenly, there the fish was—almost two feet long, its scales flashing amazing iridescent colors in the sunlight as it broke the surface of the water.

Ryan grabbed the line and lifted the fish over the side of the boat. "A northern pike, and a nice one. Good eating, too. You'll enjoy your supper tonight."

"Have to take out your own hook," Charlie reminded. "Hey!" His own reel started singing as a fish began carrying his bait away.

"Think you can handle it, Chrissy?" Ryan asked. "Not so easy to hold a fish and take out the hook at the same time."

"I'm not afraid to hold a fish." She grabbed it with one hand. "How do I get the hook out without hurting the fish?"

Charlie, still fighting his own fish, hooted. "You're worrying about hurting it? You'll be eating it in another hour or two."

Her gaze sought Ryan's. His image blurred, and she blinked away the telltale tears.

"Hold on to the fish tight." He reached over, and a moment later the hook was removed.

The fish slipped from her hold. It flopped in the bottom of the canoe, gasping for breath. *It's only a fish. Get a grip, Girl,* she reminded herself. It didn't help. "Is it too late to put it back in the water, or is he too injured?"

When there was no answer, she looked up at Ryan.

"It was a simple, single hook. The wound shouldn't be life-threatening."

Chrissy appreciated how he kept his voice low. She tried grabbing the fish but couldn't keep hold of it. Ryan picked it up. It tumbled from his hands and landed safely in its home with a splash. Chrissy watched it dart away through the clear water.

"There goes your dinner, Sis." Disgust filled Charlie's voice. "Oh! And there goes mine." The fish he'd been reeling in was swimming free.

Chrissy silently cheered for the fish. She didn't dare look at Ryan. "I just couldn't do it," she said. "It's so beautiful and incredible alive. I couldn't kill it."

Ryan took the rod from her. "No law says you have to kill fish."

Charlie snorted. "What are you so squeamish about? It's not like you don't eat meat."

"I know. If I had to kill all the meat I ate, maybe I'd be a vegetarian." She took a deep breath. "Any gorp left for my dinner, or do I have to collect edible weeds for my meal?"

Ryan chuckled. "We have other food along. Charlie and I enjoy fresh fish, but we don't make the mistake of counting on it. Fish have been known to be finicky and not bite. We have some granola bars along if you're hungry now."

She held up her hands. "Eat a bar with these hands that had a worm crawl on them and held a fish? Thanks, I think my stomach can hold out for awhile." She frowned. "Hey, what's on my nails?"

The perfectly shaped ovals had been a delicate shade of pink when she started out this morning. Now they were gray, green, and filthy. She touched the index nail of her left hand. "It's like glue." What could she have gotten into? Dirt and unidentifiable things were embedded in the polish.

A horsefly landed on her thumb. She swatted at it impatiently. "The bug goop doesn't work too well against these things, does it?"

"Nope," Ryan agreed. "Works better against the mosquitoes."

Chrissy's back straightened with a jerk. "The insecticide—that's what melted my nail polish." The polish was so soft, she could peel it off, so she did. "And to think we're putting that stuff on our skin. No wonder it keeps the mosquitoes away. How can something destroy nail polish and not kill a little old fly?" She slapped at another of the pesky creatures.

Neither man attempted to answer. Chrissy settled back against the hot metal of the canoe, shifted the bill of her purple and pink hat to better keep the sun out of her eyes, and decided to concentrate on something more pleasant than the possible fate of another fish. The canoe rocked lightly, water slapping softly against the sides. Insects hummed from the rushes. Geese honked as they flew overhead. Chrissy closed her eyes, lulled by the rocking and lakeside sounds.

She turned her thoughts to her favorite topic: Bryon. The thought of him always brought a gentling to her spirit. He was such a combination of serenity and passion. She'd sensed it the first time they'd met in a course on the famous romantic poets, Byron, Keats, and Shelley. She'd even tripped up and called Bryon "Byron" a couple times.

They'd hit it off right away. For two weeks, after each class, they talked for hours about the poets, read aloud their favorite works to each other, and discussed their own dreams to one day share their own deepest experiences in writing that would touch others. He hadn't kissed her or asked her out, but she was sure he eventually would. How could he not? Their hearts were so alike. He was everything she wanted in a man.

Then she'd introduced him to her roommate, Rose. Rose and Bryon immediately became a couple. Chrissy and Bryon remained friends. Not for the world would Chrissy try to steal him away from Rose, but she sure hoped one day God would bring a man just like Bryon into her life. Sometimes, like today, she let herself daydream about what it would be like if Bryon loved her instead of Rose.

Bryon would love this place. The two of them wouldn't be fishing. Instead, she'd be relaxing in the bow of the canoe, her fingertips trailing in the water, while he read poetry to her—poetry revealing the depth of his love for her, of course.

A tickle on the back of her hand roused her from her sweet vision. Eyes still closed, she shook her hand. *Pesky horseflies,* she thought. It didn't leave. She knew any moment the tickle would become a bite, which would turn into a large red welt. She shook her hand again, harder, opening her eyes to glare at the intruder.

"Aaah!" It wasn't a fly, but a spider—a black spider with yellow stripes. The biggest spider she'd ever seen. The legs spanned the back of her hand. Terror spun through her. She'd always feared spiders.

She shook her hand so hard it hit a thwart. The pain was irrelevant compared to the fact the spider was knocked from her hand and landed in the bottom of the canoe, right beside her.

She struggled to get away from it, trying to stand. Her feet refused to cooperate on the rounded canoe bottom. Ryan and Charlie were both talking to her, but she wasn't listening. All her attention was concentrated on getting away from that creature. It wouldn't stay still. It insisted on moving toward her.

"Kill it!" she screamed.

She felt Ryan's hand on her arm and threw herself toward the thwart that divided them, dragging herself on top of it. His arms closed around her.

And then they were in the water.

Chapter 7

Ryan concentrated on what he needed to do, which was to get himself and the canoe back to shore. He refused to think about why he needed to do these things because if he did, he'd lose his temper for sure. It was only the first day of their trip, not yet twilight, and this was the second time he was in the water because of that menace of a girl.

Don't go there, he warned himself.

The menace was already climbing up on shore. Naturally, she'd reached it before Ryan and Charlie. She hadn't stuck around to right the canoe and swim it to shore, collect the paddles before they floated off, or help Charlie retrieve his fishing pole from the bottom of the lake.

Ryan hadn't needed to retrieve his pole from the bottom. It had conveniently attached itself to his palm by way of the hook. The pole now rested in the canoe beside Charlie's. It was still attached to the hook, which was still in Ryan's hand.

Once again, he tried to turn his thoughts. *It's my own fault. I'm the one who invited her to come on this trip. What was I thinking?* The answer, of course, was that he hadn't been thinking at all. He'd been reacting like a teenager to a pretty girl, a girl who was everything he was not looking for in a companion. If he hadn't known it from the beginning, today should have proved that to him.

At least she knew how to swim. He hadn't had to rescue her from drowning on top of everything else, he thought as he and Charlie reached shore. Ryan dug a Swiss army knife out of his pocket, opened it with difficulty, and cut the fishing line.

Ryan and Charlie removed the paddles, carried the canoe ashore, and tipped it upside down to drain. It was easy to see Charlie was steaming. "Careful," Ryan warned him. "Wait until you cool down before you say anything to her."

Charlie shook off Ryan's warning hand and marched over to Chrissy. She stood near the tent, rubbing her hair dry with a towel. With a sigh, Ryan followed. It wasn't going to be easy playing referee when he felt ready to give Chrissy a piece of his mind, too, but the wilderness was no place for enemies to travel together.

"What kind of a stupid stunt was that?" Charlie's face was ruddy with anger. His clothes and hair dripped, forming spots of mud.

The worn, beige towel with which Chrissy had been drying her hair rested on her shoulders. No longer in a ponytail, her black hair framed her face in a glistening, mussed tumble. "You know I hate spiders."

"That's no excuse to tip over the canoe." Charlie punctuated his sentence by repeatedly stabbing his index finger into the air an inch from the end of Chrissy's nose.

"Someone could have been hurt. We might have lost some important equipment."

Chrissy was shaking. Ryan wondered whether it was from the cold lake water, anger, or fear.

"Did you see how big that spider was? He could have eaten me for dinner. If you would have killed it like I asked, you wouldn't have ended up in the lake."

"So now it's my fault the canoe tipped over?" Incredulity filled Charlie's eyes. "First thing tomorrow, we're taking you out of this country."

"The deal is to keep going until I say 'uncle,' not you."

"You're a disaster waiting to happen."

"That's original." Sudden tears pooled in Chrissy's blue eyes.

Ryan's chest tightened in sympathy. He wanted to draw her into his arms and reassure her. Instead, he held up both hands, one palm toward Charlie, the other toward Chrissy. "That's enough. Attacking each other this way isn't going to change anything."

Chrissy gasped and grabbed Ryan's wrist. "There's a fish hook in your hand."

Charlie told her succinctly how it got there.

Remorse filled her eyes. "I am so sorry, Ryan."

Her hand still encircled his wrist. He didn't attempt to pull away. "I've been stuck with fish hooks before. I'm up to date on my tetanus shots, so I'm not going to die from this."

She insisted on removing it for him. Since it was in his right hand, and he was right-handed, he didn't argue. At least, that was the reason he gave Chrissy for not arguing with her. If it had been a barbed hook, he might have been more cautious.

They sat on a large, lichen-covered rock at the lake's edge where there was plenty of light. A blue dragonfly hovered nearby, as if to watch the surgery. With Ryan's hand in both of Chrissy's, her head bent over his palm, a sense of intimacy surrounded them. The anger he'd felt toward her vanished as completely as morning mist evaporates in sunlight.

Ryan was surprised at the relative ease with which she removed the hook. "Didn't even hurt."

She found ointment and a Band-Aid in the emergency kit. While she was putting the ointment on the wound, he said, "Earlier today, the bull moose frightened you, but you didn't panic. You weren't afraid of the worm or the fish, and lots of women won't touch either. So what's up with spiders?"

She shrugged and kept her attention on his palm while she put on the Band-Aid. "I don't know. They've always terrified me. I guess because they give no warnings, and they move quickly. And that one. . .it was so big." A shiver made her shoulders tremble. "One good thing about swamping that canoe: I must have drowned the spider." She gave him a shaky grin.

He didn't tell her that fisher spiders don't drown, they swim. Neither did he tell her fishers could grow five-inch leg spans in the Boundary Waters nor that fishers had been seen catching tadpoles. If she knew the full truth about the spiders, Chrissy would require a sedative to get back in the canoe.

Chrissy caught her bottom lip between her teeth and glanced up at him. "Are you and Charlie going to take me back tomorrow, like he said?"

He hesitated. It would probably be the wisest thing. What if another fisher spider turned up at an inconvenient time, like when they were in the middle of a large lake with high waves or running a small rapid? But if she ended the trip now, she'd never see Curtain Falls, the ancient pictographs on the cliffs above Lac la Croix, or the route her voyageur ancestor followed. It was suddenly very important to him that she see these things. "Do you want to go back?"

Droplets flew from her hair as she shook her head. "No."

"Then you won't."

The smile that lit up her face lit his heart. He lifted one of her hands. "You're getting a blister." The angry, pink place on her palm filled him with the most absurd desire to press his lips to it.

She tugged her hand gently from his. "Yes, from paddling."

"I forgot to tell you to bring gloves." He could kick himself for that omission. "Be sure to put a Band-Aid over the blister before you pick up another paddle."

"Dinner's ready," Charlie called from near the tent. "You should be sent to bed without any supper," he grumbled to Chrissy when she and Ryan reached him.

"What is this cookstove?" she asked. "I thought this was a back-to-the-wilderness trip. Where's the firewood?"

"We could make a traditional fire if we chose," Charlie defended himself, "but the cookstove is safer. It's hard to put a traditional fire out completely. We wouldn't want a fire we started to cause a burned-over area like the one we saw today."

Ryan dropped down on a log opposite Charlie. "In

parts of the Boundary Waters, cookstoves are required. In the summer of 1999, a storm came through the area. It's known as the 'blow down,' because the winds took down over 350,000 acres of trees, mostly to the east of here. One spark, and all that deadfall would turn into flames."

Chrissy nodded. "So the idea is that it's more important to save the wilderness for everyone to enjoy than it is to let people live like Jeremiah Johnson for a few days in the forests, right?"

Ryan grinned. "You got it."

"What's for dinner?" she asked Charlie.

"Since we don't have any fish, we're having noodles and freeze-dried vegetables, boiled with dry milk."

"Smells good."

Ryan noticed she didn't mention that the meal didn't sound much like traditional wilderness fare. A red squirrel chattering from a nearby red pine acted as though he thought the meal sounded just fine. After their day of paddling, portaging, and unexpected swims, they had no leftovers to dispose of and no treats for the friendly squirrel.

Chrissy didn't object when Charlie volunteered her to clean up the dishes after the meal. He handed her a container with "Camp Suds" written on it. "Biodegradable," he said succinctly. She accepted the suds with a smile and headed toward shore.

"Wrong direction," Charlie barked. "You wash them back in the woods, beyond the traditional 150-foot border from the lake."

Ryan filled their largest kettle with lake water. "Heat this for the wash water."

Her patience seemed to grow thin, Ryan noticed, when

she was told she'd be expected to brush her teeth and do any personal lathering and rinsing beyond the 150-foot perimeter, too. Yet she did as she was told. Only body language reflected her unvoiced complaint. Soon, all three of them had washed up and changed into clean T-shirts and shorts. Ryan strung a rope clothesline between two young saplings since the clothes were still wet from their unexpected swim.

As twilight came on, the light breeze that had made the afternoon on the lake more pleasant died away, and the mosquitoes came out en force to welcome them. The small tent was good protection against the buzzing insects, so the three humans headed to bed.

Rather than carry two tents, Ryan and Charlie had opted for one four-man tent. It took up less space in the canoe than two and weighed less. Without comment, Charlie laid his sleep pad and sleeping bag down the middle of the tent. Ryan and Chrissy made their beds on either side of Charlie. Ryan set a flashlight beside the door zipper, near Charlie's head, where they could all find it if needed in the middle of the night.

Chrissy knelt on her purple sleeping bag and nibbled at her bottom lip, looking uncertain. "Um, do you think any of those big spiders will get in here?"

Charlie chortled.

Ryan frowned at him. "Don't worry. The tent is sealed pretty tight."

After they were all snug in their beds, Charlie heaved a sigh. " 'Nor Ghosts, nor Rattlesnakes, nor Spiders, nothing can prevent the fatigued Voyageur from sleeping.' "

Ryan kicked him. Trust Charlie to try to upset Chrissy

with the all-too-appropriate quote from Nicholas Garry, a Hudson's Bay Company official from two hundred years ago.

"Very funny, Charlie," Chrissy murmured from the depths of her sleeping bag.

Ryan grinned to himself. She hadn't recognized the quote. She thought her brother was only being his usual pesky self.

Chapter 8

Chrissy opened her eyes. Her entire body tensed. She tried to still the sound of her heart so she could hear better. What was that rustling noise? It sounded as though it was coming from the other side of the tent, but it wasn't one of the guys rolling over, and there was no flashlight gleam.

A grayness spoke of morning, but not full morning. She began to make out shapes. Slowly, she lifted her head, then dropped it back with a sigh of relief. The noise was Ryan, digging in one of the packs.

She lifted her head again. "Morning already?"

"Yes," Ryan whispered. "I'm going downshore to pick some wild blueberries for breakfast. Want to come?"

"Do I! What fun." She glanced at Charlie. He was snoring away. "Should we wake him?"

"Let him sleep. I'll bring your clothes from off the line. I've already dressed."

The clothes were still slightly damp, but Chrissy didn't bother to complain. What good would it do? Once outside, she understood the dampness. A mist hung over the lake. She could barely make out Ryan's form near the canoe.

Together, they put the canoe in the water and started off. Chrissy, as bow paddler, kept a close watch for boulders or fallen trees Ryan might not see in time due to the mist. She loved the way the gray shroud added mystery to the lake, the way shapes emerged slowly as she and Ryan neared them, and how something so ethereal added a hush to the sounds of morning wakening in the wilds.

Ryan guided them beside a bit of sandy shore, and together they carried the canoe onto land. "I noticed a mass of purple fireweed from the canoe yesterday," Ryan said. "Where there's blooming fireweed, there are blueberries."

"Maybe we should take some fireweed back. It's supposed to taste like asparagus. Of course, if it's in bloom, the stalks are probably too tough already."

Ryan came to a halt, an aluminum kettle swinging from one hand. "Where did you learn that?"

"Gardening is one of my hobbies. I like studying plants."

"You're one surprise after another, Lady."

The blueberries were there, as Ryan had said they'd be, plump, purpley-blue, and so ripe, they made Chrissy's mouth water to look at them. Not all of those she picked made it into the kettle. The blueberries weren't as large as the ones she bought in stores, but they were the sweetest she'd ever tasted.

"Mmm. Ambrosia. No wonder bears like these so well." She glanced about, suddenly remembering they might not be alone. The mist was rising, but she saw no telltale black humps about the bushes.

On their way back to camp with their treasure, they surprised a doe and her speckle-coated fawn nibbling at tender roots near the water's edge. Quiet joy danced across Chrissy's heart when her gaze met the lovely brown-eyed gaze of the doe. For a moment, they stared at each other, the doe weighing the danger to herself and her fawn. The next moment, the mother leapt away, white tail flying, the fawn following on legs that looked too impossibly skinny to carry it.

By the time they reached camp, Chrissy was wrapped in wonder at the gifts nature was spreading before her. "How long have you been coming to the Boundary Waters?" she asked Ryan as they carried the canoe ashore again.

"I came the first time with a scout troop when I was twelve. Fell in love with the place. My first day back home, I went down to the local newspaper office and signed on as a paperboy. I saved and saved until I had enough for this old second-hand canoe." He patted the aluminum hull. "It had a number of dents and scratches already, and I've added a few since, but it's been a good canoe for me. Someday, I'd like to get a more modern canoe—a Kevlar, maybe. They're sturdy, but lightweight for portaging."

Charlie was already at work at the campstove. The everyday odor of coffee blended with the lake and forest smells of weeds, loam, and pine. Chrissy didn't care for coffee, but she intended to take full advantage of the only caffeine she'd be offered until dinner.

Charlie was pleased with their offering of blueberries for the morning repast. Since he'd cooked the night before, Chrissy offered to make blueberry pancakes. Ryan made a syrup of purified water, sugar, and maple flavoring.

While Chrissy fried the pancakes, a gray whisky jack hopped on the ring of rocks that surrounded the camp-stove. She had to shoo him away from the frying pan more than once. She laughed at his antics, but she was concerned for him. "He's going to burn his feet."

Ryan glanced up from the kettle he was stirring. "He's probably breakfasted with lots of canoeists. Whisky jacks are also called 'camp robbers.' They have little fear of humans and lots of curiosity."

Chrissy rewarded the bird's persistence with a small piece of pancake, though Ryan insisted it was best not to encourage the jack.

"Can't remember when I've had a better breakfast." Chrissy leaned back against a fireside log after the last bite of her third pancake. "Or had a better morning, for that matter." She smiled at Charlie, then Ryan.

The look she caught in Ryan's eyes as he returned her smile felt like a hug. It stayed with her throughout the day, tugging her glance again and again to his.

Chrissy was glad to discover the night's sleep and fresh blueberries seemed to have chased away all of Charlie's thoughts of returning home. He headed to the lake with a kettle to get water for dish washing. "We'd best clear camp and head out. If we're to camp on Iron Lake as we've planned, we've a lot of miles to cover."

It was a long and exhausting day of paddling the Stuart River, streams, and lakes of various sizes. Eight portages tasked Chrissy's patience but supplied a wel-come variety for muscles wearied by paddling.

The group stopped for lunch beside a little rapid where the water laughed and dashed white against small rocks and over pebbles smoothed by centuries of the dance between water and stone. The rocks, which were so mundane in color above water, glowed and sparkled in wonderful hues on the river bottom.

While the three travelers sat on a large lichen-covered boulder and dined on jerky, wheat crackers, and fresh blueberries from the morning picking, Chrissy looked over a map of the Boundary Waters and Canada's adjoining Quetico region.

"There're more lakes and rivers in this area than land," she joked.

"There are about a thousand lakes in the Boundary Waters," Ryan told her.

The number didn't sound unbelievable to a girl raised in the Land of 10,000 Lakes. "Listen to some of the names. Lake One, Lake Two, Lake Three, Lake Four." A giggle broke her listing. "Wonder why whoever named them stopped at four. That Man Lake, No Man Lake, This Man Lake, Other Man Lake. Romance Lake, that stirs the imagination. Disappointment Lake. A fisherman must have named that."

"He probably tried fishing with you, poor guy."

Chrissy ignored Charlie's not-so-subtle reminder of yesterday's episode.

The wind picked up at midmorning, causing white-tipped waves on the larger lakes, which made paddling an entirely different and more difficult maneuver than her experience on the sluggish Stuart River. They stayed near the shores where the waves were lower, but Chrissy still felt the effort in her back and shoulders. At least the wind kept the mosquitoes, horseflies, and deerflies away.

Ryan patiently explained other paddling strokes Chrissy might need. She performed the strokes as well as she could but felt woefully inadequate for her job.

Iron Lake, their destination, was considerably larger than other lakes they'd passed over. Numerous bays and peninsulas formed a shoreline that reminded Chrissy of an inkblot. She couldn't see from one end to the other of the island-dotted lake. Her heart quick-stepped when Ryan told her the Canadian border ran through the middle of the lake.

On Iron Lake, Chrissy saw the first of other humans since she, Ryan, and Charlie had entered the Boundary Waters. She had already become so accustomed to the sounds and sights of only wilderness, the sight of other canoes, tents, and people had a jarring effect. A rush of gratitude filled her that Ryan and Charlie had chosen the route they had and had given her the gift of wilderness solitude so quickly and completely.

They camped on an island point of flat rock that ranged out into the lake. She found the rugged splendor of the glacial rock that decorated the lake far more appealing than the green sameness of the weedy river through which they'd traveled.

When the packs were unloaded and the canoe safely settled on shore, Chrissy stared in surprise at the campsite. A ring of rocks surrounded a fire pit that had obviously seen much use. She pointed to it. "There's a grate on that fire pit."

"Yes." Charlie's voice didn't register even a hint of surprise. "The park service maintains grate-covered fire pits at most of the Boundary Waters campsites. The site we camped at last night was in a specially designated primitive management area." He gave her an innocent-looking smile. "And if you need to use the latrine, you'll find it at the end of that trail." He nodded toward the woods, where an almost indistinguishable break indicated a path of sorts.

"A real latrine?"

"Well, there are no walls, but there's a box. You won't have to dig any holes tonight."

She wasn't sure which emotion took precedence—gratitude for the convenience or anger at being subjected to such a difficult first night in the forest. She decided to settle for gratitude.

Chrissy had visited a number of parks and nature preserves, but they looked like civilization compared to the Boundary Waters' primitive conditions.

Chrissy helped Ryan set up the tent, proud of herself for knowing how, though she didn't say so. When they were done, she was disappointed to see Charlie flying the food pack. Her stomach was churning with hunger. It took effort to keep her disappointment from her voice. "I thought maybe we'd make dinner. Are we going fishing again first?"

Ryan only smiled at her over the domed tent. "We have a side trip in mind."

"A side trip?" Her muscles already felt like rubber. A side trip would dismantle all her pretense of strength and Charlie would spend the evening gloating over her as the weak little woman.

"It's a surprise." Ryan's smile grew larger. "A reward for

being such a good sport the last couple days. And this time you get to ride, not paddle."

Charlie grumbled at first about replacing Chrissy at the bow, but Ryan insisted. After the first few minutes, Chrissy suspected Charlie was enjoying himself. He and Ryan made a great team. They immediately fell into a rhythm that she knew was the result of numerous canoe trips together. The canoe responded as easily to their paddle commands as a well-trained dog to its master's voice. Their combined strength carried the canoe through the waves and across the water much quicker than when she had the bow, though she wasn't about to admit it to them. Chrissy envied their skill and wondered whether she'd ever be as good as they were. For the first time she saw how her lack of experience might have tested their patience.

Chrissy was starting to love the canoe. Growing up along a lake in a Minneapolis suburb, she'd spent time in a motorboat. Occasionally, she and Charlie were allowed to take a rowboat out when they were kids. But she'd never been in a canoe. She'd never experienced this feeling of almost being part of the water they crossed. She liked it.

She saw that Charlie and Ryan brought along their fishing rods. She was disappointed but said nothing.

They crossed a large bay, then paddled along a rock and pine coast. Chrissy sat up straighter midship, stretching to see what lay ahead, when she heard the chuckling sound. "Listen, it sounds like a rapid."

"It is." Ryan's voice was filled with approval at her new skill in recognizing this common music of the wilderness. "Here is where the last bit of Crooked Lake enters Iron Lake."

They carried their canoe up onto the rocky shore and left it to rest by the canoes of other travelers. Was this what the men had brought her to see? Charlie started up a path along a steep, rocky bank. Chrissy followed, with Ryan taking up the rear.

The opposite bank was just as steep and rocky. The rapid where they'd started was only the first of three that tossed and turned through the rock-strewn gorge. The stony trail wound through dense, green forest. As the trail rose, the roar of the rapids was muted.

Eventually, the thunder of water grew loud again. Chrissy gasped in delight when, instead of the expected rapids, a one-hundred-foot-wide waterfall came into view. The water, a smooth flowing curve at the top of the falls, was soon split by large boulders and dashed into a foaming, churning fury that poured between tumbles of huge granite and on to the rapids that Chrissy and the men had portaged past.

Chrissy dropped down on a small, rocky point, drew her knees up, circled them with her arms, and drank in the pristine beauty and power before her. Charlie headed downstream a few yards with his fishing rod, urging Ryan to join him. Ryan declined and sat down beside Chrissy.

She was glad for his presence and glad, too, that he allowed her the luxury of enjoying the falls without conversation. Other tourists visiting the falls climbed among the rocks amid conversation and laughter, but as their comments weren't directed toward her, she wasn't disturbed by them.

When she thought she'd absorbed enough of the beauty to remain with her for a time, she turned to Ryan. "Thank you."

"You're welcome."

Aware of something she hadn't recognized in him before, she studied him now. What was it she was sensing? He sat without fidgeting, the tan fishing hat covering his short clipped hair, his face stubbly with two days growth of beard. He gazed at her, undisturbed, as she examined him.

It was serenity she sensed in him. Now that she was aware of it, she realized this fortifying, calming quality had been part of him from the beginning of the trip. It wasn't an attribute she expected in a man who was an award-winning athlete and loved the traditional "manly" sports. She liked the way his serenity wrapped around her fears and calmed them, liked the way it directed her focus to the beauty and consistency of the wilderness.

She leaned near him to be heard over the crashing of the falls. "I love your wild North Country. It seems easier to hear God speak to my heart here than in the city." Immediately, she wondered if she had spoken too hastily. Ryan might think her fanciful to speak of God that way.

His gaze moved to the falls, turning his profile to her. " 'Perhaps the facts most astounding and most real are never communicated by man to man. The true harvest of my daily life is somewhat as intangible and indescribable as the tints of morning or evening. It is a little star-dust caught, a segment of the rainbow which I have clutched.' "

There it was again, she thought, a sliding back of a

curtain to reveal something unusual about this man. "That's beautiful. It sounds like poetry."

A grin spread across his tanned face. "It's Thoreau. I haven't read poetry since I was required to, to pass high school English. But I read a lot of firsthand experiences with the wilderness, and much of it seems to stick with me."

The wind that had plagued them during the afternoon diminished as they traveled back to their island camp, and it almost stilled when twilight was ushered in with swaths of violet and peach across sky and lake. Loons swam in the pastel washes of color, their black and white backs and curving necks etched against the reflected light. Their eerie calls fascinated Chrissy, who heard them for the first time.

Although they had snacked on crackers, meat sticks, and dried fruit on the way to the falls, all three were starved after their long day. Charlie had success while angling below the falls and shared his fish for their dinner. While he cleaned the fish, Ryan built a fire in the grate-covered pit. "Might as well use it since it's here and built on such a safe site with water on three sides."

Chrissy complimented Ryan on the golden-fried fish. Rice and dried broccoli boiled up into a nice side dish. Ryan dug out graham crackers, marshmallows, and chocolate bars after the meal. "Since we have a regular campfire tonight, we might as well treat ourselves to some s'mores."

Chrissy couldn't remember the gooey concoction ever tasting so good. Afterward, when the songs of evening insects melded with the crackle of the firewood, Chrissy looked out over the water and wondered again what it would be like sharing this time with Bryon. Would he have a piece of poetry ready at his lips that caught the atmosphere of this place?

As if Ryan had heard her thoughts, he spoke. " 'Our Dinner Table was a hard Rock, no Table Cloth could be cleaner and the surrounding Plants and beautiful Flowers sweetening the Board.' Nicholas Garry said that when he traveled through the area almost two hundred years ago, and it could have been spoken about our meal tonight, couldn't it?"

Charlie stood up, his fork rattling against the tin plate in his hand. "Won't be clean and beautiful if we don't get these dishes washed and the food pack flying again."

His practical actions shattered the sweetness of the moment. Chrissy and Ryan helped pick things up. Since Charlie had caught the fish for dinner, Chrissy and Ryan took kettle and flashlight and went into the woods to wash the dishes. None of the three was eager to clean themselves up back in the dark forest, so they settled for a quick washing of face and hands. Chrissy was disgusted with herself when she realized she'd forgotten her toothbrush and toothpaste back in camp. She retrieved them from her pack and sat for a moment, thinking of the night sounds and rustlings in the dark forest. Knowing she hadn't the combination of energy and courage to brave them for something as unimportant as brushing her teeth, she laid down on top of her sleeping bag. Sleep stole gently upon her, blending nature's whispers into her dreams.

Rrrriiiip!

Chrissy's eyes flew open. Some strange sound had jarred her awake. What was it?

She could hear heavy breathing. A strong, earthy smell assailed her. Something large stumbled over her feet.

A bear!

Chapter 9

Chrissy knew it was a bear. All her instincts said so. Fear shot through her like a physical thing, tearing to get out. She wanted to run, but she couldn't move. She opened her mouth to scream. A hand clamped over it.

"Keep quiet." Ryan's words were a mere breath in her ear. "The bear's not after you. Charlie's unzipping the back screen. I'm going to pull you out."

Chrissy nodded to let him know she understood, but she wasn't sure Ryan would be able to distinguish the nod from her trembling.

The bear was snorting, his nose rooting along the tent floor beside her sleeping bag. The soft sound of the zipper didn't appear to distract him.

Ryan slipped his hands under her arms. A moment later, he yanked her out of the tent.

Charlie was there. He shone the flashlight in her face. "You okay, Sis?" Concern hoarsened his whisper.

She nodded, still too terrified to speak.

"Come on," Charlie urged them. "We need to find something to scare it off."

Ryan stood up and helped her to her feet. As soon as he let go, her knees gave out, and she sank to the ground.

Ryan knelt beside her and wrapped one of his arms around her waist. She leaned her cheek against his shoulder. The solid muscle reassured her.

"Your knees rubbery?" His question was asked as calmly as though they were sitting on a bench in a Minneapolis park.

She nodded.

"Mine, too. If we lean on each other, we should be able to make it."

She didn't believe his knees were the consistency of jelly like hers, but she let him think she did. By the time they were around to the front of the tent, her knees were getting some starch back, but she continued to lean into Ryan's arm.

Charlie was shining the flashlight on the flying food pack. "If we had the kettles that are in the bag, we could bang them together to scare him off."

His idea sounded so ludicrous to Chrissy, it brought her voice back. "Oh, right. Just bang kettles together and a big, tough bear will run away with its tail between its legs."

"Its tail isn't long enough to stick between its legs."

"He's right about the kettles." Ryan spoke in the same stage whisper as Charlie. "Black bears are chickens at heart. Usually a lot of noise frightens them away, but it's always best to be cautious around them."

Charlie scratched his head. "I'm afraid if I take down the food pack to get the kettles, the bear will smell the food and drag it off. Then, we'd be in a fine pickle. I can't think of anything else to make a good, loud noise. Of course, we can yell and scream; but somehow, I don't have as much faith in the frightening quality of our voices compared to clanging metal."

"What about using the canoe?" Chrissy asked. "It's aluminum."

"That's right." Ryan sounded excited.

"We don't want to dent it up too bad," Charlie warned.

"It's hit more than a few rocks in its day. It'll survive," Ryan assured him, heading for the overturned canoe. "We can use Chrissy's paddle. It's metal."

Chrissy had heard the sound of her paddle clanging against the canoe many times the last couple days, but in the stillness of night, the sound amplified. When Ryan began striking the paddle against the gunwales, where it would do the least damage, Ryan and Charlie began whooping and screaming. Charlie focused the flashlight on the tent. Chrissy covered her ears with her hands and watched.

In a minute, the bear lumbered from the torn tent door and raced into the woods as if chased by a swarm of bees.

Chrissy uncovered her ears. "It worked. I can't believe it."

"That was quick thinking, Chrissy, to use the canoe as a drum," Ryan praised.

"Bears don't normally come into a tent unless there's food around," Charlie said. "Did you bring any chocolate left from the s'mores back to the tent with you, Sis?"

Indignation raised Chrissy's ire. Of course he would blame her for the bear's visit. "I didn't. Did you?"

"Don't get your dander up. I was only asking."

"Whatever he was after, the bear's gone now." Ryan, as usual, was the voice of reason. "We'd better check the tent and see how much damage it did. Maybe it left behind whatever it was after. If so, we'd best clean it up so the bear doesn't make a repeat visit."

Chrissy sat down beside the canoe. "I, uh, think I'll stay out here for awhile, if you don't mind." The thought of the bear returning while she was in the tent drained the blood from her face.

Ryan knelt down, facing her. "Will you be okay out here?"

"Sure."

"Holler if you need us."

A few minutes later, he was back. He sat down, cross-legged, beside her on the large, flat expanse of granite. "Charlie's repairing the tears in the tent door and the floor with duct tape. It won't look too fashionable, but it should last the rest of the trip."

"Did you find what the bear was after?"

"Yep. Toothpaste."

Chrissy suddenly felt sick to her stomach. "My toothpaste. I didn't know bears like toothpaste."

"It's not your fault. We forgot to warn you about it."

It seemed to Chrissy there was no end to things about which Ryan and Charlie had forgotten to warn her. She groaned and hid her face in her hands.

"Look." Ryan shook her shoulder.

"Is the bear back?" She opened her eyes with reluctance.

"The sky's about to put on a display for us. That's the Northern Lights."

A curtain of vivid green seemingly fell out of the heavens and poured across the sky. Ribbons of yellow streamed through it. Together, the lighted colors swirled and waved where the stars normally held stage. They faded into the night, only to emerge again in a new dance, shimmering and trembling over the sky and reflecting in the lake until Chrissy felt awash in light and color.

When they finally slipped into the mystery from whence they'd come, the world seemed suddenly and completely still. It was minutes before Chrissy could make herself break the silence. "It was like a symphony. How could I hear a symphony when there was only light and no sound?"

He could only smile at her. He wanted to tell her that he had heard the music of the heavens, too. He always heard it when the lights played in the northern sky, but to share it would make him feel too vulnerable. He'd never known anyone else who heard the music. The music was in the heart, of course, not from the sky. Yet, the wonder that she had heard it was something he needed to absorb.

Instead, he told her of the lights' history. "The Ojibwa believed when a warrior died, his spirit gathered with all the warriors who had died before him. Together, they danced their war dances along the northern horizon, and their colorful headdresses are the Northern Lights."

"Mmm. I'm glad I believe God draws us unto Him to a peace-filled heaven when we leave here, and not to a place of war dances."

"You know, if it weren't for the bear, we would have

slept through the lights tonight."

"Strange, isn't it? Your North Country is such an enigma. Again and again, I've seen that in the last two days—the combination of the beautiful and the dangerous, as you told me that man said about the land two hundred years ago."

It sent a thrill through him that she remembered that insignificant piece he'd quoted her yesterday.

She tipped her head back, and he could see her profile clearly against the moonlit water. "I've never seen the Northern Lights before." Her voice was filled with awe. "Now I'll always have this experience to remember the time when the lights filled the sky, the waters, and every place around me."

He was wildly glad that he was part of this experience she would remember for the rest of her life. The depth of his joy rocked his world. This woman he had thought too fragile for the canoe trip, too dependent to stand up to life's blows, was speaking of the music and beauty of God's creation after a bear had literally stood beside her bed. She was as much a contradiction as the wild canoe country he loved.

The knowledge thrilled and terrified him.

Chapter 10

C hrissy should have been exhausted after the bear fright and spending hours out on the granite point, but she wasn't. Instead she was amazed to find the next day even more exhilarating than the first two.

They left their island camp behind and canoed northwest across Iron Lake and Bottle Lake to Bottle Portage. Ryan was a treasure chest of information about the voyageurs. Although Chrissy and Charlie's ancestor had been a voyageur, they knew little about the voyageurs' history. It was thrilling to learn that their ancestor would have followed this very portage, canoed these lakes in traveling to and from the forts in the fur country.

She tried to imagine her ancestor, dressed in traditional voyageur wear with a red sash about his waist, paddling around islands and cliffs in a thirty-six-foot birch-bark canoe filled with other voyageurs, singing lilting French songs to set the paddling pace. Would he have looked like Charlie?

They ended the muddy Bottle Portage at Lac la Croix. "It means Lake of the Cross," Ryan explained.

Chrissy liked the name. Lake of the Cross, the ultimate symbol of love.

Less than two miles from the portage, they stopped on the south shore of Irving Island. Ryan pointed it out to Chrissy, a huge hill of granite that rose steeply from the shore. "Legend has it that Ojibwa warriors used this hill to prove their strength by running from the lake's edge to the summit and back again—a couple thousand yards, I'd guess. Some early records call it Warrior Hill, others call it Running Rock."

Chrissy grinned at Ryan and Charlie. "If you two want to race each other, I'll be glad to declare the winner."

Charlie crossed his arms over his chest and drawled, "Considering the reason you joined this trip, maybe you'd like to test yourself against Warrior Hill."

She wrinkled her nose. "Maybe next time. Didn't bring my jogging shoes this trip." As they climbed back in the canoe, she realized she truly hoped there would be a next time.

Though she had teased the guys about running the rock, she was sure they could both do so if they chose. They were strong and in good shape, and their paddling and portages on this trip were ample evidence. She was surprised to find that she, who had always thought a man's eyes and heart were his only important features, was noticing the muscles that flexed beneath Ryan's long-sleeved T-shirt. Muscles weren't such an unattractive feature in a man, she decided, though certainly not the most important.

In spite of the lake's size, they saw more people and canoes than in the first two days of their trip combined. Chrissy was surprised to hear the sound of a motor.

"Motors are allowed on the Canadian side of the lake," Charlie explained.

Since there were so many travelers on the lake, Charlie suggested they claim a campsite early. Ryan and Chrissy were quick to agree. They headed toward an area Charlie called Lady Boot Bay. Both men insisted it was some of the prettiest country in the Boundary Waters. Its rocky shorelines and pine forests certainly looked beautiful to Chrissy, and there weren't too many other canoeists in the bay.

They passed a group of scouts camped on a shore half a mile from the camp they chose for themselves. The boys waved, called greetings, and generally acted as if they hadn't seen another human being for months.

After setting up camp and eating lunch, Ryan, Chrissy, and Charlie headed back onto Lac la Croix. The weather was cooler today, the sky overcast but not threatening. The temperatures had been pleasant for the portage, but they could be uncomfortable on the lake if the wind picked up, so the group brought along their jackets.

Waves rolled across the large lake, and Chrissy was glad that today Charlie and Ryan were both taking turns with her in the bow so she didn't have that duty all day. The waves weren't so high that they washed over the bow. They swelled and crested lazily, but Chrissy's shoulders felt the effort of fighting them, just the same. Without the packs, which had been left at camp, the canoe rode higher than usual in the water.

A benefit of the cooler temperatures and wind was freedom from mosquitoes and horseflies and a corresponding freedom from wearing the awful-smelling bug goop.

As they headed north out of Lady Boot Bay, Chrissy was glad Ryan was at the bow. She watched his expert stroking, the ease with which he worked. Watching him brought back memories of the evening before, the sound of his voice giving her courage when the bear loomed above her, his arm strong about her as she regained her emotional and physical strength, and the feeling of connection with him when the sky wrapped itself about them in light.

She'd spent two years crazy about unattainable Bryon, who was in love with her dear friend, and now she was tumbling for another man who, though not committed to someone else, was certainly not the kind of man she was looking for in her life. Wasn't she ever going to learn?

Well, there was no sense wrecking this beautiful trip worrying about it. She closed her eyes and breathed deeply of the lake air. She was going to enjoy every remaining minute she had in this beautiful place, and she'd enjoy Ryan's company, too.

They were coming to another island. Sheer granite cliffs made an impressive plunge of one hundred feet or more into the waters of Lac la Croix. The sharp angles on the cliff added character to its rugged face. Ryan turned to tell her, "We're coming to the Painted Rocks."

She leaned forward, eager now to see the cliffs clearly. Green moss and orange lichen added natural color. Ryan had told her earlier of the ancient images painted in a brownish-red pigment on these walls. No one knew who had painted them or why.

Ryan and Charlie directed the canoe parallel to the

sheer drops. Chrissy marvelled at Ryan and Charlie's skill in keeping the canoe from crashing against the cliffs while they all studied the pictures above them. Had someone hundreds of years ago painted the images from another canoe? Or had the artists perhaps painted them from an ice-covered lake in winter?

The pictographs were simple in nature: some moose, an hourglass shape, a couple pipe-smoking figures. Whatever could they mean? Chrissy caught Ryan's gaze and said, "I wonder whether our ancestor stopped beneath these and wondered at them. Someone has chipped in the date 1781 and the initials L. R. Were they put here later than the pictures?"

Ryan shrugged. "No one really knows. I suppose someday scientists will be able to tell."

They paddled on to another cliff. This one showed moose, hands, and men in canoes. Were they war canoes? The painted cliffs brought forth mental images of people living on these waters centuries ago. Chrissy shivered, not from fear but amazement, from a sense of the continuation of the human race through many experiences and centuries. Ryan and Charlie had told her they'd seen similar pictographs at various places in the Boundary Waters. She wondered why the painters had chosen these symbols. Had they been trying to record messages for future generations, or had they simply enjoyed painting on such a spectacular canvas?

Ryan smiled at her. "Incredible, aren't they?"

She nodded, unable to put her feelings into words. It seemed appropriate it was Ryan who introduced her to these extraordinary cliffs and to the passage that was such a part of her ancestor's life. She didn't let herself explore why this felt right.

They canoed around more islands where ancient pines clung to rocky ledges above the gray waters. They came out from a sheltered area to a shocking slap from a wave, which dumped chilling water over the bow. Chrissy saw Ryan frown. She followed his gaze and was surprised to see the pale gray clouds that had covered the sky all day were quickly being replaced by clouds that were dark, rolling, and menacing. They cast an advancing shadow on the lake, which sent an ominous chill down Chrissy's spine.

"We'd better head back," Ryan called to Charlie, who was manning the stern.

Chrissy put on the jacket that had been lying in her lap. She couldn't close it over the bulky life jacket, but it still provided a barrier against the cool wind. She held Charlie's jacket out to him, but he only shook his head. There was an impatient set to his lips as he dug his paddle into the waves. "Get on your knees," he ordered.

She did as he told her.

The lake was not merely choppy now but a rolling mass of whitecaps. Water broke from the crests into the canoe. Chrissy tied the arms of the men's jackets about the midship thwart to keep them from lying in water at the bottom of the canoe. She winced and grabbed the thwart as the waves tossed her against the inner hull.

"We'll never make it back to camp," Ryan called over his shoulder. "Let's head for the next island and make shore wherever we can."

The island wasn't far. To Chrissy it looked like nothing but cliffs, large boulders, and scraggly pines. She glanced back in the direction of the thunder clouds. The lake beneath them was leaden gray and had a pebbly look she recognized as the storm line. That storm would be upon them soon, she knew, and their fight would be against more than wind. The lightning in those clouds was at least as dangerous as the waves.

Should she be paddling, too? Would she be a help or a hindrance? She didn't understand the mechanics, didn't know whether someone paddling from the midpoint would offset what the stern and bow paddlers were struggling to accomplish. Neither Charlie nor Ryan had time to guide her now. Frustration washed over her. She wanted to help and had no idea how, so she did nothing but hang onto the thwart and pray.

"There!" Ryan's shout was barely a dent against the wind. "Between those cliffs." Again, he bent into his paddle.

The men headed the canoe toward the small, half-moon of rock-studded sand bordered by the cliffs. The bow rose on the pitching water, falling back on the waves with a slap, again and again. At times, it seemed to Chrissy they made no progress toward the island. The angry lake pushed the canoe downshore from its destination, and the men had to fight their way back. The rain struck the canoe—not in a smattering of drops but in a sheet, while the group was yet yards from shore.

At last the canoe nosed into the rocky bay, where Ryan's and Charlie's efforts could only keep the canoe from crashing against the largest of the windswept boulders. Though there was some sand on the beach, it was so spread among rocks that there was no place wide enough to beach the canoe easily. There was already so much water in the bottom of the canoe, Chrissy's legs were soaked. When the craft was finally drawn beside a short granite ledge the height of the gunwales, Chrissy yelled into the gale, "I'll get out and hold it!"

The canoe bobbed and pitched, causing Chrissy's heartbeat to race as she held onto the gunwales with one hand and with the other struggled to find a handhold on the ledge. Her fingertips clung to a small dip worn into the rock over the centuries. She could hear Ryan calling something to her, but the words were blown away and she ignored him, concentrating on the ledge. She managed to get one foot on the ledge. Water licked at her boot. Chrissy refused to look at the cold gray lake, which seemed to be reaching for her. She brought her other foot to the ledge, a surge of success bracing her spirit.

The canoe tossed, yanking the gunwale from her hand and twisting her wrist painfully. She pressed her lips together against the pain and lunged to recapture the canoe. The motion unbalanced her. Her feet slipped on the age-washed rock and she plunged into the chilly northern lake. A blinding pain pierced her head. Then, all went dark and silent.

Chapter 11

"Chrissy!" Terror struck at Ryan's core. He reached over the side, tipping the canoe dangerously. She was obviously unconscious. If he could reach her lifejacket and pull her into the canoe—

A breaker broadsided the canoe and tumbled Ryan, headfirst, into the water. The cold, even in July, was a shock. His lifejacket thrust him immediately to the surface. He grabbed Chrissy's lifejacket and pulled her into his arms. Shore was only a few feet away, but the water was deeper here than he'd expected, and the rocky bottom was slippery.

Charlie fought the waves that battered the canoe, but the craft was thrown toward the ledge. Ryan shifted Chrissy so he stayed between her and the ancient granite barrier. A moment later, the canoe was flung against them, pounding them into the rock. Ryan's shoulder took most of the impact. He clenched his teeth against the pain. Chrissy needed him. He couldn't let the pain overtake him.

The stern bucked beside them now. Ryan grabbed for it, his fist closing over the gunwale beside Charlie. Hot pain shot down his arm. His good arm remained wrapped about Chrissy's waist.

"Hold on!" Charlie called. "I'm going to get into the water and pull the canoe to shore!"

Ryan had no idea how long their efforts took, but by the time the canoe and Chrissy reached shore, Chrissy started to moan. It was the most beautiful sound Ryan had ever heard. "Thank you, God," he whispered fervently.

A small shelf about ten feet above them offered a little shelter from the rain. Using driftwood for poles, Charlie propped the canoe on its side a few feet out from the cliff to provide additional shelter. Ryan sat beneath it, holding Chrissy, hoping his body would help keep her warm. He talked to her, repeating her name, saying anything that came to mind in an attempt to bring her back to full consciousness; for in spite of the moaning that had so encouraged him, Chrissy had yet to open her eyes or speak. Prayers interspersed his attempts to reach her. Fright for her rose in his chest, strong and persistent, like the waves that rolled against the shore.

Charlie went back into a small bunch of pines and brought back deadfall, kindling, pinecones, and pine knots. He got matches from the emergency kit, which was always attached to the gunwales, and began a fire in the sand between the canoe and the cliff. It was a dismal little thing at first, but the rain hadn't drenched the wood through, and soon it picked up energy. Charlie collected more wood, piling it under the overhang where it would stay dry until needed.

When there was nothing more to be done, Charlie sat down. He ran a hand in a gentle caress over Chrissy's hair, stopping at the lump Ryan had already found on the back of her head. His gaze met Ryan's, and Ryan thought it that of a tortured man. They didn't speak. Ryan could see the fear in Charlie's eyes. He knew Charlie was blaming himself for Chrissy's accident. There was nothing Ryan could say to relieve that kind of pain. They both knew the longer Chrissy remained unconscious, the greater the chance of concussion or coma.

Darkness was falling when the rain and wind let up somewhat. Charlie and Ryan discussed their options in low voices. Ryan couldn't paddle with an injured shoulder. For Charlie to manage the canoe with the three of them on the still choppy lake did not sound wise to either man, yet they knew it was vital to get Chrissy medical assistance soon. There were people with motorboats and an Ojibwa reservation on the opposite side of the lake, but it was five or six miles across. For Charlie to set out alone was foolhardy.

Then Ryan remembered the scouts. They weren't far, just a couple miles south, near the mouth of Lady Boot Bay. They had a number of canoes, and the leader would have training in first aid.

With a last worried look at his sister and a kiss upon her cheek, Charlie headed out. He left everything from the canoe behind with Ryan except the compass, map, and paddles.

For the first time in his life, Ryan found the North Country a frightening, lonely place. His arms were stiff from holding Chrissy, but he continued to cradle her, his back against the cliff. He touched his lips to her temple. "You must wake up, Dearest." His whisper broke on the words. "You must."

He leaned his head against hers and filled the night with prayers and memories of time spent with her since the trip began. Chrissy was the most incredible combination of femininity and guts he'd ever encountered. In spite of all his arguments and intentions, he was falling in love with her.

She moaned again and stirred in his arms.

"Chrissy?"

Her eyelids fluttered open. In the firelight, he saw her flinch.

"Thank God, you're awake."

"Ryan?"

He could barely hear her.

"My head." Her eyes closed tight. "I have such a headache."

"You hit your head against the rocks when you fell in the lake."

"Mmm. Hurts."

He kept her talking, not wanting her to fall back into unconsciousness or sleep. He explained Charlie had gone for help, assuring her he would be fine, that the winds had dropped considerably. After a few minutes, he helped her lean back against the cliff so he had his hands free.

Among the things Charlie had left behind were a small tin kettle they kept tied in the canoe for emergency bailing, a couple packets of spiced tea, and the usual bottled water, gorp, and granola bars. Ryan poured some water into the kettle and set it on two rocks near the fire to heat. When the water came to a boil, he dumped in the contents of one of the tea packets. After the tin had cooled enough that it wouldn't burn hands or lips, he held it to Chrissy's mouth. "It won't be the best tea, but it'll be warm and stimulating."

He wanted to give her some aspirin from the first aid kit, but he didn't know whether that was wise since she'd struck her head.

After adding wood to the fire, he sat beside Chrissy again and slid his good arm around her shoulder. The fragrance from the spiced tea wafted up to him from the kettle in her hands. "I'm warmer to lean against than that cliff," he invited lightly.

She rested against him. "You're warmer. Softer, too."

"Are you insulting my muscles?" He pretended indignation.

"No." She shook her head, her hair catching in the stubble on his chin. "No. I don't think I'll ever belittle a man's muscles again. I've learned a lot on this trip."

"So have I."

Chrissy appeared not to have heard him. "I've been nothing but trouble for you and Charlie. You must both think women are even more worthless than you did before the trip."

"You aren't worthless. You have courage, persistence, and—"

"And a true knack for trouble."

"No. Charlie and I are the troublemakers. If you'd been a man, we'd never have included you on our trip without making sure you knew what to expect, giving you some basic training in canoeing and information about camping. It was irresponsible of us to allow you to come without preparing you."

"I tried to find out a bit for myself, but I was too proud to ask anyone. I read some of the books Charlie has that were written by people who live in wilderness areas. I didn't realize books written thirty years ago would be out of date. After all, I thought, how much could lakes and forests change?"

Ryan chuckled. "They haven't changed so much. It's people's attitudes that have changed. People are learning how to use the land without destroying it for future generations."

The moon broke through the clouds. Ryan was glad for it. Moonlight would make it easier for Charlie to find his way back.

As though Chrissy had the same thought, she asked, "How long has Charlie been gone?"

"I'm not sure. Not long."

She rubbed her head.

Ryan cupped her cheek in his hand. "Does it still hurt?"

She nodded.

Ryan drew her closer against him. He wished desperately he could remove her pain.

"I like your Boundary Waters, Ryan. They'd be perfect if it weren't for the spiders."

" 'In Nature's Wilds all is Independence, all your Luxuries and Comforts are within yourself and all that is pleasurable within your minds; and after all this is Happiness.' "

"Thoreau?"

"Nicholas Garry."

"Ah, yes, the Hudson's Bay Company man. I'm going

to have to read his diary one day."

They were quiet for a long while, long enough for most of the clouds to scuttle away and the moon and stars to reclaim the sky. "Not falling asleep, are you, Chrissy?"

"No."

"Are you worried about Charlie?"

"A little. Do you think he can find us?"

"Your brother is a good outdoorsman. He knows where this island is located, and he can read a map and a compass. He'll find us." He slid his chin lightly over the top of her head. "And he has some help, you know."

"What do you mean?"

"Remember the psalmist? 'Then they cried out to the LORD in their trouble, and he brought them out of their distress. He stilled the storm to a whisper; the waves of the sea were hushed. They were glad when it grew calm, and he guided them to their desired haven.'"

She slid her hand over his and squeezed it. "Thank you for reminding me Who is in charge. You're an unusual man, Ryan Windom."

"Unusual as in strange?"

"Unusual as in. . .nice."

Ryan would have preferred something that showed she was more attracted to him than a mere "nice," but he'd settle for that mild tribute for now. If she hadn't been injured, he'd be content to stay here for days on end, just the two of them.

Chrissy wondered whether Ryan even noticed that she still held his hand. If only it weren't for that awful headache, she'd be completely content watching the stars until they melted into the lake with morning. She hated to think of the trip ending. She'd probably see Ryan again occasionally since he and Charlie were such good friends, but there was no telling where the three of them would end up working and living.

She was crazy about him, but there wasn't much hope he felt the same about her. After all, in the last three days he'd seen her at her absolute worst: gluey dirty nails, wearing the same sweaty bug-goopey clothes for three days straight, drenched by rivers, lakes, and rain—not to mention the adorable mosquito netting she'd worn over her face the first day. She groaned and dropped her head into her hands.

"Are you all right? Is it your head?" Ryan was instantly attentive.

"I'm fine. Really." *A sloppy, smelly, damp, fine mess,* she thought, swallowing another groan.

Moonlight paved a path across the water to their shore. Chrissy hugged her knees. "Have you ever noticed that whenever you're on a lake at night, the moon creates a ribbon of light from itself to you?"

"Mmm hmm. I've noticed that."

" 'By the light of the silvery moon,' " she sang softly, " 'I want to spoon—' " She broke off in embarrassment. Would he think she was hinting she wanted him to kiss her? "When Charlie and I were kids, our folks always sang when we went on long car trips. "The Silvery Moon" was one of Mom's favorite songs. She and Dad would give each other funny little smiles when they sang it. Charlie and I cracked up at the thought of our parents as a romantic young couple."

"You have a great family."

"Yes, we do." Chrissy's gaze searched the lake's surface. "I'll be glad when Charlie gets back."

Half an hour later, a canoe slid into the wavering light. "There's Charlie!" Ryan exclaimed.

"There are two canoes."

The second carried the scout leader and one of the scouts. Ryan was delighted to find the scout leader was a physician's assistant. The man checked on Chrissy's condition, asked her questions, looked at her pupils, took her pulse, and made sure her balance hadn't been affected. "It doesn't look like there's much danger of concussion," he concluded; but he told them what warning signs to watch for, just in case. "If you're uncomfortable about it, you might stop at the Ojibwa village across the lake and see if there's a doctor there or ask if they'll contact one for you."

Ryan's and Charlie's glances met above Chrissy's head, and Ryan knew they'd be visiting the village the next day.

Ryan put out the fire, dousing it with water, raking it to spread the coals, then dousing it again until there was no hint of heat left. The canoes would travel together back to Lady Boot Bay. The scout would take the bow in the canoe with Charlie and Chrissy.

When Chrissy was ready to step into the canoe, Ryan announced, "I'm not leaving."

Everyone turned to stare at him.

"What kind of stupid joke is that supposed to be?" Charlie demanded.

Ryan didn't even look at him. His gaze caught and held Chrissy's. "I've decided not to leave until Chrissy agrees to see me when we get back, on a date, like civilized people."

Chrissy walked over to him slowly. She wasn't smiling.

Ryan steeled himself not to look away from her eyes, but he was worried. Had he offended her unforgivably, making such a demand in front of her brother and two strangers?

She stopped toe-to-toe with him, put her hands on his shoulders, and kissed him lightly. "It's a deal, Mr. Windom."

Joy surging through him, Ryan wrapped his arms around her. "Let's seal that promise properly," he whispered against her lips. This time, the kiss was long and sweet by the light of the silvery moon.

Epilogue

One Year Later

Shouldn't have to worry about falling off this craft," Ryan said, looking over the railing of the cruise ship.

"I'm holding you to your promise of at least one trip to the Boundary Waters this summer."

Ryan chuckled. "I wasn't about to risk taking a trip as important as our honeymoon in a canoe."

Chrissy looked out over the bay at the receding shoreline, but in her mind she saw the new Kevlar canoe hidden beneath a tarp behind her parents' garage. Tied around the stern seat was a huge red bow with a red construction-paper heart announcing, "To Ryan, Love Always, Chrissy." She hadn't wanted to dampen his joy in giving them this cruise by showing him his wedding present before they left, but it was the first thing she wanted to do when they returned.

Ryan kissed his wife on the tip of her nose and smiled.

The day they got back from this cruise, he'd take her to his parents' house and show her her wedding gift. He knew she'd love the new canoe with the name "Christiana" painted in his best hand on the bow. Cruise ships were okay, but nothing compared to a canoe.

Contentment filled and surrounded him as he pulled Chrissy close. Whatever the craft, with God, their love was unsinkable.

JOANN A. GROTE

JoAnn is an award-winning author from Minnesota. She believes that readers of novels can receive a message of salvation and encouragement from well-crafted fiction. Her first novel, *The Sure Promise,* was published by **Heartsong Presents** in 1993. It was reissued in the best-selling anthology *Inspirational Romance Reader, Historical Collection #2* (Barbour Publishing). JoAnn has published historical nonfiction books for children and over twenty historical and contemporary novels for adults and children, including several novels with Barbour Publishing in the **Heartsong Presents** line as well as the *American Adventure* series for kids. She contributed novellas to the best-selling anthologies *Fireside Christmas* and *Prairie Brides* (Barbour Publishing). Once a full-time CPA, JoAnn now works in accounting only part-time and spends most of her "work" time writing.

HEALING VOYAGE

by Diann Hunt

Dedication

To my husband, Jim, for his endless support and for always encouraging me to reach for my dreams. Most of all, to my mother, Mae Walker, whose sacrificial love has brought me to this place. I love you both!

Acknowledgment

Special thanks to Angela Hartman and Janelle Fosnaugh for their helpful information. God bless you, Angie and Janelle!

Chapter 1

Victoria Chaney glared down at her mom and dad from the ship's deck as its mighty horn bellowed for departure. She turned away, attempting to swallow the rising anger that threatened to surface.

Colorful streamers waved around her while confetti sprinkled to the crowd below. The ocean liner was a flurry of commotion. To her right, a young couple embraced. On the other side, a family of three waved to the crowd below. All around Victoria, families hugged and cried, and small prayer circles huddled near the ship's stairway.

Victoria clutched the railing of the *Providence* as people jostled about her, scrambling with last-minute good-byes. Their obvious excitement and enthusiasm for the trip irritated her.

Turning her attention back to her parents, she watched as her father flashed a big smile and waved his arm as if cleaning a large window. Her mother stood beside him, biting her lip, waving a tense hand, and wearing a you'll-understand-this-one-day expression.

Mom's tender smile and gentle ways always had a way of calming Victoria's fears and anger. Even now, she felt remorse curl around the corners of her heart. Yet, her stubborn will froze a frown in place. How could she forgive them for doing this to her?

The salty sea air filled her senses as large waves lapped in rhythm against the ship. Victoria shivered slightly, wishing she'd worn more than her khaki shorts and red T-shirt. She pulled her arms close and attempted to rub away the chill.

The tugboat pulled the large vessel into deeper waters. Victoria watched with mixed emotions as her parents faded with the San Diego shoreline.

One by one the passengers ambled away from the deck. Victoria continued to gaze upon the sea, allowing her thoughts to move in and out of self-pity like the rolling tide.

Sadness crept up on her. She regretted not having waved good-bye. Unbidden tears surfaced.

First, the week's training for this trip and now another three months in the Philippines before she would get the promised two hundred thousand dollars. For as long as she could remember, her parents had promised the money to her when she became an adult. Well, here she was twenty-five years old—and still no money!

A flock of seagulls screeched overhead, catching Victoria's attention. Their strong wings flapped firmly against the wind. Her gaze swept across a perfect blue sky, blown clean by the afternoon breeze. The summer sun softened the air as the ship glided along the sea like an experienced skater on ice.

Victoria sighed. After she received her nursing degree, she thought her parents would be satisfied she was an adult. When that didn't do the trick, it was always implied that twenty-five would be the magic number.

Now this, just when she had started to date a young surgeon in town who owned his practice and ran with rich, powerful people.

That's what she wanted: a carefree, wealthy lifestyle complete with friends, exotic trips, and an expensive home with the finest furnishings money could buy. The promised dollars would offer a good start toward her dream.

Why did they make her do this? She didn't care about the "ministry." She became a nurse because she enjoyed helping people. She'd take care of their bodies; let the ministers take care of their souls.

She looked toward the sky again. The sun was dipping in the west. How long had she been out here? Not that it mattered. *There's no place to go, unless you're a fish.* She didn't want to socialize with anyone. Maybe she'd go find her room. Still, her eyes lingered on the sea as if it held the answer to her problem.

Pulling in a ragged breath, she reminded herself that her parents did promise the money when she returned. When she returned. . .three months later! Victoria's throat constricted. A fresh wave of anger choked her. She hit the railing with her hands. What did her parents care about her dreams or her goals?

"It's not fair!" she said, stomping her foot.

"Did you say something?" A deep voice came from behind her.

Victoria realized she'd been completely lost in thought and hadn't noticed anyone else on the deck. She turned around and stammered as she looked into the bluest eyes she'd ever seen. "I–I. . ." She couldn't finish. An unwelcome heat crept to her cheeks.

"Benjamin Meyer." He thrust out his hand. Large dimples framed a perfect smile.

"Hello. Um, Victoria Chaney," she responded, trying to swallow the lump that lingered in her throat. She returned his handshake. His grasp was firm, confident.

"I thought I heard you say something?" he said, more as a question than a comment.

"Oh, just thinking out loud." She brushed the words away with a wave.

Benjamin looked out to sea. "It's beautiful, isn't it?" Before she could respond, he looked back to her. "Is this your first time aboard the *Providence?*"

"Yes, it is." She glanced at him, then quickly turned away.

"Where are you from?"

"San Diego."

"That's nice. You didn't have to travel far to get to the *Providence*. My home on land is in Chicago."

She thought it strange that he referred to his "home on land."

"This is a great place to serve. I've been aboard for three years now."

Startled, she swung around to face him.

"Is something wrong?" he asked.

"No, it's just that. . .well, I didn't know people stayed here that long."

Benjamin laughed.

Victoria couldn't imagine what he thought was humorous.

He stopped abruptly when he saw her expression. "I'm sorry. I thought you must have learned that in the training."

Victoria brushed imaginary lint from her T-shirt, not wanting to meet his eyes. She should have paid closer attention in the training. Directing her gaze back to him, she replied, "I guess I just missed that somehow."

Benjamin nodded. "What will you be doing here?"

"I'm a nurse." She raised her chin with a sense of pride.

"Great." A large grin spread across his face. "I'm a doctor."

Victoria couldn't believe her ears. *He is a doctor and he's been on this ship for three years? He could be building a lucrative business somewhere, making lots of money, and yet he is stuck on this floating prison going nowhere.*

"Does that surprise you?"

His question interrupted her thoughts. "A little, I suppose." She eyed him carefully. The evening breeze sent the woodsy scent of his cologne her way.

"Don't I look the type?" He leaned sideways, rested one elbow against the ship's railing, and looked down at her. A teasing smile tugged at the corners of his mouth.

Victoria guessed him to be about six-foot four. His height, broad shoulders, and thick arms would suggest he did construction work. Yet, with his hair the color of golden sand and sky blue eyes, she had to admit he seemed to belong here. Dressed in crisp brown shorts, matching polo shirt, and Reeboks, he projected a warm, somewhat relaxed personality.

She realized he'd been watching her. "I don't know

what type you are." She looked away and tucked her hair behind her ear.

Benjamin looked back to the sea. "I can't imagine doing anything else." He paused, as if remembering something. "It's amazing to look into the smiling faces of those who were once disfigured, to give medical help, supplies, and training to the poorest cities in the world." Conviction underlined his words. He turned to Victoria. "What could be more rewarding?"

Victoria felt uncomfortable and didn't know why. An awkward silence stretched between them.

"Do you have a family back home?" he asked in a friendly manner.

"I live with my parents," she said, feeling it really wasn't any of his business. Why did he ask so many questions?

He dug his hand into his pocket, plucked out a piece of cinnamon candy, and held it out to Victoria.

She declined.

Benjamin shrugged and pulled off the wrapper. "Is your father in the medical profession?" he asked nonchalantly before popping the candy into his mouth.

"No, he's a real estate developer. He's owned a very lucrative business for about thirty years now." Her shoulders straightened and her head lifted as she spoke. She wanted him to know she came from a wealthy family.

"That's nice."

If he was impressed, he didn't show it. Victoria felt irritated. Her lips formed a thin line. "Dr. Meyer, I'm tired and I really must be going. It was nice to meet you." Her words were cool, distant.

A look of surprise crossed his face. "No problem. It's been a long day. I'll look forward to running into you on the ship." That same wide grin spread across his face.

Victoria hurried off in the direction of her cabin and drew to a stop next to the stairway. Before descending the stairs to C Deck, she looked back at the doctor. Their glances locked for just a moment.

He waved good night. She returned a faint smile before turning, then quickly slipped below deck.

Chapter 2

Victoria felt better with the doctor out of view. Her hands were still trembling. Convinced the turmoil of the day had set her emotions spinning, she reasoned that once she made it to her cabin, she would relax.

A tired sigh escaped her as she searched for her room. Finally, Victoria stopped. A quick look at the paper in her hand revealed the same numbers indicated on the door in front of her. At last she could be alone and sort through her thoughts.

She put the key in the knob and opened the door.

Lifting her eyes, she looked into the smiling faces of three women. She scanned the tiny cubicle that was to be her home for the next three months. Metal bunk beds were bolted against two walls and a porthole decorated a third one. A small sink hid in a corner, a tiny closet filled the other.

Before Victoria could close her gaping mouth, a rosy-cheeked, plumpish woman with gray hair pulled into a messy topknot was the first to greet her. "Hello," she said, extending her hand, "my name is Tommie Burton."

Victoria thought it was funny this lady should have a

boy's name, but shook her hand, anyway, while looking around, trying to understand what was happening.

"I–I'm sorry, I must have the wrong room."

Tommie looked perplexed. She placed one hand on her thick hip and tapped the index finger of her other hand thoughtfully against her mouth. "Hmm. Did you get your room assignment in the mail?"

"Yes."

By now the other two ladies gathered around her. "Is that the paper?" a blond woman of about twenty asked. Victoria noticed the young woman had the bottom half of her front tooth missing.

"Oh. . .yes," Victoria stammered as she seemed to break out of a trance. "It says, 'Room C-12.' "

"This is it," Tommie said with a chuckle and smacked Victoria on the back. "You must be Victoria—" Tommie frowned for a minute, then bent over to pick up a piece of luggage. She squinted to read the tag on it.

Victoria recognized her luggage at once, but in an effort to be polite, she held her tongue.

"Victoria Chaney." Tommie turned toward Victoria. "You're going to be our roommate!" The older woman jerked her head with a snap as if she'd just made a grand discovery.

Oh, boy, Victoria thought dryly. *Another thing I missed in the training. Roommates.*

"We've been expecting you. Here is your luggage."

The other two women stepped out of the way.

The older woman was saying something over her shoulder about how wonderful it was going to be to travel and work together and what a time they were going to have, but Victoria couldn't grasp all the words. Her heart screamed with disbelief. How could this be happening? Not only did she have to endure this horrid little trip, now she had to stay with three strange women in a room no bigger than a shoebox!

Tommie continued to chatter on about her family back home. Her husband was deceased. Her children were grown and married, but still they lived nearby, and she knew they would struggle without her. She bent over to scoot the luggage out of the way and exposed her knee-high nylons. The left side had a runner. Straightening, she brushed her hands together as if to say, "All in a day's work."

Victoria sighed. No doubt about it, she had to get out of here.

"Are you okay?" the blond asked her, then quickly added, "My name is Sandy Nelson." She extended her hand in greeting. A large grin swept across her face, revealing an imperfect smile but a sincere heart.

"I'm fine, Sandy, thanks." Victoria accepted Sandy's hand and returned the greeting.

The third woman looked to be about forty, possessing a gentle face with calm, dark eyes. She pointed to a top bunk and turned to Victoria. "Is this bed okay for you? If you'd rather have the bottom one, that will be fine with me." Before Victoria could respond, the woman extended her hand. "My name is Betsy Wallace."

"Hi, Betsy," Victoria returned. "The top bunk is fine."

"You didn't know you would have roommates, did you?" Betsy said the words so only Victoria could hear.

"No, I guess I didn't." Victoria felt her irritation rising.

"You'll get used to it, I promise." Betsy grabbed Victoria's other bag and showed her where she could put her things.

Over the next hour, Victoria learned more about the three women than she cared to know. Finally, everyone prepared for bed. When Victoria started calming down, she felt her stomach growl.

"Where's the cafeteria, Betsy?"

"Oh, dear, you haven't eaten yet?" Betsy was already in bed. She adjusted her covers and grabbed a thick novel.

Victoria shook her head.

"I'm sorry. They close the cafeteria an hour after every meal is served. Dinner was served at six o'clock."

Victoria glanced at her wristwatch. A groan escaped her. She hadn't realized it was so late.

Betsy scooted out of her blanket and searched through a brown bag. "Here, eat this."

Victoria looked at the wrapper carefully, as if it contained a secret code.

"If you don't like that, there's a snack bar at the back of the ship. By the way, you'll learn all of that tomorrow." Betsy crawled under her covers once again and continued talking. "During orientation they'll conduct a tour of the ship."

Oh, goody, Victoria thought. *I can hardly wait.* She opened the wrapper of the chocolate energy bar, deciding it was better than nothing at all. She certainly didn't feel like going to the back of the ship, especially since she didn't know her way around yet.

"Thanks."

"No problem."

Tommie was already asleep even though the lights were on. Victoria glanced at her.

"I've been on the ship with her before. Sleeps like a hibernating bear," Betsy said with a laugh. "You'll never wake her up."

Right then the sleeping woman fell into a rhythmic snore that whistled on the downswing. Sandy and Betsy laughed.

Terrific, Victoria fumed.

"Is there a bathroom in here?" she asked impatiently, praying they would answer yes.

"Sorry, Tori, it's down the hall—that is, if you want the liquid toilets and the showers. Otherwise, the public rest rooms are near the back of the ship."

Victoria was surprised Betsy called her Tori. She couldn't decide if she liked it or not. "What's a liquid toilet?"

"Let your imagination work for you," Betsy said with a chuckle, then looked back at her novel.

Victoria turned and rolled her eyes. *Great, just great!* She stuffed her necessities in a bag and stomped down the hall in search of the showers.

Benjamin Meyer dropped onto his bed. His right Reebok thumped to the floor, then his left. He had little strength to finish his nightly routine before climbing into bed.

Yawning, he reached for his Bible. Morning devotions had carried him through the day, but he liked to go to sleep with God's Word echoing through his mind. The pages fanned in a whisper as he flipped through the book to Philippians 4:13, "I can do everything through him who gives me strength." He rubbed his blurry eyes.

"Thank You, Father. It's just what I needed tonight."

Closing his Bible, he placed it on the nightstand and turned out the light. He stared at the ceiling while his eyes adjusted to the dark.

The picture of Victoria Chaney filled his mind. Tall and slim, she carried a certain amount of charm. A gentle breeze had stirred a few strands of her chestnut hair, causing it to dance upon her slender shoulders. Her angular face had well-defined features. A tiny dimple peeked from the corner of her mouth with every smile, while a fringe of bangs brushed across her forehead framing emerald green eyes.

She was beautiful. Yet, he had an uneasy feeling about her. Why did she leave in such a hurry? She seemed almost irritated. Had he said something to upset her? It was almost as if she didn't want to be here. But why?

He rearranged himself in the sheets and punched his pillow into position. He wanted to get to know Victoria better. She stirred him somehow. He could get lost in her eyes, her smile, her— His thoughts stopped cold as the familiar words barged into his mind once again. *Remember your promise.*

Pulling the covers around himself, he turned toward the wall. His pulse pounded against his temples like a hammer upon wood. A sudden chill pushed from the inside out, making him feel hot and cold at the same time. He trembled as the painful images took shape in his mind.

He drew in a long, deep breath.

"Lord, please keep the nightmare away tonight." His desperate plea lingered in the stillness. A portable clock ticked the time. When at last his eyes grew heavy, the dark memories that taunted him escaped to the shadows.

He knew they would return. They always did.

Restlessness continued to plague Benjamin through-out the night, but this time it wasn't the nightmare that ran through his fitful slumber. Instead, a young woman with beautiful green eyes drifted through his dreams.

Chapter 3

Sunlight pushed through the porthole. Victoria awakened with a start. The room was empty. Had she overslept?

"Just what I need," she grumbled as she threw off her covers and jumped to the floor. Dashing to the nightstand, she grabbed her watch. Seven o'clock. Adrenaline rushed through her. One hour 'til the meeting.

Victoria rummaged through her clothes and pulled out the appropriate uniform of a dark skirt and white blouse. She ran to the showers.

By 7:40, Victoria felt herself presentable and made her way to the cafeteria. Entering the room, she saw Tommie, Betsy, and Sandy sitting together at a far right table. They all smiled, waved, and motioned her to eat with them.

She groaned. "This is like riding the Happy Day Express and rooming with the welcoming committee," she mumbled. After returning the wave, she pointed to her watch and shook her head with a shrug.

Victoria heaved a sigh of relief to find them gone by the time she got through the breakfast line. She sat down and quickly ate her meal of scrambled eggs, toast, and orange juice.

After scurrying to dump her tray, she dashed to the newcomers' room. Out of breath and feeling a bit disheveled, she slipped into an empty seat in the back.

The speaker stepped to the front to begin his welcoming speech. He spoke of the mission of the *Providence,* its history since conception, and what a privilege it was to be aboard.

Yeah, real privilege. When I could be skiing at Vail, boating in Catalina, or dining in the finest of restaurants, I'm stuck on this boat filled with do-gooders. As soon as the thought formed, Victoria felt a tinge of shame.

The speaker continued to explain that workers were there for various lengths of time. Some were there indefinitely, many were short-term, spanning anywhere from two weeks to a year or more. This trip, however, required a three-month stay because it would take approximately two and a half weeks to get to the Philippines.

A discussion arose about the accommodations. Many volunteers had roommates, while some, like the doctors who had signed on for longer periods of time, were given private cabins. Victoria grunted inwardly. No doubt healthcare would suffer if a doctor had someone like Tommie for a roommate. They'd never get any sleep! Despite Victoria's grumpy mood, she couldn't help letting out a chuckle.

She glanced around the room at the newcomers. A wide variety of ages and professions was represented. She wondered why these people had chosen to come on this trip.

With a shrug, she turned her attention back to the speaker. Fringes of white hair brushed just above his ears and bordered the lower back of his balding head. His hefty middle shook with every joke he told, and Victoria couldn't help but wonder what he'd look like dressed in a Santa suit.

He listed the various countries with which they worked and the lengths of stay for each, encouraging the newcomers to get involved with future trips. Finally, he discussed their job assignment sheets and asked for questions.

Several minutes later, the excited crowd left the room to follow the speaker on a tour of the ship. Victoria reluctantly joined them.

The massive liner impressed Victoria, though she didn't want to admit it. She struggled to listen to the guide as he described the list of attributes aboard her new home.

A balmy morning embraced them as they strolled the ship's main deck. Seasoned passengers nodded as they passed by, preparing for their day's work.

Victoria breathed deeply of the ocean's scent as the summer sun warmed her face. The speaker's voice faded, and Victoria's ears tuned to the gentle waves that bobbed rhythmically around them. She watched a pair of dolphins at play in the distance.

The group slowed its pace, arriving on the aft, or entertainment, deck. It surprised Victoria to find a small pool sparkling with clear blue water. Lawn chairs formed a horseshoe around the pool. Behind them, vending machines and game tables huddled together. Maybe this trip wouldn't be so bad after all.

As much as she hated to admit it, her new home was beautiful and the people seemed friendly.

Yesterday, frustration filled her. Victoria wanted to leave this place, get on with her life. She still felt the same today but decided to make the most of her time aboard the *Providence*. She shrugged. *It won't last forever. I'm stuck here, so I may as well get used to the idea.*

The decision made her feel better. She relaxed and tuned back to the words of the tour guide as they made their way down the stairs.

After the tour, Victoria searched for the doctor's office where she would be working. She read each room number, looking for the appropriate one.

Large, choppy waves rocked the boat. Victoria felt a little queasy as she walked toward the office. She stopped for just a moment and leaned against a wall to settle herself. She wasn't sure if she felt seasick or anxious of her new position.

Since there were many physicians on the ship, she hoped the one she assisted would be a nice doctor who kept to himself, not one who would try to strike up a friendship and pry into her life. She was obviously here for a different reason than the other passengers.

What would the others think if they knew my motive for being here? Her chest tightened as melancholy settled over her. She brushed the thought away. *After all, it's my business.*

Reaching the door marked "Ship's Doctor," Victoria took a deep breath and turned the knob. Her stomach churned. As the door opened, she stepped in and looked around the room. It appeared much like a doctor's office back in the States: same sterile bed, cabinet with miscellaneous instruments, and antiseptic smell. But boxes cluttered this room.

She spotted the doctor on the other side of the office with his back to her. He was crouching in front of a cabinet, putting things inside. Victoria coughed slightly.

Rising, he turned to meet her. A smile stretched across his face. "Well, we meet again." He stepped over to her and extended his hand.

Victoria's heart sank. She felt the blood leave her face. Reluctantly, she took his hand. "Hello, Dr. Meyer," she said with a tone implying she was less than pleased.

"I take it you didn't know you would be working with me?" A smirk played at the corners of his mouth.

"No," she admitted.

Streaks of gold ran through his hair that fell haphazardly across his forehead, giving him a youthful appearance. His eyes held hers for a moment.

She looked away.

"Yes, well, as you can see, we've got a lot of unpacking to do." Benjamin's arm waved across the pile of boxes holding new supplies that crowded the room. "This room is normally organized, but we received these in San Diego. We've got to get them inventoried and put away before we reach Manila."

"Okay," she agreed.

"Before we get started, I'd like to go over the schedule." Reaching his desk, he picked up some papers. "We'll be treating the crew and passengers on this ship from eight to twelve o'clock each day, take a quick lunch break, then leave the ship for the island and set up a makeshift office there from one-thirty to five o'clock." He handed her a sheet listing her job description.

She scanned the page while he talked to her.

"Whether we're on the ship or on the island, we will treat the same kinds of things a doctor's office back home would handle."

With a nod, she slowly relaxed in the semifamiliar surroundings. Even her stomach felt better. The room reminded her of Dr. Burke's office, where she had worked for the past two years. Dr. Burke was a good doctor, but she didn't want to spend her career there.

Dr. Meyer's voice broke through her thoughts. "We work Monday through Friday. However, we help out sometimes on the weekends if we're needed in surgery or recovery on B Deck. Of course, you know the hospital ward is located on C Deck."

"Yes, I've visited the ward. What do we do on weekends, if we're not needed?" She was hopeful there would be some fun on this trip. Maybe she'd try out the pool.

"I'm glad you asked that, Victoria. We do have outreach programs on the island, if you'd like to help out there."

Her voice caught in her throat. "Uh, thank you. I'll keep that in mind."

"Good. Do you have any questions?"

She shook her head.

"Great. Let's get to work." He passed her some scissors, and they tore into boxes and sorted through supplies for the remainder of the day.

After dinner, Victoria went to her room and gathered her swimwear. Waiting for the crowd to thin out of the pool area, she wandered to the edge of the main deck and leaned against the metal railing. It was hard to find time alone here. Like many others, she found herself standing at the railing, retreating into her thoughts.

She stood mesmerized. Satin stars poked through a velvet sky and sparkled upon the moonlit sea. The *Providence* serenely glided forward, echoing the peacefulness of the night.

In the stillness of that perfect moment, contentment descended upon her. She was surprised. Not stopping to analyze her feelings, she turned toward the pool.

It was almost deserted now. A young couple was just leaving. They smiled and said their good nights to her. Victoria responded, then placed her towel and swim wrap on a nearby lawn chair. Snapping a rubber band in place to secure her ponytail, she slipped into the warm water. The heat of the day washed away, relaxing her tired muscles.

She had put in a full day's work. Never one to be a slacker, she prided herself in working hard.

Victoria stretched her arms over her head and took several laps across the pool. The water splashed through the night air. She swam to the other side, then back. Her right hand reached for the pool's ledge. Lifting her head, she brushed the water from her face with her free hand. Legs moving rhythmically, she bobbed lightly, relaxing in the stillness.

The ship became quiet around ten o'clock. The management encouraged its passengers to get their needed rest. Victoria cherished her privacy.

A soft drink can snapped open, startling her. She looked up to see Dr. Meyer settling into a lawn chair, facing her.

Great. So much for solitude, she thought.

"Sorry if I'm interrupting you," he said thoughtfully.

She looked at him, too surprised by his presence to say anything. Why did he make her feel uncomfortable?

"Victoria?" He lifted her name like one would a delicate rose.

Despite the warm water, she felt goosebumps form on her arms. "Hello, Dr. Meyer. I didn't know you were here." She thought he looked tired.

He looked away and seemed troubled as he took a drink from the can. Something was wrong.

Continuing to tread water, she searched for something to say. "The water is nice tonight." Why did she say that? He would think she was inviting him in. How could she be so forward?

"You shouldn't swim alone." His words were short, stern. Dark shadows lined his face, making him look old in the moonlight. He took another drink, never taking his gaze from her.

She knew he was right but resented being treated like a child. "I appreciate your concern, but I think I can manage." She lifted her nose into the air with feigned confidence.

He stared at her for what seemed an eternity, then with a curt nod, he lowered his gaze.

Victoria felt a pang of guilt for her defensive attitude, but he seemed to bring that out in her.

Benjamin rose from the chair, turned toward Victoria, and stopped abruptly at the edge of the pool. Her heart leapt to her throat as his tall frame towered over her. He stooped down closer to her. Their gazes locked for a moment.

"Thanks for your hard work today."

"You're welcome." Her eyelids lowered. She felt uneasy with his nearness. He stayed there without the slightest movement.

She watched as he stared intensely at the pool. His expression changed. Color left his face. His blue eyes clouded. The veins in his neck pulsed hard with every heartbeat, while perspiration formed on his forehead. His hands trembled.

Victoria became alarmed. "Doctor, are you all right?"

Her voice seemed to shake him out of a trance. His attention focused back to her. His breathing was ragged, unnatural. "Oh, sure—sure, I'm fine." He stood, took the last sip from his soda, then tossed the can into the trash.

Victoria climbed from the pool and put on a mint green swim cover. He turned and threw her a surprised glance.

She shrugged. "You're right. I shouldn't be out here alone." The sudden compliance startled even her, but before she had time to dwell on it, Benjamin's thankful expression chased away her obstinance.

"I'll see you tomorrow."

She stood unmoving as she watched him fade into the shadows, leaving her alone once again.

Chapter 4

Victoria felt tired and grumpy the next morning. Thoughts of Benjamin Meyer and his strange behavior at the pool caused her to sleep restlessly. It was Wednesday, and morning devotions were scheduled on the main deck. That made her grumpier still. Why did she have to go? She could never find the Scripture reference. The Bible her parents had given her two years ago was still like new. *Why do these people read the Bible all of the time?*

"Good morning," Tommie called out in singsong fashion.

Victoria pulled her pillow over her head and groaned.

Tommie giggled and poked at the pillow. "Come on, Sleepyhead. Rise and shine."

I think I'm going to hurl, Victoria thought. She couldn't handle cheerfulness first thing in the morning.

"The medical group meets for devotions in forty-five minutes, Tori," Betsy chimed in with a pleasant voice.

Who made her the devotion warden? Victoria grumbled inwardly as she peeked out from under her pillow.

Betsy was making her bed, carefully tucking in the covers at the corners.

Tommie stood in front of the mirror. She shoved the last pin in her hair, securing her tight, little bun. Victoria rolled her eyes and pulled the pillow back over her face.

Someone entered the room just then and tripped over something, causing an annoying clang to reverberate through the room. Victoria yanked the pillow from her face with a start. *Sandy. Can't that girl go five minutes without dropping or knocking something over? No wonder she has a chipped tooth—probably got it tripping over something.*

Sandy apologized.

Oh, why can't I be starting my new life? Victoria's mood grew darker as thoughts of home filled her. She looked around the tiny room with the three women scurrying about, and she felt like a trapped bird. She tried to disguise her annoyance in front of the others, but restlessness and irritability claimed her. She crawled out of bed.

"Oh, Victoria, thanks for letting me use this." Sandy turned to give Victoria the handheld mirror, but the young blond stumbled and dropped it. It shattered into tiny pieces upon the floor.

"That's just great," Victoria growled under her breath. She felt anger surge through her. All the frustrations of the trip swelled within her and came bursting forth in a ball of fury. "Do you have any idea how old that is? Do you know what it meant to me? My grandmother gave that to me when I was eight years old! But what do you care? You are such a klutz!" Victoria's arms jerked angrily with every insult that spewed from her mouth.

Anger rushed through her veins as she released her mounting emotions without giving thought to the damage being done until her rage was spent.

Sandy stood perfectly still with each blow of the verbal lashing, never retorting, just grimacing. Tears gathered, then spilled over onto her cheeks.

The air grew tense. Tommie and Betsy stood motionless, mute.

Sandy lowered her head and cried. "I'm so sorry, Victoria. I'm so sorry." She crouched down and picked up the tiny pieces. Tommie and Betsy looked at Victoria, then reached down to help Sandy clean up the mess.

Victoria grabbed her things, then headed for the showers, slamming the door behind her.

When Victoria returned from the showers, the room was clean. . .and empty.

I don't know why I should feel bad. She's the one who broke my mirror—my grandmother's mirror!

Victoria felt more irritation. She skipped devotions. Grabbing her quilted bag, she closed the door behind her and left for the doctor's office.

She was the first one there. *Good. Benjamin's probably at devotions. Finally, maybe I can get some time to myself.*

She sorted through the last of the boxes and tidied the room. Her emotions subsided and remorse settled over her. She shouldn't have treated Sandy that way. After all, it was an accident. Victoria bit her lip as she thought of Sandy's face, her tears.

I refuse to get upset about this all over again. Victoria

shrugged off the thought like an unwanted touch. If only she didn't have to take this trip.

Dr. Meyer opened the door. "Good morning, Vic," he said as he entered. His blue eyes were bright and sparkling.

Her heart flipped in spite of her mood. She started feeling better.

"Missed you in devotions," he said over his shoulder as he pulled out some paperwork.

"Thanks," she said, not wanting to discuss it.

A knock sounded at the door. An elderly man clutched his stomach as he entered the room.

Victoria and Dr. Meyer rushed to the man's side and helped him to the examining table. Victoria noted his complexion resembled the color of chalk. She efficiently grabbed a blood pressure gauge, tongue depressor, and thermometer. Together she and Dr. Meyer worked on the patient, all the while attempting to calm him. After a diagnosis of seasickness and receiving medication, the man was released.

Dr. Meyer passed out suckers and cartoon bandages to a few children who came in with cuts and colds. He talked gently with each one, as a father would his children. Victoria watched with admiration.

By five o'clock, Victoria grew weary. The day had tired her, and yet in some ways, she was strangely revived. She realized again how much she enjoyed her work. *It really feels good to help others.*

"Want to grab a bite to eat?" Benjamin asked.

His words startled her. She looked up at him, confused.

"You've worked hard today, Vic. I thought maybe

you might want to go to your room, freshen up, then we could go to the cafeteria together?" His expression seemed hopeful.

"I'd like that," she found herself saying, though she didn't know why.

"Good," he said quickly, as if he were afraid she would change her mind. "I'll stop by your cabin, say, five forty-five?"

Victoria smiled. "Okay." She picked up her quilted bag and reached for the door. Looking back, she saw Benjamin still staring at her, his warm smile revealing those dimples.

She turned and left for her room.

Victoria knew when she entered her cabin the atmosphere would be cold. Her roommates probably wouldn't talk to her after how she'd behaved. She couldn't blame them.

Pausing at the door, she listened. She could hear murmuring voices. Victoria dreaded going inside. Gathering her strength, she stretched to her full height, opened the door, and entered.

"Hi, Tori," Betsy greeted cheerfully.

"Hello," Victoria said, her glance barely brushing past them, her voice thin and low. She dropped her bag on the bed.

"You've got to see this, Victoria," Tommie said, patting the seat beside her. "I bought it at the ship's store today." She leafed through a new cookbook.

Victoria glanced at it absently, keenly aware that Betsy and Sandy were looking at her. She uttered some words about the cookbook to Tommie, then prepared herself for dinner.

"Would you like to eat with us?" Sandy asked, her sorrowful, brown eyes meeting Victoria's.

"Sandy, about the mirror—"

Sandy waved her hand to stop her, but Victoria shook her head. "No, please, I need to say this." The only sound she could hear was the pounding of her heart. "I'm sorry I behaved the way I did to you. I could give you excuses for my actions, but really, there is no excuse." Victoria inwardly struggled with her pride. "I was wrong, and I hope you can forgive me." There. She said it.

"Christ forgave me of far worse. How could I not forgive you?" Sandy patted Victoria's shoulder with reassurance.

"Thank you." Victoria felt relieved but didn't want to get into a discussion on religion, so she quickly changed the subject. "Dr. Meyer and I are meeting for dinner tonight, so I won't be able to join you."

Betsy let out a whistle.

Victoria didn't miss the smiles and knowing glances exchanged by her roommates. "It's nothing like that."

"Oh, I see," Betsy said dramatically. She swung a pillow at Victoria with a teasing grin.

Victoria looked at them, puzzled.

"You really don't get it?" Betsy looked at her in disbelief.

Victoria shook her head.

"It's a date. Tori, even I can see that!" Betsy said, smiling.

"A date?" Victoria suddenly became aware of her

appearance. She absently reached for her hair as she glanced over her clothes.

"How soon will he be here?" Betsy asked as she scanned the room.

Victoria glanced at her watch. "In forty minutes."

"No problem. Sandy, plug in my curling iron." Betsy started barking orders like a mother preparing her daughter for the prom. For the next forty minutes, Victoria's roommates pampered her with creams, curls, and polish, giving her a finished look just as the knock sounded on the cabin door.

Victoria looked into the faces of her new friends. Adorned with wide smiles, they eagerly motioned for her to answer the door.

She shrugged, then opened it. Dr. Meyer's eyes grew wide as he observed her. A smile flashed across his face. "All set, Vic?"

"Yes." Victoria turned to close the door behind her. She looked at the trio once more. Tommie gave her the thumbs up sign. Victoria winked and closed the door behind her.

As they strolled down the passageway, she wondered if she felt wonderful because the women fixed her up or because she realized her roommates were becoming true friends. She marveled that even though she had behaved so poorly, they still went out of their way to be nice to her.

She glanced over at Benjamin. His hair, though slightly gelled, hung loosely across his forehead. He wore a crisp, blue-striped oxford shirt with neatly pressed navy pants. *Maybe I feel wonderful because I'm going to dinner with the most handsome man aboard the ship.*

⚓

Benjamin Meyer chewed his fried chicken and looked at Victoria. *Her hair's different tonight,* he thought, as he admired the way she had swept it back. Her peach-colored top revealed her smooth neck and velvety skin. He lifted the linen napkin and absently brushed his mouth.

I've got to stop this. I'm getting in way over my head. I don't know enough about this woman yet.

Victoria turned and looked at him.

Oh, great. She saw me staring at her. Benjamin caught his breath. He felt like a little boy getting caught with his hand in the cookie jar. Their gazes locked for a moment. He winked at her.

Victoria smiled, then dropped her focus to her plate.

He picked up his glass. The ice tinkled lightly against the glass. Taking a sip of water, he carefully placed it back on the table. He watched as Victoria toyed with her food. She ran the fork around her plate, attempting to act interested, but her mind seemed elsewhere.

"You were a great help today," he said, tossing her a smile.

A blush crept to her face, fanning her creamy cheekbones with a faint shade of pink.

He dug his fork into a piece of chicken. "So what are you doing after dinner?" He stuck a bite in his mouth.

"I thought I'd go swimming. I've been terribly warm today." She scooped a bite of mashed potatoes and lifted them to her mouth. Looking at him, she swallowed and said, "Do you want to join me?"

His breath seemed to leave him. How long had it been since he'd gone swimming? The last time was before the accident.

Just then, the scene flashed across his mind: The water gently rocking his sister's tiny form, light brown hair floating softly around the back of her head, pudgy arms hanging limply from her sides. . . .

Victoria's hand was on top of his. "Ben, what is it? What's wrong?"

He struggled to breathe. Her words brought him back to the present. "I'm sorry. I don't know, I was just. . ." His voice faded away.

Victoria removed her hand from his.

Quickly, Benjamin grabbed the napkin from his lap and placed it on the table. "I'm really sorry, but I don't feel so well, Vic. Do you mind if I head off to my cabin?"

"Uh, no, not at all. Are you going to be all right?"

"I'll be fine. I'm sorry I can't walk you back." His look met hers.

"Don't worry about it. I'll be fine," she assured him.

"I'll see you tomorrow, okay?" He stood.

"Sure."

Benjamin left the table, carrying his tray. It trembled slightly beneath his grasp.

He could kick himself. What would Victoria think of him now? He was losing his heart to her, but what could he do when the memories refused to let him go?

⚓

Betsy, Sandy, and Tommie greeted Victoria upon her return from dinner. Their eager faces made her feel even worse. She looked at them. "He went to his room. Wasn't feeling well."

Their smiles faded.

Victoria reached for her swimming suit. "Don't wait up for me," she called over her shoulder. With that, she was gone.

Chapter 5

Casting a final glance in the mirror, Victoria checked her lipstick, then headed out the door of her cabin. As she strolled through the corridor, her thoughts traveled to the night of her dinner with Benjamin. They hadn't broached the subject of that incident, though the event puzzled her still.

People had been watching them that night, and she wondered if he suddenly regretted having taken her to dinner. Their relationship had been cordial but somewhat distant since then.

She shook off her musings as the ship sounded its arrival at Manila South Harbor. Victoria climbed the stairway to the upper deck, taking in the scent of the sea. The hot morning sun threw shafts of light across the ship, making everything fresh as a new day. Victoria stood, captivated by the bustle of activity surrounding the dock.

Lifting her hand, she shielded her eyes from the blazing light and surveyed the area. Five cement piers stretched from the shoreline into the bay to accommodate incoming ships. Cruise liners and yachts lined the docks.

The smell of fish and the sea rose with the faint breeze.

Horns tooted and people called across the distance.

Victoria's curiosity took her to the ship's railing for a better view. Down the road, tourists waved for waiting taxis. Men in crisp, white shirts and shorts stood in front of hotels that lined the oceanfront, preparing for their guests.

The captain of the *Providence* hired a Filipino driver for the daily trip to the clinic site. The driver agreed to transport the needed medical supplies, equipment, and personnel via FX taxi.

The next afternoon, Benjamin and Victoria loaded the back of the black rusty FX, which resembled a pickup truck, and climbed onto the seats. Other individuals from the ship would check in with them throughout the afternoon.

The medical duo headed north up Roxas Boulevard. Victoria glanced out her window at the row of palm trees lining the street. On the other side, tall office buildings and large hotels bid them welcome.

"What's that?" Victoria asked the driver as she pointed to a walled border.

"That is Intramuros," he said, pride underlying his words. "The Spaniards built the fortified city hundreds of years ago for protection."

"What's in there now?"

"Stone arches, Spanish-style buildings, and little antique stores. Lots of places to shop."

Victoria promised herself she would come back and visit one weekend.

Their taxi sped across the mouth of the large Pasig

River and finally through a few neighborhoods. "This is it," Ben said to Victoria as the driver pulled into a tiny vacant area at the edge of the Tondo, an enormous squatter settlement. The metal door of the taxi squeaked in protest as Benjamin pushed it open and stepped out.

Victoria marveled how wealth and power swept the tourist district so clean with sparkle that most visitors were unaware of the filth and poverty which defiled the city only blocks away.

Although they set up their clinic a short distance from the settlement, the air still reeked of open sewers and garbage ditches. As Victoria climbed out of the taxi, she covered her mouth, taking only shallow breaths of the repulsive air. She closed her stinging eyes for a moment.

"A great breeding ground for disease, huh?" Benjamin said more as a comment than a question. The driver opened the tailgate of the taxi and Benjamin began removing supplies.

Victoria choked back a cough. She looked briefly toward the settlement. About every forty yards, there was a small opening in an outside concrete wall that lined the houses. The opening stretched about three yards across and led into a corridor between the homes. Power lines sagged dangerously in the middle, crisscrossing through the corridors. Television antennas poked above rusted roofs. Gray shacks and mud stretched as far as her eyes could see. Victoria sighed heavily, then turned her attention to organizing their outdoor clinic.

Islanders quickly lined up for medical attention. Benjamin and Victoria spent the afternoon giving vaccinations, cleaning and bandaging wounds, checking pulses, throats, ears and eyes, and dispensing vitamins and medicines.

Before they knew it, the day had ended and the medical team found themselves loading equipment back onto the taxi and returning to the *Providence*.

By the time Victoria had eaten dinner and reached her room, she was exhausted. She chatted briefly with her roommates about their first day on the island, then climbed wearily into her bunk.

As tired as she was, though, she couldn't sleep. Thoughts of Benjamin filled her. Scenes of the day flashed through her mind as she thought of his compassion for these people. His kindness touched her deeply.

Her thoughts drifted to the Tondo. Tiny lean-tos made of assorted materials connected like dominos along a rutted dirt path. Malnourished children played lazily in the dirt. Victoria had never seen such poverty.

She thought how the world was a vast array of contrasts just like the Philippines. The rich brushed past the poor every day in every city, many never extending a helping hand.

A wave of guilt swept over her as she realized that was the lifestyle she had wanted—to be rich and carefree, giving no thought to the needs of others.

Victoria turned to the wall, bringing the sheets just under her chin. She wanted to get home where life was comfortable and the plagues of society were nothing more than a flashing commercial that a few cents a day would resolve.

⚓

The next day grew hotter. The stagnant air hung in thick layers, but Victoria found herself growing used to it.

Volunteers from the *Providence* brought water bottles to help cool the medical teams.

Victoria took a long drink of her water as a young woman staggered up to them, carrying a child around four years of age. The thin little girl lay limply across her mother's arms.

The mother spoke quickly in English, "Please, my daughter, my Claudia, she is very sick." Tears streaked down the mother's face. Her arms trembled and her large, frightened eyes pleaded for help as she looked at Benjamin.

Benjamin and Victoria reacted quickly, lifting the little girl to the portable examining table. He asked the mother questions relating to her daughter's recent behavior and symptoms.

A line of patients grew behind the mother as Victoria and Benjamin worked on the little girl. Victoria watched as growing concern lined Benjamin's face. The way he handled the fragile patient went beyond compassion. What was it?

He lifted his gaze to Victoria. She looked at him, and for an instant, something flickered across his face. Was it raw pain she saw staring back at her? Victoria sensed she had stumbled upon something very personal.

Benjamin broke into a sweat. He sighed deeply and swiped his arm across his forehead.

The waiting patients talked among themselves, while the mother held her breath, anticipating an answer.

"Doctor?"

He grimaced. "Dengue fever, I think." He glanced at the little girl once again. "We'll have to take her to the ship."

Victoria knew only a little about dengue fever. She knew it was transmitted by infected mosquitoes, could reach an epidemic, and made the victim very sick. Though rarely fatal, it was always a concern. She looked at the girl's mother with compassion.

"Check in the next patient while I talk to the mother," Benjamin said.

Placing the last box in the doctor's office for the night, Victoria stood and faced Benjamin. He looked tired and spent. "I'll go to the ward tonight and check on her, Ben. You try to get some rest."

Victoria turned to leave, but he grabbed her wrist. She spun around to face him.

"I need to talk to you, Vic."

"Yes?" She glanced at her wrist. He released his grip.

"We've got to go to their home."

"Whose home?"

"Maria and Claudia Garza's."

Victoria stared at him. "Why?"

"We need to let Mrs. Garza know how Claudia is getting along." He flipped through his patient charts, then looked back at Victoria. "Will you go with me?"

Without hesitation she replied, "Certainly, I'll go. When?"

"Tomorrow. I've asked another doctor to cover for me while we're gone." He returned the patient charts to the desk. "I'll meet you here at eight o'clock in the morning."

"Okay," she answered, her voice gentle with concern.

"Victoria, please pray for Claudia. Dengue fever causes severe pain in the bones. I've put her on analgesics to relieve the pain, but she's so young, so frightened. . ."

Victoria reached out and touched his arm. "Benjamin, you are doing all you can. She'll be fine. And I will. . .pray." The words came out before she could stop herself. How could she pray? She didn't even know how. But she would. She must. For Claudia and for Benjamin, she would pray.

↙⁎

Benjamin and Victoria left the taxi in the area of their clinic and headed toward the Tondo. The stench of the area swelled with every step as they worked their way along the dirt paths that stretched up to the makeshift homes. Victoria grimaced at a mauled rooster to the right of her.

"Cock fighting," Benjamin answered her unspoken question. "It's a popular pastime among the men in the area."

They continued forward until they came to the crumpled form of a man along the filthy roadway. Victoria gasped.

The drunkard lay in his own vomit at the side of a ditch. The man turned in his sleep, still clutching an empty, dirty bottle. Victoria covered her mouth as her stomach lurched.

Benjamin felt for the man's pulse. "He'll have to sleep it off," Benjamin said as he reached for Victoria's hand to help her step around the man.

She felt strangely comforted by the firm grasp of Benjamin's hand.

They walked farther down the road, then Benjamin stopped. "This one belongs to the Garzas," he said, as they looked at the walls of weathered plywood scraps and cardboard that reached up to a roof of rusted, corrugated iron.

The sight sickened Victoria. *How can people live like this?* She wanted to scream, to run away.

Benjamin turned to her. "You gonna be all right?"

"I'm fine," she lied, swallowing the bile in her throat.

"Good." He looked toward the house and took a deep breath. "Okay, let's go."

Benjamin took three steps forward and Victoria followed closely behind. He tapped lightly on the plywood panel that appeared to be a door.

Maria opened it and invited them in.

Once Victoria's eyes adjusted to the dimly lit area, she looked around the tiny hovel consisting of two rooms and a dirt floor. In one room lay four tattered blankets. A corner held a small pile of clothing. The other room held a little gas burner for cooking and a large, heavy cardboard box, which served as a table. Weak lighting came from a dull lightbulb hanging in the corner and sunbeams that squeezed through cracks in the bumpy walls. Tiny insects roamed in and out of crevices.

A young boy and girl with swollen stomachs and skinny arms and legs looked up at them through sad eyes. Victoria thought them to be about seven to nine years old, but with their health condition, she wasn't sure.

"Sarita and Marlon, this is Dr. Meyer and Nurse Victoria," Maria said. Her words were calm, but Victoria noticed Maria nervously wringing her hands.

"You going to make Claudia better?" the little girl asked.

Benjamin scrunched down in front of her and smiled.

"I'm sure going to do my best." He patted her arm.

"Claudia is doing well?" Maria lifted her anxious expression toward the doctor.

Benjamin motioned her away from the children. Victoria visited with Sarita and Marlon while Benjamin talked with their mother. Maria whimpered, but when she turned around, peace glowed from her face.

"Maria, we would like your permission to examine your children."

Maria nodded approval and answered their questions while Benjamin and Victoria checked the children.

Once they were finished, Benjamin gave Sarita and Marlon each a coloring book with Bible story pictures and crayons and showed the curious youngsters what to do with them.

He looked at Maria. "With some healthy food, they'll be good as new," he said with a smile. "And we've brought you some food, Maria."

She licked her lips slightly and looked down at the bag he was opening. She grabbed her children's hands, and they watched as the doctor placed bread, rice, fresh fruit, some canned goods, and a can opener on the box.

Tears slid down Maria's face as she and her family watched the doctor place the food on the box. Before anyone could say anything, Maria looked at her children. "You see? I told you God would provide. He always takes care of us. Do you see now?"

Her little ones nodded in agreement. The girl tugged on Maria's dress.

"Yes, Sarita?"

"Mama, God will bring Claudia home, too."

"If God wills, Sarita. We'll pray for Claudia to come home." Maria smiled at her daughter, then looked back at Benjamin and Victoria. "Thank you for everything. You have been God's hands to our family."

Benjamin smiled and Victoria blinked back tears. "We will be passing out clothing and more supplies at the clinic tomorrow afternoon. Be there early so you can provide for your family," Benjamin advised Maria.

"Thank you," she said before starting to pray out loud. Victoria looked around, feeling awkward, then closed her eyes.

"Oh, God, thank You for Your faithfulness. Always when we are hungry, You take care of us. Please help our neighbors who are sick. Teach us how to take care of our families. Thank You for kind people like Dr. Meyer and Nurse Victoria, who give their lives to help others. May we learn to do the same. Amen."

A broad smile flashed across Maria's face, revealing rotted teeth. She held up canned goods. "I will share with my neighbors."

Hot, stubborn tears pushed through Victoria's lashes and splashed onto the dirt floor. She quickly turned to wipe her face.

She edged out the door as Benjamin said their good-byes. Silence followed them to their waiting vehicle.

"How do they exist?" Victoria asked when they climbed back into the waiting FX taxi.

"Maria works sewing dresses."

Victoria felt hopeful. "She does? I didn't know she had a job."

"She makes about fifty cents an hour," Benjamin said

dryly. "Those dresses are sent to the States and sold for much more."

Victoria's stomach knotted. How many times had she purchased such dresses, never giving thought to the real price being paid by one so young, so lonely, living in a dark cardboard room.

Chapter 6

Benjamin sat beside Claudia's bed, adjusting the ice bag on her head. She cried and cradled her skull with her hands. Severe headaches accompanied dengue fever. Her temperature had risen to 105 degrees but was coming down. Benjamin bathed her face, arms, and legs with tepid water. They were on day five of the illness. It usually lasted six to seven days. He prayed she would come around soon.

Wet hair stuck to her cheek and he gently pulled it away. Her dark lashes and tiny face reminded him of his sister, Emily. Same age, same helplessness. Only this time he was there, trying to help. He would do his best to get her through this. Oh, why hadn't he been there for Emily?

He bowed his head and closed his eyes hard, trying to shut out his thoughts.

A gentle hand touched his shoulder. "Ben, let me stay now, please?"

He looked up to see Victoria standing over him. She was a welcome sight. Relief swept over him, chasing away his painful memories. He was so tired.

Victoria squeezed his arm. "You're exhausted. Let me take over, Ben."

He stood, stretched his aching legs, and faced Victoria. They were so close, he could smell the fresh, clean scent of her shampoo. "Her fever hit 105 earlier. I've been bathing her with cool water. It's dropping now."

Victoria glanced at Claudia. "I'll keep at it." She turned back to face him.

"Thanks." They stood motionless for a moment.

"I rested this afternoon, and I'm ready to watch her."

Her caring expression warmed him. His heavy burden seemed to lighten. He reached for her hand. "Thanks, Vic," he said, giving her fingers a quick squeeze. "See you in the morning."

He had that same look when he looked at Claudia, Victoria thought, as she watched Benjamin leave. *Something has happened to him. Something terrible.*

Claudia stirred on the bed. Victoria turned to her and bathed her with the tepid water. Touching the child carefully, Victoria tried not to aggravate the pain.

Wringing the water from the wet cloth one last time, Victoria placed it on the small tub. Claudia finally settled back into her bed, weakness pulling her into a fitful sleep once again.

Victoria watched her absently. Images of Claudia's home life and her family's poverty flashed through Victoria's mind. Their great faith puzzled her. How could Maria appear so happy in such a dire existence? It made no sense. No sense at all.

These people on the *Providence* paid their own way to

be here. Not only that, but then they had to work the whole time. Why would anyone want to do that? If they had extra money, why wouldn't they want to spend it on something fun for themselves?

Nothing made sense anymore. People giving up security, money, and a bright future to help others who lived in cardboard houses. People in cardboard houses giving thanks to God for His faithfulness extended through those who sacrificed to come on the *Providence*.

She could never do this for very long. She had a dream, and this was not a part of it. No, she would follow her dreams and enjoy her wealth. After all, God had placed her in a well-to-do family and they had the means to help her. Was that so wrong?

Victoria browsed absently through a magazine, throwing occasional glances at Claudia.

A light rustling of sheets caused Victoria to look up. She felt the little girl's forehead. The fever was almost gone. Claudia's eyelids fluttered open.

"Nurse?" she asked in a broken whisper, her voice hoarse with little use.

"Yes, Dear?"

"Thank you." Claudia closed her eyes and fell back to sleep.

Tears stung Victoria's eyes. She lovingly stroked the sleeping girl's hand. Her chest tightened. Love flooded through her for this child unlike anything she'd ever experienced. *Is this how Ben and the others feel? Is this what pulls them to serve here?*

Looking warmly at Claudia, Victoria found herself thinking she could come back and serve on this ship someday. The thought surprised her. Things were changing. *No, I am changing.*

"How's Claudia doing, Tori?" Betsy asked as she pulled a stiff brush through her hair.

Victoria stretched and yawned. "She's doing better. Her fever finally broke." The early sun warmed their room as it streamed through the porthole into the cabin.

Sandy tucked in the corner of her blanket and turned to Victoria. "I heard you come in. I looked at the clock and it said five. I was sure that was wrong, but it wasn't, was it?"

Victoria smiled faintly. "Unfortunately, no."

Tommie placed her hands on her hips and chimed in with a motherly tone, "Young lady, you can't continue this schedule. Although it is admirable, you must keep up your strength."

"I know, but I couldn't let Ben handle it alone."

Tommie heaved a sigh and shook her head.

Betsy grabbed her purse and headed for her job in the schoolroom as a teacher's aide. They would be sorting through the books in preparation for fall classes. "Just take care of yourself, okay, Tori?" Betsy nudged her in a sisterly fashion.

"Yeah," Victoria smiled.

Sandy grabbed her handbag and prepared to leave for her secretarial position. Stumbling on her way out, she quickly straightened herself. She turned around to Victoria and Tommie and shrugged.

"Have a nice day, Sandy," Victoria said with a smile.

"You, too." Sandy closed the door behind her.

"Well, I guess it's my turn. I had better get to the kitchen, or we won't be having lunch today." Tommie grabbed her cookbook and glanced back at Victoria. "Take care, Hon, okay?"

"Will do, Tommie. Thanks." Victoria watched as the older woman scrambled out of the door. She was really growing fond of her new friends.

Looking around the room, she sighed. The time showed eight o'clock, and Ben told her she could come in at ten this morning. She jumped down from her bunk and looked in the mirror. After a moan, she muttered, "It'll take me that long to get presentable."

She quickly ran a brush through her hair, grabbed her bag, and headed out the door for the showers.

Victoria sighed with pleasure as the steaming water spread over her. It felt good to relax after staying up all night. She let the hot water wash her weariness down the drain with the soap bubbles.

Her thoughts drifted to the first day on the ship, her parents, and her attitude. She regretted having parted on such terms. She knew they were trying to help her, but she was angry they had gotten in the way of her dreams. Was that so wrong?

And then these people. . . Her roommates were kind to her when she didn't deserve it. Why?

Then there was Benjamin Meyer. One day, she caught him eyeing her as she fumbled to find the appropriate Scriptures during morning devotions. He turned quickly when she glanced up at him, never mentioning it.

What would her new friends say if they knew her real reason for being on the ship? Their hearts were full of compassion, kindness, and mercy for others. But hers? Filled with herself, her wants, her goals.

Victoria reached for the shampoo. She scrubbed her scalp hard as her thoughts rambled on.

Maria Garza and her family had touched Victoria's heart in a powerful way. Maria's prayer rang in Victoria's ears long after it was over, especially the words, "Thank You for kind people like Dr. Meyer and Nurse Victoria, who give their lives to help others." Shame covered her.

Maria possessed nothing of earthly value and yet possessed so much more. . . .

Victoria thought of her own life. She had so much for which to be thankful. Still, she was always searching for more, wanting more, needing more to be happy.

She stood in the hot water 'til it turned lukewarm, then shut off the knobs. They squeaked from constant use. Had God really made the difference in the lives of these people?

Grabbing her towel, Victoria patted her wet skin. She thought God was just Someone you talked about on Sundays. Although her parents had changed, started going to church, and reading their Bibles when she was in high school, Victoria had thought they were just getting old and sentimental. She never really believed there was much to it. Now she wondered.

She shrugged into her clothes and combed through her hair. Benjamin acted like he cared for her, yet sometimes he pulled away. She knew God was important to him. What if he knew the truth about her—that she didn't come to serve on the ship for the right reasons?

Why did she care what he thought? She couldn't let him get in the way of her dreams. Only a few weeks to go on this trip, and it would soon be over. She would go back to the happy life she had so carefully planned out for herself.

Victoria grabbed her things, then exited the bathroom. As she walked down the narrow passageway, a disturbing thought haunted her. When she returned home to claim her money, she would be happy—wouldn't she?

↙

Benjamin Meyer rose from his kneeling position by the bed. He closed his Bible and prepared to leave, knowing God had heard his prayer. The answers would come, but he would have to be patient. Healing was on its way. God is always faithful.

↙

When Victoria peeked through the large doors of the hospital ward to check on Claudia, she gasped. Benjamin stood next to Claudia, who was sitting up and sipping broth.

"You're better, Claudia." Victoria smiled as she slipped into the room.

A weak smile stretched across the little girl's face. Benjamin carefully placed the bowl of broth on the small table next to her and stepped out of the way.

Victoria reached Claudia's bed and grabbed her hand. "I'm so glad you're better." Victoria's words were tender, motherly. Tears stung her eyes.

"Thank you for helping me, Nurse Victoria." Claudia's eyes were wide, unclouded. "I told Dr. Meyer I got scared last night. I was so cold, and I was afraid. I wanted my mama."

Victoria squeezed the little girl's hand slightly.

"But I looked over, and you were here. I wasn't alone. Mama always says Jesus sends people to help us when we're in trouble. When I saw you, I knew He had not forgotten me, and I was not alone. Thank you, Nurse Victoria."

Victoria's tears fell upon Claudia's hospital gown as they embraced.

"Dr. Meyer says you both were praying for me. He says I can go home today, too."

Go home, Victoria thought. *Claudia lives in a shelter of discarded scraps. How can she want to go there?*

"I can't wait to see Mama and Sarita and Marlon."

"Well, you had better get some rest so you'll be able to leave when your mother gets here after work this afternoon." Benjamin tousled her hair.

Claudia giggled and snuggled under her covers.

Benjamin and Victoria turned to leave the room. Another doctor stopped Ben outside the door, and Victoria continued on. Claudia's words ran through Victoria's mind. Had God really used her? How could He? Her life represented selfishness and greed. The people on this ship offered mercy.

Victoria reached her empty cabin and closed the door behind her. She peered out the porthole, her thoughts drifting to the new condo she had considered moving into when she returned home. The excitement she once felt over living there had dulled. The picture of the condo faded as a sudden image of the Garza home interrupted the scene. Victoria felt her wants slipping away—or were they changing? She knew a decision had to be made. Yet, she wondered if the price was too high.

Chapter 7

Benjamin and Victoria waved good-bye to Maria and Claudia as they made their way off the ship. Benjamin exhaled slowly and turned to Victoria. "What do you say we get back to the office?" He cast her a smile, warming her with his dimples once again.

As they worked late into the afternoon, Benjamin seemed preoccupied.

"Ben, are you okay?"

His face looked flushed when he turned to her. "I need to talk to you, Vic. Could we meet on the Promenade Deck tonight after dinner?"

"Certainly," she said, puzzled.

"Thanks." He turned and busied himself with paperwork.

Victoria wondered what could be on his mind.

Footsteps echoed behind her, causing Victoria to pull her gaze from the sea and turn from the ship's railing. Dressed in a gray T-shirt underneath a gray-striped button-down shirt and jeans, Benjamin edged toward her. His shirt hung open in a casual style. She decided he looked very *GQ*.

Victoria's heart fluttered. She took a deep breath, inhaling the familiar rustic scent of his cologne.

"Hey." His greeting was friendly, but his expression seemed pensive.

"Hello," she managed to squeak.

She turned back toward the water and Benjamin joined her. They rested their hands on the metal rail as they listened to the murmur of the sea. Victoria waited for his words to come. She had no idea what they would bring but sensed it would affect her somehow.

"I've been struggling with something for over thirteen years now." Benjamin's words lifted gently through the night air. "Finally, I feel free, and I wanted to share it with you." He turned to face her.

Victoria looked into his eyes, realizing the seriousness of the moment.

"I had a sister. Her name was Emily. She was four years old at the time. I baby-sat her one day while Mom and Dad went to a banquet." He took a ragged breath.

"Being seventeen, my mind was on other things than little sisters. I turned on a video for Emily, and she sat watching cartoons." His eyes were glazed, distant. "I called my girlfriend. We talked awhile. I peeked into the living room where Emily sat and saw her head above the couch from time to time, so I thought nothing of it.

"The last time I checked on her, I still saw the top of her head but thought it strange she hadn't moved. I asked my girlfriend to hold on. I put the receiver down and walked farther into the room. Emily's favorite doll sat on a stack of pillows on the couch.

"I looked around the room and began to panic. Running through the house, I called her name, searching every corner. That's when I noticed the back door was ajar." Benjamin stopped for a moment. His jaw tensed.

Victoria stood frozen, knowing difficult words would come.

He looked back to the sea. "We had a pool," he said barely above a whisper. "The gate was open." He turned to Victoria. His face grew ashen. "She was floating, face-down."

Victoria gasped. "Oh, Ben."

"I pulled her out of the water and screamed for our neighbors. People gathered in my backyard as I worked to revive her." A long pause filled the air. He stared past her, as if reliving the event. "It was too late. She was gone."

Benjamin placed his quivering hands on the railing. Victoria covered his hands with one of her own. "I'm so sorry, Ben."

He looked at her. "I've blamed myself all these years. I vowed then and there that I would never get involved with anyone. I'd devote my life to service in helping others. In a way, I think I was denying myself any possible happiness because of what I'd done."

Victoria looked into his eyes. They seemed clearer somehow.

He grabbed her hands. "Vic, you have changed all that. I fell in love with you the moment I met you." He looked at her intently.

"I've battled with my vow and my feelings for you. Then, when Claudia Garza got sick, the Lord began to deal with me. I realized it wasn't my efforts that made her well. Life belongs to Him. All we can do is our best and leave the outcome to Him.

"Life is hard. Things happen that we can't fix. What's done is done. I can't change the past, Vic. My vow will not bring Emily back." He took a deep breath. "I guess what I'm trying to say is, God has brought me healing. I've finally learned to forgive myself."

A sudden warmth radiated throughout Victoria's body as he looked at her. His gaze traveled to her lips. He lowered his head, and she moved toward him. His strong arms claimed her as his lips tenderly covered hers. She relaxed in his arms, surrendering to the moment.

When they pulled apart, his hands grasped her arms gently, firmly, as he looked into her eyes. "I love you. I knew it from the moment I met you." His voice was thick with emotion.

Victoria felt hot tears forming. She pulled away.

"Is something wrong?"

She turned and looked straight ahead. The words were waiting to be said, but her mouth refused to free them. Her life was becoming a muddled mess. Things were not supposed to be like this. She was supposed to do her duty here, then ride off into the sunset, money in hand.

"You don't know me, Ben. Not really," she finally managed.

"I know that you're beautiful. I know that you didn't want to be here, but you've worked hard helping the people."

"But you don't know why I didn't want to be here, do you?"

He shook his head. "I guess I don't. It's not always convenient to come work on this ship. You probably—"

Victoria turned to face him and placed a finger on his mouth to quiet him. "Let me share my story before I lose my nerve."

He nodded.

Bravely, she told him how her parents made her come, the money, her dreams. Benjamin never interrupted but listened intently.

"So you see, I'm not the nice little Christian who people think I am. I have other goals for my life." She looked into his eyes. Pain looked back at her.

"I'm sorry to hear that, Vic." His voice came out brokenly. "I was hoping. . ." His words trailed off.

Victoria looked down and rubbed her fingers nervously.

"Although this is not an easy life, the rewards are great. Reaching out to others, filling them with hope, introducing them to Christ. . .well, there's nothing better. Jesus Christ is the reason we're here. Apart from Him, our lives are lived in vain." He waited a moment, then added, "He can give your life meaning, too, Vic. I can lead you to Him, if you'll let me."

She bristled at his words. *Who does he think he is? My life has meaning!* She flipped her hair angrily over her shoulders. "Things are just fine for me, thank you. If I wanted to find Him—which I don't—I would do it on my own!" she said with a voice that dared him to challenge her.

Benjamin's face paled. Victoria didn't like the way he stared at her with such sorrow in his eyes. It made her weak. She felt her resolve loosening its tight grip.

No, she must stand up for herself. Not much longer to go now. Her time here was almost spent. *I have to get out of here, away from these people. I want to go home where life is easier.* Images of the Tondo flashed through her mind. Then Maria's family, her generosity. Victoria's head hurt from thinking.

Her dream was just around the corner. Why was everyone trying to take that from her?

"Well, I guess there's not much more to say," Benjamin said with a sigh. "We have different ideas about how we want to spend our lives." He inhaled a ragged breath. "I'm sorry, Vic—more sorry than you could ever know." He tipped her face toward him. The sadness she saw there snuffed out her anger like a quick puff of air on a flickering candle. Regret closed in on her. She struggled to hold back the tears. Benjamin gently ran his fingers along the side of her cheek. "If only. . ." His words faded as he dropped his hand. "Good night, Vic."

Scarcely able to breathe, Victoria stood speechless as the echo of his footsteps carried Benjamin into the night.

The life she had dreamed of was only weeks away, yet a heavy ache clutched her heart. She groaned. This was the worst pain she had ever known.

Chapter 8

Benjamin looked at the clock again. Only five minutes later than the last time he checked. The red numbers blinked three o'clock. He pulled in a long breath, then released it in a frustrated sigh. Flipping off the covers, he turned on the light.

Reluctantly, he crawled out of bed and got dressed. The early hour covered the ship with calm—a calm that was lost on Benjamin. His heart ached with every step as he made his way toward the Promenade Deck.

Stopping in front of the railing, he took a deep breath of the morning air. Glistening stars reflected upon the water. He stood perfectly still, listening to the ocean's stirring as the water splashed against the sides of the ship.

How could he have been so wrong about Victoria? He knew she didn't want to be on the ship at first, but he thought she had changed. Never once had he considered she wasn't a Christian. His heart beat hard as he began to pace.

"Lord, I've finally worked through the pain that has followed me since Emily's death. Must I endure more?" His sneakers thumped against the shiny deck, swabbed clean by yesterday's work crew. He looked around, making sure he was alone, and continued pacing.

"Why did I have to meet her? I would have been content carrying on with my work, serving You." His steps carried him back and forth as he thought through the problem.

"How could I have been so blind? I thought I could read people." He jerked his hands forward in frustration.

Stopping in front of the railing once more, he stared out to sea, unseeing. "I've been a fool." His words darted toward the distant horizon. "Victoria must think me nothing more than a country doctor with no ambitions." His face grew hot. "And to think I poured my heart out to her."

Shadows of pride and embarrassment masked the love he felt for Victoria, giving him the determination he needed to forget her and get on with his life.

He felt himself relax as he listened to the sounds of the sea. Lifting his head, he stared at the heavens. "I will forget her, Lord. You're all that matters. Grant me strength for the time left on this trip." He glanced at his watch. Four o'clock. No point in going back to bed now. He decided to get showered and go to work. He left the Promenade Deck and wondered if his sudden determination came from God or if pride pushed him forward.

꙳

Victoria felt her stomach tighten just before she entered the office. Reluctantly, she opened the door and stepped inside. "Good morning, Ben."

Benjamin swung around to face her. "Morning, Victoria." He shoved some paperwork in her hands. "I'm afraid we're lagging behind a little. I would appreciate it if you could bring this up to speed before we go inland this afternoon," he said, using his professional voice.

She looked down at the papers, then back to Benjamin. "Yes, of course." She shifted nervously, then went over to the desk to sort through the paperwork.

"Oh, by the way," he called over his shoulder as he leafed through some files, "I thought you might like to know the ship is extending its stay in the Philippines due to the number of needy people here."

"Yes, I had heard that. The captain said they're planning to stay until the end of October now."

Benjamin kept his gaze away from her.

Victoria tried to sound pleasant, to offer a truce of some sort, but his actions told her their relationship would be strictly professional from this point forward.

She cast a furtive glance at him. Dark circles shadowed his eyes. His face looked pale and rigid, his jaw tense. *So that's how it is to be—cold and formal between us now. He even called me Victoria. He hasn't done that for a long time.* Victoria looked at the papers but saw nothing. She winced inwardly. She knew she'd hurt him and didn't know what to do about it. A fresh pain stabbed her. *Seems like I cause hurt everywhere I go.* Thoughts of her parents' faces as the ship pulled away from the dock filled her.

All I want to do is enjoy life. What's wrong with that? Just then the Garza family entered her mind. Their home, their love. . .their faith. Victoria closed her eyes for a moment. She wanted to shut it all out. She wanted to run away, far away. Forget these people, their faith, their God, and most of all forget Benjamin Meyer.

"I've got to talk to Dr. Schroeder, I'll be back in a minute."

Victoria nodded.

He turned and left the room.

Turmoil twisted her insides. Confusion met her at every turn. She thought of the money waiting at home, the ease and comfort that awaited her. Then she thought of the passengers on the *Providence*, those who sacrificed so much just to make this trip a possibility so they could help others. Guilt made her uncomfortable.

She shifted nervously in her seat. *What's wrong with doing what you want to do in life?* She picked up some papers and shuffled them noisily upon the desk. *I don't belong here. If I can just get through the next few weeks, every-thing will be fine. I'm not like the others, and I never will be.*

Victoria shoved her thoughts behind and clenched her teeth as she set out to tackle the bulky paperwork piled on her desk.

⚓

"Nurse Victoria!" Claudia Garza shouted, running as fast as her little legs could carry her. Victoria smiled as she watched, thankful the tiny patient was growing stronger every day.

Victoria squatted to Claudia's level. The four year old ran into Victoria's open arms. After a warm hug, she put Claudia at arm's length. "Let me take a good look at you."

Claudia smiled and stood like a soldier for the inspection.

"You are positively beautiful, young lady," Victoria said with a smile. "Looks like you've been following doc-tor's orders."

Claudia nodded enthusiastically.

Victoria glanced up and saw Benjamin watching them.

He smiled. Kindness filled his eyes. When she looked at him, he quickly turned his attention back toward a patient.

"I think a sucker is in order for you today," Victoria said as she rose.

Claudia clasped her little hands together. "Thank you, Nurse Victoria!"

Victoria grabbed a bag from the desk and pulled out a sucker. She squatted in front of Claudia and handed her the sugary treat, then gave her a hug. Claudia stared at the treasure for a moment as she bit her lower lip.

"Is something wrong, Claudia?"

Claudia glanced back in the direction of her mother. Just then Victoria noticed Sarita and Marlon standing behind Maria. "Oh, I see. How are you Sarita, Marlon?" Shy eyes greeted her as they sheepishly stood behind their mother. "Would you like a sucker, too?"

They nodded in unison. Victoria retrieved two more and handed them to the children. Eagerly, they ripped off the wrappers and popped the suckers into their mouths.

Victoria laughed, then looked toward Maria Garza. "Maria, how are you?"

The woman smiled. "I am fine, thanks to you and the kind doctor." She cast a glance toward Dr. Meyer, then to Victoria. "I have so much food, I give some to my neighbors. They come here and bring their friends and families."

"You gave away some of your food, Maria?" Victoria asked, incredulously.

"I'm so thankful for food to share."

Victoria was speechless. She thought of the food given to the Garzas. While the *Providence* offered a generous supply, she felt guilt when she thought of her ingratitude for her own bulging cupboards back home.

The line of people had dwindled and Benjamin turned toward Maria. "So good to see you, Maria." His dimples made Victoria's stomach flip-flop.

She turned away. She had fallen in love with Benjamin, but now it was too late. He said they had different ideas about life, and he was right. She had to get over him.

Victoria went over to the table and grabbed some bottled water. She drank some of the cool liquid and replaced the cap. The air was hot and muggy, but the sky shined pure blue, not a cloud anywhere. She fanned herself. Lifting her shoulders, a sigh escaped her.

Benjamin interacted with the children of the Garza family, and Victoria laughed in spite of herself. *He has a way of making everyone he meets feel special.* An unfamiliar longing filled her heart.

She twirled a pencil between her fingers. She could feel her own wants slipping away, but that would change once she got home and received her money, wouldn't it?

Benjamin's deep, pleasant laugh caught her attention. *He's so handsome, so kind, so. . .godly.* Victoria's selfishness blared at her as thoughts of Benjamin's goodness came to her mind. She shifted with uneasiness.

The Garza family said their good-byes, and quitting time settled upon them.

↵

Victoria couldn't eat dinner. Thoughts swirled in her head. She felt sick. Indecision followed her. Scenes of her life's dreams and goals shamed her.

She paced the deck. An evening fog caused her a slight

chill. Going to her room, she grabbed a sweater. Tommie, Betsy, and Sandy were in giddy moods, laughing and teasing one another. Victoria had to get away. She longed for solitude.

Finally, when the ship settled down for the night, Victoria found her way into the chapel. A wooden cross hung on the wall. She stepped cautiously through the small room, like one embarking on unfamiliar territory, running her fingers over the tops of the wooden pews as she slowly passed the rows.

Reaching the altar, she stood trembling. Her heart pounded as her soul struggled between life and death. She hadn't intended to come in here, but something—or Someone—drew her in. Why? She didn't deserve mercy, love, or grace. Yet in her heart, she knew God was offering those very gifts to her. Would she accept? Could she accept?

Dropping to her knees, she bowed at the altar. "Why are You doing this for me? I don't deserve it." Her hushed words echoed through the stillness. Tears squeezed past her lashes, making wet trails down her cheeks.

"You, more than anyone, know how I am, my selfishness, stubbornness, pride. How can You love me?"

His answer filled her. *"I have summoned you by name; you are mine."* The awesomeness of God's love flooded her soul. Her arms clasped the altar as tears freely flowed and heaven touched earth once again.

"Oh, God, I've been so wrong. Please forgive me for my rebellion, for choosing my way instead of Yours. Forgive me of all my sin and change my life. I want Your goals for my life, Your dreams." Anguished cries filled the room, but she didn't care. All Victoria wanted was for God to fill her, change her.

"It doesn't matter what the future holds, Lord. With or without money, with or without Benjamin Meyer, I'm Yours. My life is in Your hands."

She didn't know how long she stayed there. The tissue box placed beside the altar was almost empty. Peace settled upon her, and she knew she was no longer the same. God had met her in the ship's chapel, and the course of her life had changed forever.

A light feathery feeling touched her heart. She felt she could float on thin air. Inhaling deeply, she slowly drank in her first breath of new life. The air smelled fresh and clean, like the sea on a summer day. Everything around her looked brighter. Victoria smiled. *So this is what Mom and Dad have been trying to tell me. I'll have to call them.*

She gathered the used tissues, stood, and made her way to the door. Tossing the tissues into a wastebasket, she glanced once more at the cross. "Thank You," she whispered with more gratitude than she had ever known. She slipped through the doors, beginning the journey into her new life.

Chapter 9

G reat, another sleepless night." Pacing the ship's deck in the evening was becoming a familiar routine. Benjamin stopped at the metal railing and raked his fingers through his hair with a sigh.

Why can't life ever be easy?

"I'm sorry. I know You know what You're doing." He directed his words toward heaven. Moments ticked by as he waited, listening for an answer. "Help me to let her go." A light breeze lifted his whispered words and carried them out to sea.

The island noises drifted toward the ship. He gazed at city lights that sparkled in the distance like tiny fireflies.

Benjamin tried to focus his thoughts on the workings of the *Providence,* the people the workers helped, the miracles taking place in their midst, but every thought brought him back to Victoria.

He took a deep breath and moved aimlessly along the rail. Before he knew it, he found himself in front of the chapel door. Knowing it would do some good to go in and talk with the Lord, he slipped inside.

Lost in thought, at first he didn't notice the muffled

cries coming from the front of the room. He settled into a back pew to pray. Then he heard her. Whispered groans, then sobs, anguished cries. Surprised, Benjamin looked up and saw a woman crumpled before the altar. He didn't want to disturb her. He knew he had stumbled upon holy ground.

Standing, he turned to leave the sacred place when he glanced at the woman once more. The clothing looked familiar. His eyes narrowed in on her. "Victoria." Her name escaped him in a whisper. Hope surged through him. God was breaking through to her heart. *Thank You, Father.* Faint tears formed. He stood perfectly still for a moment.

He wanted so much to present the gospel message to her, to introduce her to the Savior, but her words echoed through his mind. *If I wanted to find Him, I would do it myself.* No, he had to let Victoria find Christ on her own. Benjamin's burdened heart lifted to the Lord. "She's in Your hands, Father. Give me the strength to leave her there."

Reluctantly, Benjamin turned and slipped from the room.

Victoria felt refreshed from her shower. She opened the door to her room and placed her bag on the floor. Pulling the towel from her wet hair, she bent over and rubbed it vigorously with the heavy cloth. She straightened, picked up her comb, and started working through the tangles.

Streaks of sunlight poked through the porthole, washing the room with brightness. *Everything seems cleaner today,* Victoria thought with a smile.

Tommie, Betsy, and Sandy roused from their sleep.

"Morning, sleepyheads," Victoria teased.

Betsy squinted to see the clock, then looked toward Victoria. "It's only six, and you've had a shower already?" she asked in disbelief.

"Amazing, isn't it?" Victoria replied with a laugh.

Sandy sat up in her bed and yawned. Tommie threw off her covers in the bunk below.

Betsy pulled herself from underneath the blankets and staggered toward her clothes. Tommie and Sandy followed.

Humming cheerily, Victoria made her bed while the other three women adjusted to the morning. She glanced up in time to catch her roommates exchanging a curious glance.

"You okay, Tori?" Betsy asked.

Victoria smiled at her. Sandy and Tommie stopped their morning routine and stared at Victoria now, too.

"I'm glad you asked," she said. One by one, she looked into their faces. "Last night, I was miserable. I couldn't eat, couldn't sleep." She sighed and lowered her head. "You see, I've been playing a game." Everything grew still, except for the sounds of hushed breathing.

Victoria lifted her gaze back to her friends. Tommie's face held the compassion so typical of a mother. Sandy listened shyly, as if she shouldn't be eavesdropping. Betsy nodded, encouraging Victoria to continue.

The trio listened intently as she revealed the story of her dreams, the money, her parents' insistence on the trip. The small group offered supportive glances and pats to Victoria as she revealed her true self. Cords of love and understanding bound them together.

Victoria finished by saying, "I found myself standing

in front of the chapel doors last night. I made my way to the altar, and there I met Jesus."

Tommie pulled a hankie from the pocket of her flannel nightgown. A surprised gasp escaped Sandy, and Betsy smiled, reaching over to hug Victoria. "Tori, that's wonderful."

Tears spilled from Victoria's eyes. "I've been so blind, so selfish," she said, shaking her head. Then she looked at the three of them. "But your witness, your love for me when I've been completely unlovable, spoke volumes to my heart."

Victoria faced Sandy. "The way you forgave me when I reacted so cruelly over the broken mirror became a turning point for me, Sandy. It made me see myself more clearly." Victoria's voice cracked. Sandy's eyes filled with tears. She reached over to hug Victoria.

After the embrace, Victoria gazed toward the porthole. "The people on this ship with their selfless love and dedication to others, then Claudia Garza's family with their faith in such dire circumstances. . ." Her words trailed off. She blinked and turned back to her roommates. "I could no longer live the same way. I had to make a decision to either continue with my selfishness and be miserable or allow Christ to work through me and find peace."

She shrugged and lifted her palms. "So, here's the new me," she said with a smile, wiping away fresh tears.

By now all four women were a heap of hugs and tears. Victoria had never known such joy.

"Mom?" Victoria held the receiver snug against her ear so she could hear every word.

"Victoria?" her mother replied excitedly.

"Yes. How are you?"

"We're fine, Dear. How are you?" The phone wires crackled.

"Hey, Kiddo," her dad's voice called from an extension. Victoria could imagine his handsome smile.

"Mom, Dad, I'm sorry I've only written a few times and haven't called 'til now."

"It's all right. We know you're busy," her mother replied.

"We've missed you so much." Her dad's words held tenderness.

Victoria took a deep breath, trying to gather her nerve. "I have something to tell you—I asked Jesus Christ to come into my life."

Her mother gasped. Her father's voice nearly burst through the phone. "Well, praise God!" Victoria could almost hear him slap his knee.

Tears followed. Her parents talked excitedly about her news.

The conversation continued with talk of the *Providence* and the work being done there. They filled Victoria in on bits and pieces of home life.

Victoria glanced at her watch. "I've been talking far too long. This will cost a mint!" She realized it was the first time she'd ever worried about spending too much money. "I just wanted you to know—oh, and Mom, Dad?"

"Yes?" they said in unison.

"Thanks for the trip. I love you."

"We love you."

"Bye."

Benjamin looked across the room and watched Victoria dining with the captain. Her countenance glowed. He was certain she had made peace with God, but she said nothing to him. He desperately wanted to bring it up but knew he had to wait. She would tell him when she was ready.

Would the change he sensed in her affect their relationship, or would she still think he was a "country doctor" with no ambitions? Although she had been more lighthearted at work, she acted as though they were nothing more than friends.

Lost in thought, he rubbed the evening stubble that had formed on his jaw. He couldn't help staring at Victoria. She was standing now, shaking hands with the captain. She turned, caught Benjamin's eye, and waved.

He returned her wave and watched as she left the room. His heart pounded hard. Did he dare hope she would be in his future?

Victoria took her usual evening trip to the Promenade Deck. She couldn't believe the end of August had already arrived. Where had the time gone? She had learned so much, and there was more yet to discover.

She paused when she saw Benjamin leaning against the railing. They both did a lot of thinking in this spot. She approached him and tapped him lightly on the shoulder. "I've been wanting to talk to you privately."

Benjamin turned a surprised face toward her. His grin revealed the dimples that made her heart race. "I'm glad to hear that. I've been a jerk and I was afraid you'd never be my friend again." His eyes searched her face.

She placed her hand on his arm and shook her head. "You haven't been a jerk, and I'll always be your friend, Ben." She moistened her lips and took in a slight breath. "I have something to tell you."

He arched his brow. "Oh?"

Victoria explained to him the details of her experience in the chapel and her conversion. Benjamin stood speechless, watching, listening.

She shrugged. "So that's it. I've notified my parents that I've decided to stay on the *Providence* indefinitely. Their gift will support me for some time." She smiled. "The captain has cleared the way for me. That is, if you don't mind me continuing as your assistant?" She looked to him for approval.

"Mind?" he almost shouted. In one giant swoop, Benjamin lifted her into his arms and twirled her around. They laughed together until he finally put her down.

"I take it you don't mind," she said between gasping breaths.

He grew serious. "You know how I feel about you." He tipped her chin until their gazes locked. "I love you, Victoria Chaney. I've been miserable without you."

A solitary tear trickled down her face, and Benjamin kissed it away. Victoria closed her eyes with the tenderness of the moment. She loved him, she knew that now. "Thank You, Lord," her mouth formed the unspoken prayer.

Benjamin brushed the hair from her face. She reluctantly opened her eyes, afraid she would wake up from this dream.

"Say you love me, Vic." His eyes pleaded for the words.

"I love you, Ben," she whispered against his ear. He kissed her forehead and feathered light kisses down her cheek. His lips sought hers, finally claiming her with a tenderness and love she had never known.

He gently pulled away from her and placed his hands on her shoulders. "Vic, I want to do something before I lose my nerve."

"What?" she asked with a light chuckle.

Benjamin scooted a chair up to her. "Sit here, please." Wide-eyed, she obeyed.

Once she was seated, Benjamin knelt down before her and took her hands into his. Victoria shivered from the cool sea air—or was it just excitement? The night was perfect as the moon cast a romantic glow across the deck.

Benjamin's serious blue eyes penetrated her soul while he said the words she'd only dreamed of hearing. "Victoria Chaney, would you do me the honor of becoming my wife?"

The words caught her by surprise. She gasped. "Oh, yes, I'll marry you, Ben!" She pulled her hands free and threw her arms around him.

He lifted her with ease, and they embraced. Could he feel the drumming of her heart? Benjamin slowly lowered her feet to the deck. "I don't think I've ever been this happy in my life." His hand rubbed the side of her face. "Vic?"

She could hardly focus. Her contentment had muted everything to a dreamy state.

"I know this is sudden, but we're adults and, uh, well, I was wondering if you would consider a short engagement?"

She pondered his words. "I've got an idea. . ." And before either took another breath, they said in unison, "Let's get married on the ship!"

Chapter 10

The bright October sun found the ship's deck sparkling from the good swabbing it had received the day before, compliments of the passengers who scurried around to help make this a perfect day for the ship's doctor and nurse.

The weather cooperated as the humidity held off, and a gentle breeze stirred from the waters, cooling the guests as they strolled onto the deck and took their seats on padded folding chairs.

The *Providence* anchored a pleasant distance from the Manila shoreline, shutting out the harbor noises. The fresh scent of the sea surrounded the wedding guests while the sun glistened upon the calm waters, making this a perfect setting for the sacred ceremony.

The captain, dressed in a crisp white uniform adorned with brass buttons, took long strides toward his place at the bow. A hush settled over the crowd as the ship's intercom echoed the strains of "The Way You Look Tonight."

The groom and groomsmen filed in to the left of the captain. Benjamin Meyer led the way dressed in a white suit with black bow tie, and the three groomsmen wore ebony suits and matching ties. The young doctor's wheat-colored hair lay neatly combed into place, and his blue eyes sparkled like the sea. He squared his broad shoulders and stood tall, awaiting the arrival of his bride. Benjamin looked toward his parents and threw his mother a wink.

On the opposite side, Mrs. Chaney cast a warm smile toward her soon-to-be son-in-law.

In the back, the bridesmaids and flower girl stepped quickly into place, with Victoria and her father standing close behind them.

"You look beautiful," her father whispered as he squeezed her hand.

A gathering of fine netting around a small ring of tiny pearls formed her headpiece. She'd pulled her hair up into a stylish twist with slight curls framing her face.

Victoria's simple satin gown began with a scooped neck. Capped sleeves tipped delicately over her narrow shoulders. The dress hugged her tiny waist, revealed her shapely figure in a tasteful manner, and fell into a flowing skirt with a petite train brushing lightly against the deck.

She smiled at her father. "Thank you, Dad. I love you." Threatening tears were cut short as the ceremony began.

A slight murmur rippled through the crowd. Cameras clicked and flashed. Dressed in muted pinks, blues, and yellows, Sandy, Tommie, and finally Betsy made their way down the narrow aisle. They stepped to the captain's right side.

Light chuckles swelled through the crowd as they watched a shy Claudia Garza dropping flower petals from a tiny basket onto the ship's deck. Victoria's mother had purchased the soft pink dress adorned with delicate ruffles and lace for Claudia. Maria had told Victoria she was sure her daughter would never take off the lovely dress.

Finally, through the intercom, organ music majestically hailed the "Wedding March." Evelyn Chaney stood to face her daughter. All eyes followed Mrs. Chaney's gaze toward the back, where Victoria stood beside her father. His black suit complemented glistening silver hair. He smiled tenderly toward his daughter.

"I love you, Sweetheart." He paused for a slight moment as if seeing the image of his daughter growing from infant to womanhood in the span of a heartbeat.

Victoria smiled at him with understanding. Her fingers gently squeezed his arm.

"Shall I take you to your groom?"

She nodded. The crowd faded as she looked at Benjamin through tunnel vision. Her heart drummed a steady rhythm. When she reached Benjamin, he took her hand and drew her closer to his side in front of the captain. The rest of the ceremony passed in a blur.

Violin concerti and happy chatter filled the air. Victoria felt she had drifted into a beautiful dream.

"Did you hear what I said, Mrs. Meyer?" Benjamin asked as he grabbed his wife's hand and stepped away from the guests.

Victoria lifted her gaze toward him.

"I said, I love you." His voice was husky, low. He looked at her tenderly.

Warmth filled her. "I love you," she whispered, her voice quivering with every word.

Benjamin leaned his head down into the side of her

hair, brushing quick, secret kisses against the side of her face.

"Hey, you lovebirds," a voice cut through their longing. "Will you cut the cake?"

The happy couple looked up and smiled, allowing others to lead them toward the cake table.

The afternoon surrendered quickly to evening, when finally Victoria and Benjamin turned toward their cabin.

"Victoria?" a voice called from behind her.

She turned to face Sandy. "Yes?" She smiled at her friend.

"I wanted to give this to you, personally," Sandy said as she extended a package toward Victoria.

Victoria looked at her, puzzled. Turning her attention to the package, Victoria opened it. Lifting off the wrapping, she looked at the most beautiful hand mirror she had ever seen. It was antique, much like the one her grandmother had given her, except it had intricate designs bordering the mirror itself.

Victoria gasped. "Sandy, this is beautiful! How did you ever find it?"

Sandy beamed. "Some of the locals helped me. I know it's not from your grandmother, but do you like it?"

Victoria reached for her friend and hugged her tightly. "I love it! Thank you so much."

Sandy's eyes lowered. "You're welcome."

"I'm so glad you're my friend, Sandy."

"Me, too." She answered shyly, then turned to leave.

Victoria explained the mirror story to Benjamin as they walked to their cabin. They reached the door and Benjamin opened it, then turned to his bride.

"Well, Mrs. Meyer, I believe this is where I lift you over the threshold," he said with a twinkle in his eye.

"You'll never make it through this narrow opening with me in this dress!" she said with a laugh.

"Oh, you just watch me." Before she could blink, he scooped her into his strong arms and pulled her inside.

Laughing, he placed her feet on the floor once again. He turned and closed the door behind him, then reached for her, pulling her into a warm embrace. Gently, his hands caressed her face, holding her for just a moment. His fingers traced the outline of her chin and moved in a circle around her lips. Benjamin leaned forward, and Victoria felt the warmth of his lips upon her own.

"Vic," he whispered, "I'm so thankful God brought you on this voyage."

She couldn't speak. Emotions she had never known before stirred within her.

"I love you, Vic." His tender words gently embraced her heart. Victoria reached up and cupped his chin. Then Benjamin kissed her as a groom claiming his bride.

Victoria's heart floated into a sea of thankfulness.

God had changed her dreams and her world, making them better than she could have ever imagined. Her heart was content. She squeezed her arms tighter around Benjamin and snuggled her head against the crook of his neck, knowing the voyage of their lives had just begun.

DIANN HUNT

Diann lives in Indiana with her husband, Jim, who is an elementary school principal. They have one daughter, one son, a son-in-law, a fifteen-month-old granddaughter, and a dog. Feeling God has called her to this ministry, Diann gets up early (most of the time) to write before her day job as a full-time court reporter. She has sold magazine articles, but *Healing Voyage* is her first published novella.

A Letter to Our Readers

Dear Readers:

In order that we might better contribute to your reading enjoyment, we would appreciate you taking a few minutes to respond to the following questions. When completed, please return to the following: Fiction Editor, Barbour Publishing, Inc., PO Box 719, Uhrichsville, OH 44683.

1. Did you enjoy reading *Love Afloat?*
   - ❏ Very much. I would like to see more books like this.
   - ❏ Moderately—I would have enjoyed it more if _____
   _____

   _____

2. What influenced your decision to purchase this book?
   (Check those that apply.)
   - ❏ Cover
   - ❏ Back cover copy
   - ❏ Title
   - ❏ Price
   - ❏ Friends
   - ❏ Publicity
   - ❏ Other

3. Which story was your favorite?
   - ❏ *The Matchmakers*
   - ❏ *By the Silvery Moon*
   - ❏ *Troubled Waters*
   - ❏ *Healing Voyage*

4. Please check your age range:
   - ❏ Under 18
   - ❏ 18–24
   - ❏ 25–34
   - ❏ 35–45
   - ❏ 46–55
   - ❏ Over 55

5. How many hours per week do you read? _____

Name _____

Occupation _____

Address _____

City _____ State _____ ZIP _____

E-mail _____

If you enjoyed

LOVE AFLOAT

then read:

Once Upon a Time

*Four Modern Stories with All the
Enchantment of a Fairy Tale*

A Rose for Beauty by Irene B. Brand
The Shoemaker's Daughter by Lynn A. Coleman
Lily's Plight by Yvonne Lehman
Better to See You by Gail Gaymer Martin

Available wherever books are sold.
Or order from:
Barbour Publishing, Inc.
PO Box 721
Uhrichsville, Ohio 44683
http://www.barbourbooks.com

You may order by mail for $6.97 and add $2.00 to your order for shipping.
Prices subject to change without notice.

If you enjoyed

LOVE AFLOAT

then read:

TAILS
of LOVE

*Pets Play Matchmakers in
Four Modern Love Stories*

Ark of Love by Lauralee Bliss
Walk, Don't Run by Pamela Griffin
Dog Park by Dina Leonhardt Koehly
The Neighbor's Fence by Gail Sattler

If you enjoyed

LOVE AFLOAT

then read:

Resolutions

*Four Inspiring Novellas Show a
Loving Way to Make a Fresh Start*

Remaking Meredith by Carol Cox
Beginnings by Peggy Darty
Never Say Never by Yvonne Lehman
Letters to Timothy by Pamela Kaye Tracy

If you enjoyed

LOVE AFLOAT

then read:

LESSONS *of the* Heart

Four Novellas in Which
Modern Teachers Learn about Love

Love Lessons by Kristin Billerbeck
Beauty for Ashes by Linda Goodnight
Scrambled Eggs by Yvonne Lehman
Test of Time by Pamela Kaye Tracy

Available wherever books are sold.
Or order from:
Barbour Publishing, Inc.
PO Box 721
Uhrichsville, Ohio 44683
http://www.barbourbooks.com

You may order by mail for $6.97, and add $2.00 to your order for shipping.
Prices subject to change without notice.

If you enjoyed

LOVE AFLOAT

then read:

Montana

A Legacy of Faith and Love
in Four Complete Novels by Ann Bell

Autumn Love
Contagious Love
Inspired Love
Distant Love